UNHALLOWED

RATH & RUNE BOOK 1

JORDAN L. HAWK

CONTENT ADVISORY

This book contains the following: references to past child abuse, references to past parental death, references to past house fire, violence, death (including references to past death by fire), suffocation, on-page sex, and bats (which remain unharmed, no need to be concerned about the bats).

Widdershins always knows its own,
In blood and spirit, breath and bone.

CHAPTER 1

*T*he monster boarded the train in Boston.

He found an unoccupied seat at the back of the rail car. Warm May air drifted in through the open window, along with the tang of burning coal. Men and women crowded the platform outside, the plumes in the women's hats bobbing in the breeze.

A small girl tugged urgently on her mother's skirts, demanding attention. The monster stiffened, expecting the woman to backhand the child. Instead, she smiled indulgently, bending down to better hear her offspring's excited babbling.

"Pardon me," said an affable voice practically in his ear.

He jumped, then cursed himself. Inattention wasn't something he could afford, ever. Certainly not now, when so much hung on the outcome of this journey.

A smiling man, his face flushed from the heat, stood looking down at him. "Is this seat taken?"

He thought about lying, but he'd be caught out when no companion appeared. "No."

The man stowed his suitcase, then dropped into the seat. "Dave Moore," he said, thrusting out his hand.

"Vesper Rune." Ves shook reluctantly, withdrawing his own hand as quickly as possible. The last thing he needed was a gregarious seat-mate, but a quick glance around the car showed no other empty seats. It seemed he was trapped, at least until the next stop.

The train whistle screamed, and a few moments later, it lurched into movement. Ves turned to the window, suppressing a flinch as he caught a glimpse of dark hair and brown eyes reflected in the glass. Fortunately, his reflection was distorted, and he was able to look through it and pretend to be deeply interested in the passing scenery.

Alas, that wasn't enough to dissuade his seatmate. Mr. Moore launched into a long monologue concerning his business (traveling brush salesman), his family (wife and three children), and the weather (warm). Ves murmured where it seemed polite, but his thoughts were only half on the other man's idle conversation, until he asked, "So where are you headed, Mr. Rune?"

Resigning himself to an unwanted conversation, Ves said, "Widdershins."

To his surprise, Mr. Moore paled. "Widdershins? Is that…I mean, do you hail from there?"

"No," Ves said, and hoped Moore didn't pry any further into his origins. It was tedious to lie all the time, and he was becoming sick of it. But what choice did he have? *I was raised in an insane cult* was the sort of answer that only invited even more intrusive questions. "I'm visiting on business."

Moore seemed marginally less concerned, though a frown still creased his brow beneath the brim of his hat. "I see. You won't be there long, I hope?"

The task Mr. Fagerlie had given him was simple enough. With any luck, Ves and his brother would be leaving New England behind forever in only a little over a week's time. With the curse lifted, they'd be free to go anywhere they pleased, live as they chose.

"I'm not planning on staying," he replied. "May I ask why?"

Moore worried at his lower lip with his teeth. Then he leaned in, dropping his voice to a whisper. Ves stiffened, hoping the cologne he'd splashed on this morning covered his natural scent. "They claim the town was founded by a man fleeing the witch trials, back in colonial times. I don't know if that's true, but it's said those who live there even today scorn the laws of both man and God. I wouldn't linger any longer than you must, if I were you."

Ves barely kept from rolling his eyes. What a bunch of rot. Widdershins might be a small port town, but it was still a town, which meant people and their prying eyes. It wasn't like the countryside where he'd grown up, where the remoteness of farmsteads meant their inhabitants had the privacy to engage in activities that would make Moore's blood curdle were Ves to name them aloud. Nothing Widdershins had to offer would be stranger or more horrible than what had surrounded him growing up.

Nothing would be stranger or more horrible than himself, when it came down to it.

But of course he couldn't say that out loud. "Thank you for the warning, but I'm sure I'll be fine."

Moore still seemed uncertain. "What sort of work do you do, Mr. Rune?"

Here, at last, was a chance to secure some peace and quiet. "I'm a bookbinder and conservator," Ves said, and immediately launched into a long dialog concerning the importance of margin width in rebinding. As predicted, Moore's eyes began to glaze over within seconds.

"How very interesting," Moore said hastily, when Ves paused to draw breath. He retrieved a newspaper from his suitcase, signaling an end to the conversation. Ves suppressed a smile of triumph.

Moore settled himself, unfolding the paper. The front page occupied him through the stop in Revere, but as the train pulled out of that station, he angled it in Ves's direction. Ves glanced down and saw Moore was indicating the daily update on the speed and visibility of Halley's Comet.

"What do you think about all this?" Moore asked. "That French astronomer says we're all going to die when the earth passes through the comet's tail next week. That it's the end of the world."

"It isn't," Ves said shortly.

"But how can we be certain?"

Ves turned away without answering. Because he knew what Moore —what most people—didn't.

The end of the world was supposed to have happened eight years ago. And it had been Ves's purpose to help bring it about.

🐚

"He wouldn't have just *left*," Sebastian said as he put down his bottle of beer.

Irene sighed, and Arthur groaned loud enough to be heard over the noise of the crowd. Over the years they'd worked together in the library of the Nathaniel R. Ladysmith museum, they'd developed the tradition of going to The Silver Key bar for drinks at least twice a week to wash the dust from their throats after closing. Ordinarily their conversation ranged from baseball to whatever film was playing at the Nickelodeon, but for the last two months only one subject had been on Sebastian's mind.

"Not this again," Mortimer Waite said, the corner of his lip raised in a sneer.

Sebastian tried not to glare. Mortimer had become engaged to Irene over the winter holidays, when they met at one of his family's parties. Ever since, he'd taken it upon himself to assume he was invited wherever Irene was, whether he was actually wanted or not.

"People *leave*, Sebastian," Irene said, far more tactful than her fiancé. Irene Endicott was short, plump, brown-skinned, and the most fashionable person Sebastian had ever met. She wore her sleek hair in a shocking bob that she claimed was all the thing in Paris, and the cut of her skirts was slim enough to show off the roundness of her thighs. At work, she kept to the sober colors suited to their profession, but as soon as they left she'd donned a bright red hat topped with enormous plumes. "Even librarians."

"They disappear," he corrected.

"He had been thinking of finding a different profession," Arthur Fairchild said tiredly. He was paler than Irene, though not nearly as pale as Sebastian, his hair in messy curls and his worn sack suit well out of date. "All of his things were packed up and gone. His landlady received the key in the mail, and Mr. Quinn his resignation the same way. I agree it was abrupt and out of character for him to simply walk away from his position at the library without a word, but these things do happen."

"He probably ran off with a woman," Mortimer said disinterestedly. "Or a man."

Sebastian took a swig of beer. "Kelly O'Neil was born in Widdershins. He wouldn't have just moved away. You of all people ought to know that, Mortimer. Your family has been here since the 1690s."

Mortimer only shrugged and swirled his wine in his glass.

Irene frowned at Sebastian. "Why are you so upset about this? You weren't *friends*, were you?"

The emphasis she put on the word "friends" indicated she meant something quite different. "Good God, no!" Sebastian exclaimed, affronted.

"I suppose O'Neil had some taste, then," Mortimer murmured in a low voice.

Irene shot Mortimer an annoyed look, then turned back to Sebastian. "I'm just asking. If you weren't sleeping with him, why are you so upset he left without a word?"

"Because he wouldn't have done that. Not to me and Bonnie. After Mother died, he came around every few days to see how we were doing." Kelly had been Mother's assistant, when she worked in the library's bindery, then succeeded her as binder and conservator after her death.

Of course, Mother had originally hoped it would be Sebastian, not Kelly, who came after her. He'd refused. They'd fought over it—one of the only times his mother had ever raised her voice in anger to him.

When Sebastian proved intractable, she'd passed her experience on to Kelly instead. And now he was gone, too, taking that knowledge, that link to the past, with him.

"Sebastian thinks this is one of his little wooden puzzles," Mortimer said with a smile that bordered on a smirk. "Pieces he can put together to form a figure, or take apart to reveal...what? Foul play?"

Arthur glanced from Mortimer to Sebastian, then back. "I hate to even think it, but...is it possible he stole something, a valuable book perhaps, and took it with him when he left?"

"Then the curses would have gotten him," Irene replied, taking a long pull from her own beer. "Unless he had magic of his own. Or some kind of amulet to keep them off. He wasn't a sorcerer, was he?"

Outside of Widdershins, their conversation would have sounded like madness. Here, Irene didn't bother to keep her voice down.

"Not that I'm aware of," Sebastian said. "Surely he wouldn't have stolen a book, though."

"Perhaps we should conduct an inventory, just to be certain," Arthur suggested.

Mortimer groaned loudly. "Do you know how many volumes are in the library? It would take forever to inventory the entire place."

Arthur finished off his drink. "We'll discuss it further tomorrow. Now, if you'll excuse me, my wife will be wondering where I've gotten off to."

"How is Laura?" Sebastian asked.

"We had a bit of money come in—a bequest from a relative of hers —so happier than she has been for a while," Arthur said with a rueful smile.

Sebastian winced. It wasn't that a librarian's salary was poor, but Arthur had lost almost everything in the 1907 Panic and been beholden to the charity of relatives ever since. "I'm glad. Hopefully everything is turning around for you."

"I think it is."

Mortimer stretched dramatically. "I should leave as well. The family is holding a dinner at *Le Calmar*," he said, naming Widdershins's most expensive restaurant. Arthur's eyes narrowed, but Mortimer ignored him and instead turned to Irene. "I asked them to keep a place for you, in case you changed your mind."

"No, thank you," Irene said firmly.

Mortimer bowed over her hand, kissed her on the cheek, and left along with Arthur. Irene watched her fiancé go, then sighed and turned back to Sebastian. "You don't think O'Neil stole anything and then fled, do you?"

It was a reasonable explanation. Or, as Mortimer had pointed out, Kelly might have left town with a woman, or a man. Or a traveling circus for all Sebastian knew.

Sebastian was probably worrying over nothing. Being ridiculous. Allowing his emotions, his grief over his mother's death cloud his judgment.

"No," he said. "I don't. Arthur's wrong to even suspect him."

"Mortimer is probably right, you know. People do leave, even those born here."

He took the opportunity to redirect the question. "What do you see in him? Mortimer, I mean. He's a terrible bore with an inflated sense of his own self-importance, just because he's a third cousin to the head of the Waite family."

"He's not a bore," Irene objected. Then she considered. "Not much of one, that is. He doesn't chide me for caring about fashion, or for my weight—"

"There's nothing wrong with your weight."

"Yes, Sebastian, I'm quite aware of that. My point is, some men can be annoyingly backwards when it comes to what society so quaintly terms the 'New Woman,' as if my ancestresses hadn't been independent for centuries."

"Yes, well, they were also powerful sorceresses who could incinerate people."

"And they never hesitated to use that to their advantage," she agreed. "Mortimer is entertaining, and joining forces with one of the old families will be of advantage to the Endicotts. Of course, the Waites feel the same about us. It's a very sensible arrangement."

"If it makes you happy," he said dubiously. Not for the first time since meeting Irene, he found himself grateful not to be from a prominent family. It seemed to be a great deal of hassle for not much reward.

Irene finished her drink and stood up herself. "Go home and get some sleep, Sebastian. Work on one of your puzzles, or read a book, or do something to take your mind off O'Neil. He's gone."

Sebastian followed her out. While she went to her waiting automobile, he turned away toward the trolley line. The evening breeze ruffled his hair, and the smell of seared fish from one of the restaurants reminded him he hadn't yet eaten.

He might not have been romantically involved with Kelly O'Neil as Irene had suggested, but Sebastian thought they'd been friends. Or could have been, if they'd spent just a bit more time together. After Rebecca Rath died, Kelly had grieved almost as deeply as a member of the family.

Was there actually something sinister about Kelly's abrupt resignation? Or did Sebastian just not want to think that his mother's chosen successor would run off, abandon his post, as though all of her effort and training meant nothing?

The effort and training that would have been poured into Sebastian, if he'd just agreed to follow family tradition. But he had refused. Let her down.

Sebastian hunched his shoulders as if at a chill, even though the air remained warm. He hoped he was just being ridiculous. That Kelly was off safe and happy somewhere.

But he couldn't make himself believe it.

CHAPTER 2

*V*es's first impression of Widdershins was of its age.

Not that Boston didn't have more than its share of colonial architecture. And of course Widdershins had electricity and more modern buildings. But gambrel-roofed houses dominated much of the town, surrounded by gnarled, ancient oaks whose hoary limbs seemed to conspire to shield them from casual sight.

Much of the city went about its business like any other. But he caught furtive glances from behind curtained windows, and had spotted at least one cloaked and hooded figure scurrying down an alley. No one else had given the figure so much as a glance, though, which made him feel even more uneasy. He hadn't imagined it, had he?

The boarding house whose advertisement he'd answered looked to date from the early eighteen hundreds, as did much of the neighborhood. Judging by the size of the houses, it had once been affluent, but many were either slowly sliding into disrepair, or had been broken up into apartments or boarding houses.

"The rooms are eight dollars a week, paid upfront," the landlady said as she led Ves up to the third floor apartment. "Four rooms in the suite, furnished including bath and a gas stove." She paused outside the door and gave him a look. "I'd apologize for the steepness of the stairs, but it looks as though they aren't giving you much trouble."

Ves flushed, suddenly conscious of how he must appear, with his heavy steamer trunk balanced easily on one shoulder. It was a stupid mistake; he should have at least pretended to struggle with the weight, or to be out of breath from the climb. He was acting suspicious, drawing attention to himself, at the very time he most needed to be discreet.

Her eyes traveled over him slowly, taking in his thickly muscled thighs, the breadth of his shoulders. The tip of her tongue touched her lower lip. "Been a while since there's been a man around here who could take care of himself. I'm glad you decided to answer my newspaper ad, Mr. Rune."

Ves's face heated even more as he realized her implication. Her eyes slid over him again, lingering somewhere below his waist, as though in curiosity. "That's very kind of you, ma'am," he managed to say. "But I should like to set this down. It was a long walk from the train station."

"Oh! Of course." She hastily unlocked the door and flung it open.

A faint musty air hung in the small parlor, as if no one had lived in this suite for some time. Even so, it was nicely appointed, the furniture worn but not to the point of shabbiness. The mismatched couch and chair looked comfortable, and the rug had only a single small stain that he could see, even after she switched on the light. The generous fireplace was cold now, but had he been staying until the fall, it would have offered comfort in the cooler months. A large mirror hung above the fireplace, and he looked quickly away, before he could catch more than a glimpse of his reflection.

"I'll leave you to settle in," the landlady said from the doorway. "But if you need anything—anything at all—my apartment is on the first floor. Room one. Just knock, anytime of the day or night."

"I will," he said, though he was certain he'd be doing nothing of the sort.

She shut the door, leaving behind only a trace of her perfume. Lilacs.

Ves put down the trunk and went immediately to the windows to draw the drapes securely closed. A part of him still cursed himself for letting Nocturn become so careless…but if his brother hadn't been spotted, then Fagerlie would never have found them, and their only chance at escaping the curse would have passed them by along with the comet.

But that had been sheer luck—or destiny, if such things still applied to them. If you turned your back on destiny once, did you get a new one?

The closed drapes plunged the rooms into dimness, but Ves saw in the dark as easily as in daylight, so he didn't bother to turn on any more electric lights. With the prying eyes of the outside world blinded, he went to the fireplace and, without looking too closely, lifted the mirror off its hooks, turned it around, and propped it on the mantle. Then he went to the bathroom and bedroom, removing the mirrors there and setting them against the walls, their faces turned so they reflected only the odd, yellowish wallpaper. The tiny mirror in his shaving kit, only big enough to show a fraction of his face at a time, would suffice for now.

The mirrors dealt with, he carried his trunk into the bedroom and set about unpacking. It didn't take long, consisting of little beyond hanging up his suits and putting other various articles into the dresser. He had no mementoes, no photographs, no reminders of any past.

He wished he had a photograph of Noct. The brothers had never been separated before, not like this. Ves knew Fagerlie would be taking good care of him—that was part of the bargain—but he couldn't help but worry.

As soon as the curse was broken, they'd have a photograph taken together. Then, once they found somewhere new to settle, Ves would start collecting something inexpensive. Paintings, perhaps, or post cards, or tea cups. Something to give color to his surroundings, something Mother would have disdained as childish, pointless.

Soon. All he had to do was pass the interview tomorrow. After that first step, it would be simple. He'd soon be rejoined with Noct. Then the comet would pass, and the curse would be lifted, and everything would finally be made right.

Sebastian came to a halt in front of his sister's house. Of course, she insisted it was *their* house, that he was always welcome. That he shouldn't feel like a tenant. But somehow, he couldn't help it.

Perhaps it was simply that the house was so different from the one they'd grown up in. That house had been something of an architectural nightmare, with hidden passages and doors that went nowhere. Sounds carried oddly inside, and their favorite game as children had been to find places where one of them could whisper and the other make out the words clearly even if they were on a different floor.

That house was nothing but ashes now.

He took out his key and let himself into the small reception hall. The dark parlor lay to his right, but light spilled from the sitting room directly ahead.

Flickering light. Flames.

Sebastian's heart began to pound. Where was Bonnie? The children? How far had the fire spread?

He broke into a run—perhaps there was still time to extinguish the flames. Perhaps—

Bonnie looked up from her knitting as Sebastian burst into the sitting room. She rocked Clara's cradle with one foot; the infant slept soundly, her little face scrunched as though concentrating on her dreams. Three-year-old Tommy sat on the floor nearby, playing with wooden blocks. He, too, looked up at Sebastian, his eyes wide and slightly alarmed.

A bayberry candle burned on the table near the doorway, scenting the air. With a snarl, Sebastian snatched it up and flung it into the safety of the hearth. "Are you mad?"

Bonnie arched a brow and lowered her knitting. "Not that I've noticed. Are you?"

Sebastian gaped at her. "Why on earth would you have an open flame right there in the house? We have electricity!"

"Because I wanted a nice scent." Irritation snapped in her hazel eyes. "I was right here, keeping an eye on it, Sebastian."

"It was irresponsible!" The smell of bayberry gave way to burning wood, the clear air to stinging smoke. Screams rang in his ears. Sebastian ground his nails into his palms, struggling to keep his thoughts in the present.

Bonnie set aside her knitting and rose to face him. "You're acting like a lunatic, and you're frightening Tommy."

Guilt flashed through him when he glanced at the toddler. Tommy stared up at Sebastian, lips parted as though he wasn't quite certain whether he should start crying or not. "Better frightened than hurt," Sebastian said, but he lowered his voice as he did so.

Bonnie sighed, irritation giving way to pity, which was even worse. "All right, Sebastian. I won't burn any more candles."

She was saying it to humor him, that was clear enough. But she hadn't been there that day. Hadn't returned to see the house they'd grown up in wreathed in flames, while the fire company struggled to put it out. She hadn't heard the screams coming from inside. She hadn't stood in the street, helpless against the overwhelming heat and smoke, while their mother died in agony before her very eyes.

Sebastian had.

Clara began to cry, her little fists waving. Bonnie reached for the buttons on her dress. "Will you put Tommy to bed, while I feed the little one?"

"Of course." Sebastian lifted Tommy from the floor with a grunt. "You're getting heavy."

Tommy tucked his head into Sebastian's shoulder as Sebastian carried him to the front set of stairs. He shared a room with his brother, eleven-year-old Willie, who was already asleep after a long day of school and chores.

As Sebastian laid him down beside Willie, Tommy yawned. He curled into his bigger brother, thumb slipping into his mouth as he did so. For a moment, Sebastian looked down at them, illuminated in the light from the hall. They were so innocent. So untouched by the horrors of the world. If anything happened to them...

Even the thought made his heart ache. He would die before he let them get hurt.

Sebastian slipped out and shut the door, before going back downstairs to double-check that all the doors were locked. Satisfied, he retreated to his room. The chamber had originally been servants quarters, long before Bonnie and her children moved in, and sat directly above the kitchen. Come full summer, the heat would be ferocious. For now, it was pleasant, the night breeze stirring the curtains and bringing with it the fishy scent of the ocean.

Boxes of dissected pictures, along with the newer jigsaw puzzles, sat in one corner. He'd assembled most of them more than once, but found himself reluctant to let them go, even as he added to the pile with every visit to the shops. Of more interest was a new puzzle box he'd acquired from the toymaker's store. One-of-a-kind and made with exacting precision, it hadn't been cheap. But Sebastian had few expenses outside of the rent he paid to Bonnie and the drinks he got with his friends. Similar boxes clustered on his shelves, alongside wooden purses that could only be opened by knowing a certain trick, and even a book whose wooden leaves each contained their own puzzle to unlock the next.

He sank down on the edge of the bed. He knew he ought to go down and find something to eat for dinner, but couldn't summon the energy to do so. The sudden burst of fear he'd experienced seemed to have drained him completely.

Bonnie meant well. But she didn't live with his nightmares. Or his guilt.

He should have risked it. Despite the wall of furnace-like heat, the flames wreathing the door…he should have pushed through anyway. Saved their mother, or died in the attempt.

Sebastian stared up at his ceiling for a long time, trying not to think.

CHAPTER 3

$\mathcal{V}$es stared up the flight of marble steps leading to the Nathaniel R. Ladysmith Museum, a ball of nerves knotted in his belly. It was mid-morning on a Wednesday, and only a few people went in and out of its great doors: a small herd of school-children, shepherded by a harried teacher; two scholarly looking men arguing over some point of science; a young woman with intent eyes.

A newsstand nearby did a brisker business in papers and magazines. The *Widdershins Enquirer Journal* was prominently displayed, the name of the museum itself in the headlines. FAMED LADY ARCHAEOLOGIST SAILS FOR EGYPT ON BEHALF OF LADYSMITH was emblazoned just beneath the header in huge type. Below, a photo showed a woman standing on the docks, two children in front of her and flanked by a pair of smiling men. A tall man in the back seemed to be attempting to hide from the photographer.

Ves had a vague recollection that a female archaeologist had been the one to excavate Nephren-ka's tomb some years ago. Not that his family had allowed newspapers to enter the house—the brothers were meant to concentrate on their studies, not be distracted by the outside world. But the news had reached his mother somehow. She had screamed and thrown things, wild in her fury that the ancient pharaoh had been brought to America, his many sorcerous secrets fallen into other hands. And as usual, her rage had eventually turned to the two targets nearest at hand: her sons.

When her fury abated, they slipped away into the deep woods. Beneath the ancient trees, he and his brother listened to the whispers only they could hear. A low murmur of comfort and belonging that seemed to drift down from the trees and rise up from the rich loam, echoing in the chatter of squirrels and the song of birds. The voice of the All-Mother, Lord of the Forest.

The voice was the only thing Ves missed about Dunhollow. The song of belonging, of being a part of something greater, had always been there for him, even on the darkest days. And yet, he could only hear it due to his tainted blood.

He dragged his eyes away from the newspaper and back to the museum before him. He couldn't afford to wool-gather, not today. If he didn't get this job, then he wouldn't be able to give Fagerlie what he wanted, and the curse would never be lifted.

Ves and Noct would be stuck like this for the rest of their lives. Forced to hide. No friends, no lovers, no nothing.

Ves straightened his shoulders, checked his Oxford style bag, and started up the steps. He passed by the statue of a portly man with an extravagant walrus mustache; the bronze of the mustache was a slightly lighter color, as if worn by hands touching it for luck. Above the door hung a small banner: COMET PARTY AND LECTURE, *Beginning 8:00 pm, May 18. Inquire Within for Tickets.*

One week. Plenty of time.

Once inside, Ves approached a ticket-taker for directions. She instructed him to wait in the grand foyer while someone was summoned to guide him to his destination. As he waited, he took the opportunity to examine some of the exhibits. Most of those in the foyer consisted of extinct animals, the larger the better. An Irish elk stood foremost, its fearsome antlers spanning over ten feet from side to side. A small sign pointed to the right, indicating the wing housing the artifacts from the Nephren-ka expedition. Ves wondered if his mother had ever set foot here during one of her long absences. She'd occasionally left them in the care of their grandfather, vanishing sometimes for days, other times for months on end. When asked where she went, her only reply had been that she worked to bring about the return of those who had once ruled the earth and not to question her.

Not asking too many questions had been one of the cardinal rules for as long as he could remember. He was meant to obey, to prepare for his glorious purpose, and nothing more.

"Mr. Rune?"

Ves started and turned. The man in front of him was a few years older, perhaps thirty to his twenty-five. His blond hair was parted to the side and neatly slicked down, a match to his trim clothing. Ves had to look up a few inches to meet the hazel eyes peering through silver-rimmed spectacles.

Ves's mouth went dry. The man was handsome—tall and lean, with beautiful long fingers. An electric shock went down Ves's spine, stirring the flesh to either side.

No—he had to keep control of himself. He couldn't give himself away, not now, not when he was so very close.

"Y-Yes," he stammered like a fool.

The man regarded him coolly, the corners of his mouth turned down, as if something about Ves's appearance put him off. "I'm Sebastian Rath, the chief archivist of the Ladysmith library. You're here to apply for the bindery and conservatory position?"

Rath didn't offer his hand, to Ves's disappointment. Which was mad; he tried not to touch people if he could help it. He didn't dare. Still, he couldn't help but wonder what those long fingers would feel like against his skin.

This wouldn't do. Ves forced his breath to even out. "I am," he managed to say, proud his voice didn't shake.

Rath nodded once, shortly. "Mr. Quinn—the head librarian—has been informed you're here. If you'll follow me, I'll take you to his office."

Ves followed Rath to a discreet door marked STAFF ONLY. Rath made no effort to play tour guide, only led the way through a confusing tangle of corridors that soon had Ves utterly lost. Had the museum's architect ever planned a building before undertaking this one? And why had anyone ever approved the design to actually be built?

They eventually arrived at a door with a small sign reading LIBRARY. It opened into a space that struck Ves with an impression of vastness, disorienting after the ordinary dimensions of the hall outside. To one side stood a large desk, a librarian stationed behind it. A few reading tables were placed in the open space, and beyond were the stacks. Despite the feeling of space that Ves couldn't quite shake, the tall shelves quickly obscured his line of sight, so it was impossible to actually gauge the dimensions of the room.

"Mr. Quinn's office is through here." Rath led the way through a door set behind the desk, which opened onto a hall that seemed to branch and intersect itself unnecessarily. They passed several closed doors and a staff room, where a woman who looked to be of Indian heritage sipped a cup of tea. Something about the layout of the corridor—corridors?—made Ves feel faintly dizzy, and by the time they reached the head librarian's office, he'd lost all sense of direction.

For the first time, he wondered if the task set him by Fagerlie wasn't as easy as he'd assumed it would be.

Rath knocked lightly on the heavy oak door set with a brass plaque that read Mr. X. Quinn, Head Librarian. Rath stuck his head inside. "Mr. Rune is here for the interview, sir."

"Send him in," said a deep, hollow voice.

Rath ushered Ves inside, then shut the door as he departed. A large desk dominated the room, its wooden panels inlaid with swirling patterns that drew the eye. The man seated behind it looked more like a funeral director than a librarian. He dressed in a dark suit, his black hair slicked back from a high forehead. Gray streaked his temples, matching his strange, silvery eyes. His skin was so pale that the overall effect was that of a movie actor stepped from the screen, three-dimensional and speaking, yet still rendered in black and white.

Mr. Quinn gestured with one hand to the chair across from him. "Do have a seat, Mr. Rune."

The leather creaked under Ves as he sat. Something about the windowless room made the hair on the back of his neck prickle. Shadows seemed to gather more thickly than they should in the corners, deadening sound as well as sight. A human skull, weathered by the elements, perched at the corner of the desk, staring at Ves with empty sockets. On the wall behind Mr. Quinn, a glass case displayed what appeared to be a heavy dictionary, its cover battered and stained with what looked disconcertingly like blood.

Quinn touched one spidery hand to a stack of paper in front of him. Ves recognized the top sheet as the cover letter he'd typed up when applying for the position. "Vesper Rune," Quinn mused. "Lately of Boston. My sister and nieces live there. Tell me, Mr. Rune, were you born in Boston?"

The question had nothing to do with the position on offer. For a moment, Ves considered lying—but sticking as close as possible to the truth meant fewer chances to make a mistake. "I'm from Dunhollow originally. It's in the northern part of the state, off the Aylesbury pike. A tiny place; most people have never heard of it."

"And what did you do after leaving Dunhollow, Mr. Rune?"

Took his brother and ran. Hid. Waited for the end of the world, and when that didn't come, began his search for some way to break the curse. "I sought out a post in the rare book trade. My grandfather was both bibliophile and antiquarian, and though he seldom traveled, he had correspondents all over the world. Often the books they would send him were in deplorable shape. He taught me how to repair torn pages, remove dirt and stains, and rebind volumes as needed."

"The rare book trade." Venom dripped from Mr. Quinn's voice. "I suppose removing library marks was part of your job, once you arrived in Boston?"

Ves winced internally. A great deal of the rare book trade was fueled by theft from libraries, and the public institutions of Massachusetts had been particularly devastated over the years. Dealers looked down upon librarians for "hoarding" books, which they felt should rightfully be sold from one rich man to the next, rather than remaining within a single institution. Librarians, of course, had their own opinions concerning the thieves.

"No sir," Ves replied carefully. "My understanding is that's usually handled by the thieves themselves. But I never knowingly worked with a book I believed to have been stolen, and as soon as I had the opportunity to take a position at the Boston Public Library, I did so." He reached for his bag. "I've brought letters of recommendation both from my previous employers, and from Mr. Edward Fagerlie, for whom I did private work."

Mr. Quinn accepted the letters, his strange eyes scanning them swiftly. If he blinked even once the entire time, Ves didn't see it. "Impressive," he said at last. He placed the letters atop the rest of the paperwork, then opened his desk drawer and took out a small pouch of black silk.

The squarish bones that tumbled out of the pouch onto the green leather blotter were marked on each side with strange symbols. The bones might have come from a sheep or some other animal, but Ves was almost positive they had once resided in a human hand.

"These belonged to my predecessor," Mr. Quinn remarked, though whether he meant the crude dice or the bones themselves, Ves couldn't bring himself to ask. Quinn examined the symbols, a faint frown creasing his forehead. "Are you certain, Erasmus?" he murmured. "Very well."

He swept the bones back into their pouch and tucked them into the drawer. "You have the job, Mr. Rune—on a *trial* basis. Not everyone is fit to serve the library and by extension Widdershins. A final decision will be made within the next three months, depending on various factors. Is this agreeable to you?"

Ves would be gone long before the three months ran out. "It is. Thank you, sir."

"Mr. Rath will give you a brief tour of the library. You start work at eight o'clock sharp tomorrow morning. Tardiness is unacceptable."

Knowing a dismissal when he heard it, Ves rose to his feet. "Of course. I look forward to working here."

As he turned to the door, Mr. Quinn said, "One last thing, Mr. Rune. An observation of interest, if you will. Do you know how the librarians of old protected their books from theft?"

Ves's heart quickened its pace. Quinn would never have hired him if he truly thought Ves was up to no good. He didn't know anything— couldn't know anything. "No, sir."

"Curses." Quinn smiled abruptly, the expression stretching his face in a way that made Ves more uneasy than reassured. "Of course, few believe in curses these days. No matter. I merely wished to remark that, though books have been stolen from the Ladysmith in the past, none of them have ever been taken directly from the precincts of this library. Isn't that interesting?"

It was just that Ves's past in the rare book trade had made the head librarian suspicious. That was all. The talk of curses was just that— talk. Clearly Mr. Quinn had gone a bit dotty in the head, sitting here in the semi-dark with his skull and his knuckle bones, and his bloody book mounted on the wall.

"Very interesting, sir," Ves agreed, and shut the door behind him.

CHAPTER 4

*A*fter leaving Rune with Mr. Quinn, Sebastian hastened to the small staff room nearby. Irene was just finishing up her cup of tea when he entered.

"I don't like him," Sebastian announced.

Irene arched a brow. "Like who?"

"Vesper Rune, the new binder," he snapped. "We just walked past."

Irene's curiosity turned into a frown. "What's wrong with him?"

Where to start? The man looked more like a prize fighter than a bibliophile. Though a few inches shorter than Sebastian, he probably outweighed him by thirty pounds. The slim line of his suit had shown off Rune's wide shoulders and muscular thighs to good effect.

Rune's features were pleasant, his hair dark brown and his skin olive. Thick lashes framed wary brown eyes. Overall he gave off an air of reserved control. Perhaps he had been a fighter of some sort, or even a soldier; he had that air of discipline about him.

In short, he was far too good looking. But that would sound stupid if he said it aloud, so Sebastian settled on, "It's too soon to hire someone. What if Kelly comes back?"

"Mr. Rune hasn't been hired yet," Irene pointed out. "And he likely won't be. I can't believe Mr. Quinn even considered bringing in an outsider."

Sebastian felt his spirits lift. Still… "You're an outsider."

"I'm an Endicott," she corrected him.

"Even worse."

She shot him a look of annoyance. "My point is, the library holds secrets. Rare books of arcane knowledge, which could be devastating in the wrong hands. Rune probably doesn't even believe in sorcery. And I doubt a random outsider will be willing to take the Librarian's Oath."

"*Widdershins knows its own, in blood and spirit, breath and bone. I swear on my life to defend the library, the town, and the maelstrom,*" Sebastian murmured. It probably *would* sound rather mad to anyone who hadn't been born here, let alone not versed in the arcane arts. "You're probably right."

Irene's gaze became unfocused. "Still…I wonder why Mr. Quinn advertised the position outside of Widdershins? Perhaps he knows something we don't."

Sebastian didn't reply. The head librarian kept his thoughts to himself, so it was impossible to guess whether he was motivated by prophecy, dark knowledge, or whim at any given time. Or perhaps the director or board had suggested hiring from outside Widdershins to expand the pool of talent within the town.

As he mulled it over, footsteps sounded in the hall behind him. Vesper Rune appeared from around the corner, unaccompanied, his expression giving nothing away. "Mr. Rath? Mr. Quinn said you would give me a brief tour of the library, so I'll be ready to start work straightaway in the morning."

Sebastian's heart sank. Bad enough to have seen Kelly laboring behind his mother's desk, but now an outsider would be there. If only Sebastian had done as she wished—

But it was far too late for that now.

"You're hired, then?" Irene asked in surprise.

A frown flickered over Rune's lips, there and gone. "On a trial basis, yes."

"Huh."

Rune lifted a brow at her rudeness. "And you are…?"

"Irene Endicott, Librarian." She thrust out her hand; looking startled, he shook it.

"Vesper Rune," he said, "binder and conservator. At least for the next few months."

Perhaps Kelly would return by then. Sebastian straightened his shoulders. "I'll show you the bindery first."

The door was unprepossessing, with only a brass plaque reading BINDERY AND CONSERVATORY to indicate what lay beyond. Sebastian opened it and led the way into a room much larger than the door would have suggested. Light streamed through the glass dome of the ceiling, as well as the tall windows along one wall. Long tables offered plenty of space to do work, a book press, and other various tools. Cabinets lined the walls, concealing supplies within. There was also a desk and two chairs.

"I'm sure this all seems quaint to you, compared to Boston," Sebastian said as Rune turned in a slow circle, taking it all in. "The Ladysmith handles a much smaller volume of books and periodicals. Many of our acquisitions are quite old, and require conserving in various ways, from repairing tears in pages to rebinding if the damage is too great."

Rune wandered over to the table where the piled periodicals awaited binding. "I'm familiar with the job requirements, Mr. Rath."

Sebastian's cheeks burned. He'd managed to sound as if he questioned the man's intelligence and competence alike. "Of course." He cleared his throat awkwardly. "Ordinarily there isn't so much of a backlog, but the work has been piling up since Mr. O'Neil disappeared."

Rune turned to him in alarm. "Disappeared? I thought he resigned."

Sebastian bit his lip. "He sent a letter of resignation through the post. No one knew he meant to leave until then. His things were gone from his apartment, so presumably he moved elsewhere."

"Without asking for references?" Rune asked dubiously.

Sebastian shrugged. He didn't want to discuss this any further with the man who'd come in to replace Kelly. "If you've seen enough in here, follow me, and I'll give you a brief tour of the rest of the library."

Ves trailed after Rath, keeping his eyes steadily on the back of Rath's blond head, rather than letting his gaze stray to his shoulders or seat. It was easier than it might have been otherwise, since Rath had made it clear he didn't think very highly of Ves.

Gods only knew what had put the man off. Over the years, Ves had come to suspect that some people simply had better instincts. They realized upon meeting that there was something profoundly wrong about him, even if they couldn't put their finger on it. Perhaps Rath was one of those.

The librarian, Miss Endicott, had seemed more curious, even though her manner was rather off-putting. She was clearly one of the "New Women" the newspapers wrung their hands over, with her startling bobbed hair and fashionable clothing. She looked Indian, and her accent was British, though blunted enough to suggest she'd spent some years in America.

Well, it didn't matter what anyone thought of him. He would only be here a short time. Just long enough to memorize the floor plan of the library, replicate it, and pass it off to Fagerlie. What he did with the information was his business; the only thing Ves cared about was having the curse lifted from himself and Noct.

A week from now, they'd be on a train to San Francisco, or Seattle, or Portland. Somewhere out west, where they could start over.

Rath led him past the first line of stacks, and his heart plunged.

He'd expected the task Fagerlie had given him to be easy. The work of a day, maybe two. But this place was *huge.*

Stack after stack of books marched off into the gloom. Even so, a large square room or two would have been easily mappable. Instead, he quickly saw the library seemed to be made up of interconnected rooms, which struck out in directions that made no sense, so that the walls met at bizarre angles. Random shafts of light fell from above, striking tables or shelves seemingly without any planning or thought to convenience. Most of the illumination came from the electric lights, and when they reached a winding ramp, Ves realized they were headed underground.

"What the devil is this place?" he asked, startled. "Surely it can't have been originally intended to be a library."

Rath paused. A distant lamp cast his face half in shadow, giving a sinister cast to his thin smirk. "It's a labyrinth," he said, sounding pleased at Ves's discomfiture. "And yes, it was always meant to be the library."

A labyrinth? Gods of the wood, his task suddenly went from simple to daunting.

"But it makes no sense." Ves gestured vaguely. "Why is it partially underground? The damp and mold must wreak havoc on the books."

"It is *mostly* beneath the ground," Rath corrected. Then he sighed. "Very well. A history lesson, since you don't seem to have familiarized yourself with the founding of our fair institution." Ves stiffened at his tone, but didn't interrupt. "Construction on the museum was completed in 1859. The Ladysmith is the only example of public architecture by Alexander Dromgoole, and the last project he designed before being taken to the State Lunatic Hospital at Taunton. This was before our own Stormhaven Lunatic Asylum was built." Rath paused. "Unfortunately, Stormhaven fell into the sea some years back."

"I...see." Ordinarily such a scandal might be kept quiet, at least within the hallowed halls of the architect's own work, but Rath delivered it as though he expected it to enhance the museum's reputation, rather than the reverse. "So you're saying Dromgoole was losing his grip on reality when designing the museum? But then why did no one simply redraw the plans?"

Rath shrugged. "Mr. Ladysmith was adamant no one alter Dromgoole's work. And as it was his money funding construction, he got his way. It's said Dromgoole's final descent into madness came while working on the library."

That Ves could believe. The layout made less sense the farther they went. Ceilings changed height without warning, what appeared to be nooks turned out to conceal main passageways, and the light was generally so dim that only the addition of reading lamps on the tables offered any hope of actually perusing the books. Before the installation of electricity, they must have relied on lanterns, which seemed a rather hazardous practice for a library.

And everywhere were the books: the shelves overflowed with tomes, pamphlets, and periodicals. There were even books chained to a few of the tables, accompanied by signs suggesting they not be unchained FOR THE SAFETY OF YOURSELF AND OTHER PATRONS.

"The collections are ordered according to area of study," Rath explained as they walked. "Each collection has a specific librarian assigned to it, to aid in research. Do you see that?"

He stopped and pointed at an archway. A small bas-relief crowned it, featuring a rather threatening rabbit. "That is the Natural History of North America collection—well, part of it, it extends to several rooms. But we librarians casually call it the rabbit room. There's the star room, the flower room, the lion room, etc. I assume the library in Boston had a similar organization."

"It did not," Ves assured him.

"Did it at least have a bat room?"

"I…no?"

Rath grinned, showing a flash of good humor previously hidden under his general disapproval of Ves. "Ha! I didn't think so. Let me show it to you."

Confused, Ves followed him to an oversized door. "This room used to be called 'the chimney' because of its shape, but now we just call it the bat room."

Ves understood the comment about the shape as soon as he stepped inside. The narrow width of the room was all out of proportion to its height. It must jut out of the body of the museum like some strange tower. The books were all encased in glass-fronted cabinets, and sturdy iron ladders were set on rails, so they could slide back and forth to reach the books. A door from the upper floor led to a narrow iron spiral staircase. A shallow fountain burbled in the center of the room, and a good many natural tree branches had been nailed at varying heights.

Ves frowned, not understanding, until his gaze reached the shadowy recesses near the ceiling.

"Gods of the wood!" he exclaimed. "Those are bats. You have bats in your library!"

"Big brown bats," Rath said smugly. *Eptesicus fuscus.*

Perhaps disturbed by their voices, one or two of the bats stretched out leathery wings and blinked. One yawned, displaying tiny, sharp teeth. The occasional soft squeak or chirp drifted down, though most of the bats seemed to be sleeping.

"But why?" Ves asked. "That is, they're very cute—they are bats, after all—but surely they don't belong in a library."

"Perhaps in a place like Boston, where people aren't open to unconventional ideas. Mr. Quinn read an article, oh, three or four years ago about two libraries in Portugal that have had bats living in them since the 1700s." Rath smiled up at the bats. "They eat insects, you see. Beetles, moths, all sorts of things you don't want chewing up books. They live in here during the day—this is the American History Collection by the way—and at night we put canvas covers on the furniture, leave the door open, and let them do what bats do best. They return of their own accord by morning, though if one or two remain in the stacks during the day no one truly cares. The junior librarians are tasked with cleaning the bat room each day, so in a way I'm glad they weren't here when I first began. Come along."

He walked out, as though he'd said nothing extraordinary at all, and Ves scrambled to follow him. Had he just been hired by a library or a madhouse?

The rest of tour was as normal as it could be, given the structure of the labyrinthine place. "The rarest of the books are kept here, under lock and key," Rath said at last, when they'd reached what Rune hoped was the most remote of the rooms. The shelves here were all against the walls, with each bookcase bearing a locked grate of iron bars to prevent their removal. Ves stepped closer, peering through the bars. Most of them bore no titles on the spine, but he glimpsed Von Junzt's *Nameless Cults* in the original German edition, alongside *De Vermis Mysteriis* by Ludvig Prinn.

Ves's skin prickled. Doubtless the librarians assumed these to be nothing more than valuable rare books, but to him it was a staggering collection of the darkest tomes of sorcery and madness. Necromancy, the secrets of the arcane arts, the truth of the things humanity shared its world with…all of it was here.

His mother would have done literal murder to get her hands on these. They'd made do with Dee's English translation of *Al Azif,* half a copy of *Cultes des Goules,* and a version of *Livre d'Eibon* patched together from copies written in Greek and Latin. Most of those had been in terrible shape; charred or water-stained, or simply falling apart from centuries of use.

That was how he'd learned his art, first by watching his grandfather, then taking over from him when Grandfather's arthritis grew too bad and his eyesight too poor. Removing broken covers and replacing them with new, stitching partial manuscripts into a whole, painstakingly wiping away stains and repairing tears…

It had been one of the few things that had brought him moments of joy. One of the few things he could actually do well, without fear of constant berating. He'd failed Mother and Grandfather in every other way, so it had been nice to have something to cling to, to feel proud of.

"Mr. Rune?" Rath asked.

Ves realized he'd been staring blankly at the books. Heat rose to his face. "Forgive me. I was wool-gathering."

Rath's gaze sharpened. "Do you recognize some of the titles? I thought the Boston Public Library had no interest in such…subjects."

Could Rath know the truth about the world? Mother had divided humanity into sorcerers and sleepers. The first were worth paying attention to; the rest were unworthy, ignorant. Asleep with their eyes open.

"One of my friends worked in the reading room," Ves lied. He couldn't afford to have friends. "He'd occasionally get odd requests, and I thought I recalled that book on cults as one of them."

It sounded reasonable, at least. After a moment, Rath's shoulders relaxed. "I see. Given the rarity of these tomes, we obviously don't make them available to just any visiting scholar who manages to obtain a pass."

"Is there much demand?"

The corner of Rath's mouth quirked. "You'd be surprised." He turned to the door. "That concludes the tour. Unless you have any specific questions, I should return to my own duties."

Ves had plenty of questions, beginning with, *is everyone here insane?* But that would only draw unwanted attention. "I look forward to working with you," he said instead.

Rath glanced back over his shoulder, his hazel eyes cool. "I'll see you in the morning," he replied, rather than offer the same sentiment in return.

Prick.

Ves followed him silently back through the labyrinth. He'd wondered why Fagerlie went to all the trouble of hiring him to map out a floor plan of the library, but now he thought he understood.

Fagerlie must want the books of sorcery in the final room. He'd pose as a visiting scholar, perhaps bring a friend with him. They'd slip away into the stacks, find the restricted room, and pick the locks. Then they'd either smuggle a few selected books out under their coats, or one of them would hide until after closing, let a gang in through a side door, and make off with the entire lot.

Either way, it didn't concern Ves. He and Noct would be away from Widdershins by then. Though it would have been amusing to see the look on Fagerlie's face when he found out about the library bats.

CHAPTER 5

That evening after work, Sebastian took the trolley to Kelly's apartment building. Or to what had been his apartment building, before he vanished.

No one else took Kelly's departure seriously, but Sebastian had been uneasy from the start. He'd come here the day after Mr. Quinn announced he received Kelly's resignation letter, hoping to talk some sense into the man. Kelly was already gone, though, and the landlady said his things were cleaned out and the key returned via the post. She hadn't seemed particularly worried, and so Sebastian had left without asking further.

He should have come back again before now. Started looking into the disappearance on his own, instead of just hoping Kelly would send word, or maybe even reappear one day.

But now Kelly's position had been given to someone else. Sebastian had waited too long.

The tour with Mr. Rune had left him uneasy. The fellow had been far too interested in the books in the restricted section. Possibly his curiosity was simply that of a man who professionally conserved old tomes…or he might not be as ignorant of the arcane arts as Sebastian and Irene had assumed.

This was what came of hiring outsiders. It was impossible to guess their motives.

The soft light of the stacks had flattered Rune. Brought out the glow of his olive skin and cast the shadows of his thick, long lashes over his cheekbones. His unoiled hair had looked soft, and Sebastian had felt a sudden impulse to run his hands through it.

His blood quickened, and Sebastian bit his lip, hoping a flash of pain would quell the beginnings of arousal. There was something about Rune that Sebastian couldn't put his finger on, something beyond mere good looks, that drew him like an iron filing to a magnet. Which was absurd; he barely knew the fellow. Besides, Sebastian was going to find Kelly. Then Kelly would come back, and Rune would leave, and everything would be as normal as it could be.

God.

He climbed off the trolley at the corner of Merry Cat Lane, just before it reached the commercial district along River Street. The lane was lined with apartment buildings catering to families saving to buy their own houses, and bachelors whose salary was meant to support a wife and children. Kelly had lived in one of the newer buildings, constructed only two years previously in 1908, on the site of an older building destroyed during the Dark Days.

Yet another thing Rune wouldn't understand. The world had nearly ended in 1902, and the force that meant to destroy it had converged on Widdershins. The librarians had been on the frontlines of the fight to save humanity.

Well, most of the librarians. Sebastian himself hadn't. When he should have been fighting by the sides of his fellow librarians, he'd been healing from a broken leg in the basement of a house in Boston, bored out of his mind.

Sebastian entered the apartment building, pausing to hold the door open for a young woman whose hat was so large it barely fit through the entryway. Irene would be jealous.

His shoes tapped softly on the marble floor as he crossed the lobby, past the mailboxes and telephone, to the landlady's apartment.

She failed to answer his knock. No light showed beneath the door; she must be out for the evening.

Blast. He'd hoped to gain entrance to the apartment himself, assuming it hadn't been let out yet. He glanced up the stairs, then shrugged. Time for the direct approach.

Kelly had lived in apartment 4A, on the second floor. A knock on this door brought the sound of footsteps almost immediately.

Sebastian's heart fell; he shouldn't have expected it to still be empty months after Kelly vacated so abruptly. The door swung open, revealing a short man dressed like a clerk, a look of irritation stamped on his features. "What do you want?"

Sebastian pressed his lips together at the man's rude greeting, but kept his own voice calm. "Pardon me for disturbing you. I'm Sebastian Rath; my friend Kelly O'Neil rented this apartment before you. I wanted to know—"

"The landlady has his mail," the man interrupted. "I don't want it."

"His mail?"

"Yes, his mail. Bills, mostly. I guess he didn't want to let any creditors know where he was going." The man's lip lifted in a sneer. "So if you're here to collect, you're out of luck, because I'm not paying another man's debts."

He started to shut the door, but Sebastian grabbed it before it swung closed. "I was just wondering if you found anything in the apartment when you moved in."

The new tenant's eyes narrowed suspiciously. "Like what?"

"I...I don't know. Personal effects. A diary. A button torn from a coat during a struggle. Bloodstains—"

"Bloodstains!" the man exclaimed. "The landlady said he just moved! Was he murdered? I'm not living with a ghost—"

"No, no," Sebastian said hastily. "At least, I don't think so. I'm just trying to find him."

"Well, I don't know where he is." With that, the door shut firmly, though Sebastian thought he heard the man muttering about ghosts as he threw the lock.

Sebastian's shoulders slumped. Well, that had been spectacularly unhelpful. Maybe he ought to hire a private detective, since he clearly wasn't one himself. How much did their services cost?

"You looking for Mr. O'Neil, then?" asked a voice. The door to 4B had swung open at some point while he questioned the new tenant, and a red-faced woman with a baby in her arms leaned out.

"Yes." Sebastian turned to her. "I'm Sebastian Rath."

"Mrs. Pickman. Come inside to talk—I've got something on the stove."

The apartment was crowded with children, toys, scattered clothing, newspapers, and furniture. Mrs. Pickman navigated her way through with the ease of long practice, pausing only long enough to put the baby in a cradle just outside the tiny kitchen. Though all the windows were open to allow the May breeze to enter, the heat and steam from the stove turned the air close and damp.

"Do you know where Mr. O'Neil went?" Sebastian asked as he followed her to the kitchen. "He was a friend of mine, and I'm trying to find him."

She picked up a wooden spoon and stirred the pot on the stove. The scents of beef and cabbage wafted from the pot, and Sebastian's stomach reminded him he hadn't eaten since lunch.

"That I don't know," she said as she stirred.

Sebastian's heart sank. "Oh."

"But there was something odd about the way he moved out."

He took an involuntary step forward. "What happened?"

She glanced over her shoulder at him. "I wouldn't call Mr. O'Neil a friend, exactly, but he was a good neighbor to us. Over for dinner every now and then, and he'd watch the little ones if I needed to pop out for a moment. So when I heard a lot of thumping coming from his apartment one night, I went to see what was going on."

Mrs. Pickman stopped stirring and turned to him. "I was still expecting little Betsy, there," she said, nodding to the baby in its crib. "Close to my time, and she loved to kick, so I didn't sleep much the last few weeks with her. That's the only reason I heard the noise. I thought it was strange, so I waddled out into the hall, meaning to knock on Mr. O'Neil's door and make sure everything was all right. Instead I find the door propped open and two men taking everything out in boxes. I demanded to know what they were about, and one of them said Mr. O'Neil had moved and they were collecting his things."

Sebastian frowned. "In the middle of the night?"

"That's what I said." She pointed the wooden spoon at him. "It was gone three in the morning then, and I've yet to hear of a hauling company that works those hours. But the bigger of the two told me to mind my own business if I didn't want a smack."

"He threatened a pregnant woman?"

"Can you believe it?" She grinned suddenly. "So I made a sign as soon as his back was turned, and he dropped a box on his foot before he made it out the front door." Her smile faded. "I asked the landlady the next morning about it, and she said all she knew was that Mr. O'Neil had paid his rent for the month and anything else was none of her concern."

"I see." Sebastian didn't like the sound of any of this. "And you had no warning he was moving out?"

"None at all. I'd last seen him that very morning, in fact. We spoke about the Daylight Comet, so you'd think he would have mentioned leaving if he intended it." She shrugged. "Sorry I can't tell you more."

"You've been very helpful," he assured her. "Thank you for your time, Mrs. Pickman." He took out his card and handed it to her. "If anything else of interest occurs to you, please telephone or send word to me at the Ladysmith."

Once back out on the street, Sebastian walked slowly toward the trolley stop, his hands tucked into his pockets. The sun lingered in the west, and the air smelled of coal smoke, fish, and the ocean. Technically, nothing Mrs. Pickman had told him was absolute proof that Kelly hadn't left of his own volition. His rent had been paid, his furniture removed, and his letter of resignation mailed. One could easily argue that everything Sebastian had learned was in fact evidence Kelly left of his own accord, even if he'd done so rather abruptly.

It was the abruptness that made no sense. Arthur said Kelly had spoken to him about leaving—but why hadn't he said anything to Sebastian? And why wouldn't he mention his departure to his neighbor?

Of course it was possible that Kelly had decided to leave between speaking to Mrs. Pickman in the morning and the time the movers took his things that night. Possible, but not plausible. Kelly had been careful, meticulous. He was a planner, not someone given to sudden whims. It was what had made him good at his job.

Sebastian tightened his jaw. He was more certain now than ever that something bad had happened to Kelly. And, since it seemed no one else intended to help, it was up to him to find out what.

CHAPTER 6

*E*arly next morning, Ves walked to a café near the museum. Halley's Comet burned in the dawn sky like a distant, angry eye. Strange to think that something so far away could influence the arcane workings of the earth.

As he walked, he pondered what Mr. Rath had said about the former binder—O'Neil, wasn't it?—who he seemed to think had disappeared. It was quite possible the fellow had simply gotten fed up with his life and job, abandoned his post, and moved away. Or he might have stolen something.

O'Neil wouldn't be the first to commit such a crime. While Ves was at the library in Boston, one of the librarians had been caught smuggling a rare first edition out beneath his coat. When police went to his apartment, they'd found it full of other volumes the man had taken, awaiting a contact from the New York book trade to come fetch them. In the end, the librarian had confessed to stealing hundreds of valuable books over the last five years.

Perhaps O'Neil had taken a book whose absence would be noticed sooner rather than later, and had left town with it accordingly. Maybe Rath knew, or suspected, or was even in on the scheme. It would explain why the archivist seemed so disgruntled with Ves coming in as a replacement. He didn't want to risk inviting a stranger to join him in stealing from their employer.

There was one other possibility, of course. Fagerlie wanted a man inside the Ladysmith Library. And not just any man; one who would be motivated to do whatever Fagerlie wanted, without asking too many questions himself. Ves was a binder and conservator, so that was the position the library would need to fill.

Surely he was just being paranoid. The rare book trade was often cut-throat in the metaphorical sense, but not the literal. Though Fagerlie was a sorcerer; clearly he wanted access to some awful tome that resided deep within the Ladysmith.

Still, that didn't make him a murderer. Noct was a sorcerer as well, after all.

Once inside the café, Ves ordered a coffee and pastry, then went to a table with a man sitting alone at it.

The man held a paper in front of him. His hair and mustache were both iron-gray, as was his suit. At a glance, he looked like nothing more than a perfectly ordinary, even boring, man exiting middle age: comfortable waistline, gold pocket watch, and all. His hair, which had been long enough to pull back into a tail the last time Ves had seen him, was short and trim now.

"Mr. Fagerlie," Ves said in greeting as he sipped his coffee.

Fagerlie didn't put down his newspaper. "It says here a man died by suicide, due to his fear of the comet's approach."

Ves took a bite of the pastry. The taste of fresh strawberries burst on his tongue, wrapped within layers of dough. "That's a shame."

"He was a fool." Fagerlie lowered the paper to peer at Ves above it. "Comets herald the deaths of kings, not bankers from Ohio." He paused. "In other cases, of course, they predict victory. The same comet that we can see in the sky this morning watched over William the Conqueror's conquest of England."

And the subjugation of the people already living there. But Ves didn't say that aloud. Mother would never have tolerated such talk, and he doubted Fagerlie would be any more sympathetic.

"I start my new position this morning," he said. "So I can't linger for long. I'd like to get an early start."

Fagerlie finally put the newspaper aside. "Well done, my boy," he said with an avuncular smile. "I knew you could do it."

"The job isn't as simple as you would have had me believe," Ves said. "The library is a…a maze. A labyrinth. It's going to take a while for me to accurately reproduce the floor plan."

Fagerlie sat back, smile still in place. "If it was the few rooms of some county library, I wouldn't have needed a man on the inside to map it, would I?"

Ves ground his teeth together. A warning would have been useful, some sort of idea what he was agreeing to…but it was too late to argue now. Instead he said, "Do you want the rooms labeled as to their function?"

"Not necessary. Just bring me the map, and I'll take care of the rest." Fagerlie sipped his coffee. "Don't worry. Do your part of the job, and in six days' time the comet—and I—will set you free."

Morning light streamed through the glass dome that formed the bindery's ceiling. After Ves's tour of the library the day before, unless there was some hidden nook he hadn't seen—likely—the bindery was the best-lit room in the place.

It seemed wrong, somehow. Surely a monster like himself should be relegated to some dark corner, hidden away and unseen. The bindery was too bright, too beautiful.

If Mr. Quinn knew what he'd hired, he'd run screaming. They all would.

A piece of paper awaited on the blotter of his new desk. Ves picked it up and unfolded it to reveal a few typed lines.

Mr. Rune,

Your presence is unwelcome here. Leave while you still can.

"The devil?" he murmured aloud. His first thought was that he'd stumbled into particularly vicious intra-office politics. Or that someone was playing a joke on him. Except Rath had said Ves's predecessor disappeared.

Then again, it seemed likely Rath himself had left the note, given his animosity.

Ves crumpled the note and tossed it into the wastepaper basket. He'd be gone in less than a week. It hardly mattered that someone had taken an immediate dislike to him.

He set about familiarizing himself with the workroom, relieved when he discovered his predecessor had kept the place neatly. Ves picked up one of the books awaiting rebinding and opened it. Inside the front cover was the library's bookplate: *Nathaniel R. Ladysmith Museum Library* in a banner above an engraving of a book and skull. Beneath, a smaller banner read: *W.K.I.O.*

The title page bore an embossed seal with a similar design. The final blank page at the back of the book had been stamped with a simple ink stamp of the library's name. No doubt there were tiny marks in pencil on specific pages as well, a final check to identify stolen books.

The bookplate could be steamed off. A skillful hand could smooth away the embossed seal using a hot iron and patience. Javelle water would remove the stamp, and if it left behind a spot that looked suspiciously clean, a bit of tobacco juice or tea would return the stain. As an employee of the library, O'Neil would know exactly which pages were marked with pencil, so it wasn't even a matter of patience to find and remove those.

"Settling in, Mr. Rune?" Rath asked from the doorway.

Ves started. The sunlight through the glass dome turned Rath's hair to gold, and sparked off his silver-framed glasses. He wore a blue vest whose color brought out the hidden sapphire in his hazel eyes, and held a battered book that looked rather the worse for wear.

Had he been the one to leave the ominous note? "Yes," Ves answered, careful to keep any emotion from his face. "Thank you, Mr. Rath."

Rath snorted but made no further comment, only carrying the

book over to one of the tables. "This is the personal diary of Glen Parry, a man from Widdershins who fought in the Revolutionary War. An invaluable account we were recently fortunate enough to acquire from his family. As you can see it is very badly in need of repair." His fingers lingered a moment on the mildewed cover; they were long and elegant, the opposite of Ves's own broad, blunt hands.

"Of course. Is there any urgency?" Ves asked.

"Dr. Norris of the American History Department wishes to examine it as soon as possible, and I fear his rough handling will cause further damage if he receives it in this condition."

Rath's eyes met his as he spoke, and Ves understood this was a test. Rath didn't seem to believe he could do an adequate job at repairing this crumbling, damaged volume with its signatures falling out and its cover ruined.

He'd definitely been the one to leave the note.

What Rath didn't know was that Ves's entire life had been a series of tests. And yes, he'd failed so, so many. But this he could do.

"I understand," Ves said, letting a feral edge slip into his smile. "You may count on me, Mr. Rath."

Ves's grandfather had taught him that the art of binding wasn't merely concerned with basic repair or replacement, but beauty as well. There was nothing quite so satisfying as beginning with a stack of loose folios and ending with a handsome volume.

He examined the diary Rath had left with him with a careful eye. Its condition was indeed poor. What sort of barbarians had let a book reach this state of deterioration? A good thing it had come to the library, where it would be treated with the respect it deserved.

The rot-damaged cover would need replacing. As the work within was one-of-a-kind, he decided to favor the most durable materials at hand: morocco leather, dyed red with cochineal, half-bound with cloth, and vellum corners.

Though the library bindery had all the needed tools at hand, Ves had brought his own small kit with him as well, wrapped in a leather pouch. The awl, needle, thread, binder's knife, and bone folder had all been gifts from Grandfather, and the only mementos he'd taken from his childhood home.

He removed the signatures from the old binding with his knife, marking them alphabetically near the fold with a soft pencil so as not to confuse their order. After, he went through them carefully, removing any bits of cut thread and separating the sheets. Torn pages were mended with application of paste and thin onion-skin paper on either side of the leaf. Some pages were sadly mildewed in places, so he prepared a solution of oxalic acid and washed them with a damp sponge, followed by a solution of dilute hydrochloric acid and a rinse in cold water, before placing them to dry.

The motions of his art soothed him, and for a few hours all worry vanished. At lunchtime, Ves left the bindery behind and made his way to the library proper. Miss Endicott stood behind the desk near the entrance, her expression rather fixed. The man across from her looked as though he counted his age in the triple digits, but his reedy voice carried in the silence.

"The cover was green," he said.

Miss Endicott's smile grew a trifle strained. "Our periodicals are generally bound in green half-calf. Can you recall anything further?"

He nodded, his few remaining wisps of white hair bobbing in time with his skull. "Oh yes. It had the word 'journal' in the title."

Which narrowed it down to one of several hundred potential publications that Ves was familiar with, having handled their binding in Boston.

"The *Journal of Research on the Lepidoptera?*" Miss Endicott suggested.

"No, no, it was outside my normal field of study," the old man said. "I don't recall the exact subject, but it looked very intriguing."

"Do you recall the volume number?" she asked with increasing desperation. "The issue? The year?"

"I'm afraid not."

Her smile had become a rictus. "I shall look into the matter, and send the journal along when I find it, Dr. Leavitt."

Dr. Leavitt tottered off. Miss Endicott sighed and glanced over at

Ves. "The exciting life of a librarian. I hope your day is proving more fruitful?"

"It is, thank you." He inclined his head and was about to continue on his way, when she spoke again.

"Would you like to join us for lunch? A group of us are going to Marsh's. It's a little restaurant a short walk from the museum—cheap, but the food is good, especially if you like fish."

Would Mr. Rath be among those dining out? Not that it mattered —Ves didn't socialize with anyone, ever. His enforced work ethic had endeared him to his supervisors, though never to his fellow employees. "I brought something from home," he said. "I thought to take the opportunity to stretch my legs and familiarize myself with the library beyond the bindery."

"Suit yourself," Miss Endicott said with a shrug.

To his surprise, Ves felt a pang. Miss Endicott seemed nice enough, even if she was Rath's friend. What was her story? How had she come to these shores and found herself working at the Ladysmith? She seemed as though she'd be interesting to talk to; doubtless she'd seen so much more of the world than Ves had.

He tamped down on his curiosity. He'd see the world for himself soon enough, once he had the map in hand and the comet overhead. Everything else was just a distraction.

Once Ves was farther into the stacks and out of Miss Endicott's sight, he took out a small notebook. He counted off steps in his head and made a rough sketch of the room he was in, then proceeded to the next one. It would take far more than one lunch hour to complete the map, though hopefully he could stay late on Saturday and make good progress. If anyone asked what he was doing, he'd simply pretend a fascination with architecture.

It was odd Fagerlie hadn't been able to find any floor plans of the library on his own, now that Ves considered the matter. He'd assured Ves that he'd checked city hall, but any architectural drawings that had originally been submitted were either lost or destroyed. Even so, given how utterly unique the structure of the library seemed to be, it was odd no architectural magazine or journal had taken any interest in it.

Then again, perhaps the architect—what had Rath said his name was? Dromgoole? Perhaps Dromgoole simply wasn't well known enough to catch anyone's attention. The library was closed to the public, allowing only museum staff and visiting scholars, so likely it was simply obscure.

Even after his tour of the day before, not to mention the map he was making, Ves got lost twice in fifteen minutes. The rooms met at disorienting angles, and archways that seemed like they ought to lead to a specific chamber failed to do so. Sound traveled oddly as well, voices echoing from distant parts of the library. Once, a set of footsteps approached; Ves paused in his work and waited for the walker to appear, only to have the steps fade away before reaching him. All in all, the effect straddled the line between unsettling and intriguing.

"Binder," whispered a voice in his ear.

Ves came to an abrupt halt. The room he was in was marked by the bas-relief of a disgruntled sheep and seemed to house the Astronomy and Physics Collection. A feather duster sat on a reading table, abandoned when some librarian halted the eternal battle against dust to go to lunch. There didn't seem to be anyone in the room with him.

"Hello?" he asked uncertainly.

No one replied. And now that he thought back, he wasn't entirely certain it was a voice after all. Perhaps it had only been an odd creak, some noise of the foundations settling.

Perhaps. But his earliest memories were of the woods, or the force that lived in them, whispering to him in something other than words. A voiceless language, spoken in the wind through the branches, the piping of frogs. Those whispers had comforted him, curled around him and allowed him to sleep.

There was no comfort in this whisper. And just as the presence of the All-Mother, the Black Goat of the Woods, had walked in the forest outside of Dunhollow, perhaps something walked here.

Or it could be a flight of fancy. He put his notebook away and rubbed his eyes. It was time to return to the bindery for the afternoon. If he was lucky, he might be able to stay a bit past closing and sketch some more. The bats would be interesting to watch as they went about their work.

Though that would mean being in the library alone. After hours.

The thought shouldn't have made his skin crawl. He was the most frightening thing here, after all.

Even so, perhaps he'd hold off. See how much he could get done during the day. If his time grew short, of course he'd stay late, but until then it might be best to keep more regular hours. It would be less suspicious, anyway.

Not entirely satisfied with his reasoning, Ves turned and hurried back the way he'd come.

CHAPTER 7

That evening, Sebastian returned to the apartment house where Kelly had lived. His hopes to speak to the landlady and either collect Kelly's mail, or discover if he'd left a forwarding address, were dashed when he discovered she was still out. In desperation, he wrote a note to contact him at the Ladysmith and slipped it beneath her door. He probably should have left one the last time he visited, but he'd hoped to be able to speak to the woman directly.

As he boarded the trolley, two men dressed in plain workman's clothes jumped on so close behind him, one clipped Sebastian's heels. Sebastian reflexively murmured an apology, even though it hadn't been his fault, and found a seat near the front.

It hadn't been easy seeing Mr. Rune in Kelly's place, using techniques that were surely inferior to those Sebastian's mother had taught her apprentice. Ordinarily, satisfying the whims of the American History Department was considered the lowest of priorities in the library, but the diary had given him an excuse to test Mr. Rune's mettle. The fellow would surely botch the job somehow, and Rath could present it to Mr. Quinn. Mr. Quinn would let Rune go after his trial period was up if not before, and then…

Sebastian changed trolley lines at River Street. What outcome was he actually hoping for? If Rune left, it wouldn't magically bring Kelly back from wherever he'd gone.

It wouldn't bring his mother back from the dead.

Sebastian took off his glasses and cleaned the lenses with his handkerchief. Mr. Quinn would just hire someone else. Maybe even another outsider.

If he could just *find* Kelly, at least then he'd know. He couldn't believe the man had just up and left without notice.

Or possibly he just didn't want to believe it.

The trolley arrived at Sebastian's stop. He climbed off and started down the tree-shaded road that would take him to Bonnie's house. It was only the scuff of a shoe that made him look back over his shoulder and spot the same two men who had gotten on behind him back at the stop near the apartment. Apparently, they changed trolley lines at the same time as he did without his notice.

And now they were walking down the same street.

It might be coincidence. Most likely they were perfectly ordinary fellows going about their business, and he was being paranoid to even consider they could be following him. Likely they'd be deeply offended if they knew his thoughts.

The sidewalk was deserted now, except for them. And the men began to walk faster.

Sebastian broke into a run.

"He spotted us!" one of them yelled, dashing Sebastian's last hope of simple paranoia.

He bolted down sidewalks cracked by the roots of old trees, his heart pounding in his throat. He had to get to safety—but he couldn't lead them to Bonnie's house. If the men knew where he lived, it would put the rest of his family in danger.

He ran blindly, unsure where to go. Their feet pounded on the sidewalk behind him, but neither called for him to stop. That alone chilled him to the bone.

What did they meant to do with him when they caught him? And catch him they would. Already his lungs burned; Sebastian had never so much as set foot inside a gymnasium, while both of these men looked as though they worked with their muscles for a living.

Perhaps he could throw them off with a sudden turn. He darted down another street at the next crossroads, hoping to encounter someone he could call out to for help. No such friendly strangers appeared, but he spotted a narrow lane between two houses—an unused carriageway perhaps. If he could duck down it, maybe he'd find somewhere to hide.

Sebastian rushed into the lane—and ran full tilt into an unyielding body.

❦

Ves stared down at Sebastian Rath in shock. He'd stepped out into the lane for just a moment, hoping to get a breath of air without having to socialize with his fellow boarders, who had collected on the back porch for a game of cards. He'd barely taken two steps before Mr. Rath plowed into him at a full run.

The collision didn't so much as rock Ves on his heels, but Rath bounced off Ves's chest and fell to the ground. "No!" he cried out, flinging one hand up as if to ward him off. Then he blinked, hazel eyes wide behind his spectacles. "Mr. Rune?"

Something had frightened the man, that was clear enough. "What's wrong?" Ves asked.

"Two men—following me—"

Ves stepped past Rath and onto the side walk, just as the men in question reached the lane. They both seemed slightly out of breath, and one hung onto his crusher hat to keep it from blowing off his head. Both pulled up suddenly at the sight of Ves's imposing figure.

"Can I be of assistance, gentlemen?" Ves asked, folding his arms over his chest. Though he wasn't especially tall, Ves knew his build usually caused people to hesitate before crossing him.

"You see a man run through there?" the one with the hat demanded, pointing at the lane.

Ves arched a brow and hoped Rath had the sense to stay back out of sight. "A man? You'll have to be more specific than that."

The other glowered, no doubt realizing Ves was deliberately

playing the fool. "Glasses, blue vest. Looks bent, if you take my meaning."

"I haven't seen him," Ves said.

It was an obvious lie, but delivered with such conviction the men hesitated. Now they had to make a decision: either pretend to believe Ves and depart, or start in with the threats. The skin along either side of his spine rippled, his vision expanded, and he silently prayed to gods he no longer worshipped that they were wise enough to leave.

A burst of laughter sounded from the card players. The realization that Ves could call for help seemed to decide them. Both men glared at him, but turned and slunk back the way they'd come. Ves watched them until they turned the corner.

"Thank you," Rath said shakily. "You didn't have to do that."

Rath was right. In fact, it had been incredibly stupid of Ves to get involved. If the men had decided to escalate the confrontation—if they'd brought out a weapon and attacked Ves—

Well. It would have quickly become obvious that he wasn't nearly as human as he pretended to be.

Then he would have been the one on the run. Not that he doubted his ability to get away, but then he would never be able to show his face in Widdershins again. He couldn't do Fagerlie the favor he'd promised, and his one chance at lifting the curse would be gone.

Bad enough he might have ruined his own life, but he would have destroyed Noct's too. He'd been a fool. An idiot. He should have left Rath to whatever mess he'd gotten himself into.

But it was hard to truly regret his actions with Rath looking at him with something akin to admiration. Nothing bad had happened; so as long as he was more careful from here on out, there was no harm done.

Ves shrugged uncomfortably. "They looked as though they meant to give you a beating." He paused. "A sentiment you're likely used to inspiring in others."

Rath gaped at him for a moment—then laughed. "To be honest, I'm normally a very nice fellow."

"So the problem is with my face in particular?"

"I…no." Rath took off his spectacles and rubbed his hand over his eyes. Then he put them back on and looked down at Ves with a wry expression. "It's a very nice face, actually."

Ves's heartbeat sped up again, albeit for a very different reason than before. Rath's cheeks were flushed from the chase, his hair disheveled. He might look similar if passion had quickened his breath rather than fear.

Ves shoved the thought away roughly. "Then why the less than warm welcome? The note you left on my desk?"

He regretted the words as soon as they were out. He wasn't here to make friends.

Rath's expression was one of genuine puzzlement. "Note? What note?"

"The one telling me to leave before it's too late," Ves said, suddenly no longer sure Rath had been behind it after all. "I assumed it was from you."

"No. It wasn't." Rath shook his head in confusion. "That's...troubling." He squared his shoulders. "I can see why you might think I left it, though. I've been less than welcoming. I owe you an explanation, since you were kind enough to save me just now. But not here. Would you care to go for a drink? Or do you have a room here?"

Ves didn't go out for drinks. But he couldn't imagine Rath's reaction if they went up to the room and he saw the mirrors turned to the walls. Ves wouldn't be able to explain.

Of course, he could simply tell Rath to go to hell and leave him here in the lane. He had no further obligation to the archivist.

But he was curious. Why were the men chasing Rath? And why had Rath seemingly changed his mind about Ves?

And if Rath hadn't left the note, who else didn't want a new employee working in the bindery?

He'd satisfy his curiosity, then leave. Surely no harm could come from one drink.

"I'm not familiar with the bars in the area," he said. "So I'll allow you to lead the way."

"Here we are," Rath said, setting two beers down at the corner table where Ves awaited him.

Ves had never been in a bar before, though of course he didn't admit that to Rath. He'd read about them, though, and The Silver Key didn't seem far off from the descriptions in books.

Life in the cult had been circumscribed, all knowledge controlled. Since leaving, Ves and Noct had both read voraciously, absorbing everything from Homer to Dickens to the latest pulps. But their lives had by necessity remained narrow, confined only to each other's company. Ves normally went no farther afield than work or the grocers.

So he looked around now with avid eyes, comparing reality with illustrations from the pulps. A long bar, its surface sheathed in gleaming copper, ran along one wall. Tables crowded most of the remaining area; the clusters of folk around them looked to be mainly clerks and shop workers of various sorts, interspersed with a few men in rough overalls. A young woman in the opposite corner hunched over a sketchbook, her table littered with pastels and charcoals, her hand flying over the paper. The smell of spilled beer and fried fish hung in the air.

"Thank you, Mr. Rath," Ves said a bit stiffly. He lifted his glass and took a tiny sip, before setting it back down. The beer was good—too good. He had to be careful not to get carried away and drink too much.

Rath sat down across from him. "Call me Sebastian, please. You did save my skin, after all."

Bands tightened around Ves's chest. This encounter suddenly felt far more dangerous than the one with the ruffians. What had he been thinking to come here?

He ought to be rude. Brush off Rath's unexpected attempt at friendliness. Get up and leave, and forget about finding out what was going on. It was none of his business, surely.

But he would be gone in a few days. Surely there could be no harm in enjoying a single drink in a bar, or calling the handsome archivist by his first name.

"Vesper," he said. "Or Ves, if you prefer."

"Ves," Rath—Sebastian—said with a pleased smile, so different from the chilly demeanor he'd shown at work.

Ves took another sip of his beer. "Are you going to tell me why those men were after you?"

Sebastian glanced around, as though reassuring himself they couldn't be easily overheard above the murmur of voices all around. The silver rims of his glasses glinted in the dim lighting. "I should probably begin with an apology. As you said, I haven't been exactly welcoming."

Ves shrugged. "I came to work, not to make friends."

The crease between Sebastian's brows suggested Ves had been a bit too candid. "Still, I might have been kinder. We don't have many outsiders among the librarians."

"Outsiders?"

"People not born in Widdershins. Not to suggest we have some sort of prejudice against them," Sebastian added hastily. "Outsiders come to the city often. Many leave after a short time, but some find a true home here."

"A man on the train ride here warned me against the town," Ves said, just to see Sebastian's reaction. "He said something along the lines of the inhabitants obeying the laws of neither God nor man."

Rather than take offense, Sebastian laughed aloud. "He isn't wrong, exactly. Surely there are some laws you care to flout?"

Ves's entire body warmed. He focused on the taps behind the bar, rather than Sebastian's face. "What does this have to do with why those men were chasing you?"

"Ah. Yes." Sebastian's hazel eyes shaded toward gray as he frowned. "Indulge me in a bit of history, if you will. My family have been the binders and conservators for the Ladysmith library since the Civil War. First my great-uncle, then my mother. She expected me to follow in her footsteps, since I'd wanted to work in the library from childhood on. I chose not to."

The statement was simple, but from the regret in Sebastian's voice, Ves suspected it papered over a chasm of pain.

He trained his gaze on his beer, to avoid Sebastian's gaze. "I did something similar. My family had my entire life planned out for me from the moment I was born. Even though I never wanted it, I still sometimes feel as though I let them down."

"Perhaps you understand, then." Sebastian spread his hands ruefully. "I tried, but I never had the talent. Or, to be honest, the interest. I'm perfectly happy combing through dusty old records, peering at some dead man's terrible handwriting in an attempt to assess a document's importance. But ask me to discuss proper margin width and I'm bored to tears."

Ves drew himself up in shock. "But maintaining the correct margin width for the text is of utmost importance, especially in rebinding! I know some binders commit the atrocity of bleeding pages willy-nilly, so as to have paper scrap to sell, but you will never catch me doing so."

"Er, yes," Sebastian said, seeming a bit taken aback. "I must say, I didn't realize you had so much hidden passion."

Heat crept into Ves's cheeks, and he hastily drank some more of his beer. "Forgive me."

"Not at all. It's good to see a man so invested in his work." Sebastian lifted his own glass in a salute. "When Mother realized I was devoting myself to archival studies and no words of hers would dissuade me, she found someone far more motivated than I to join her in the bindery. Kelly O'Neil."

Unease touched Ves, like a cold breath on his neck. "The man you said disappeared. The one who resigned abruptly without asking for references for his next position."

Sebastian nodded. All the humor was gone from his expression now. "Indeed. He took over when my mother died. It seemed odd that he left, let alone mailed his resignation to Mr. Quinn rather than facing the head librarian himself."

Having met Mr. Quinn, Ves was less certain of that. He seemed the type to view finding a new job as an abandonment rather than a natural progression.

Ves listened attentively while Sebastian outlined his own quest to find out what had become of O'Neil. His first reaction was that the archivist was simply letting his own emotions cloud his judgment. Mrs. Rath had trained Mr. O'Neil when Sebastian refused to become a binder; surely it was his own guilt over not obeying the dead woman's wishes that had caused him such distress when O'Neil left. But Ves's unease grew stronger as Sebastian told him of the strange midnight removal of furniture, then of the two men who had followed him today.

"You're certain they followed you from the apartment?" Ves asked.

Sebastian hesitated. "They got on at the trolley stop there, at least. And they changed trolleys with me, then tried to chase me down. I suppose they might have been thieves, but look at me—surely I'm not that tempting a target."

Tempting was definitely a word Ves didn't want to consciously associate with Sebastian. His lips were damp from the beer, and a bit of foam clung to the corner of his mouth.

Ves's trousers felt suddenly tight, and he tore his gaze away from Sebastian's mouth. "I, er, that is, no." His face felt on fire, and he took another swig from the beer, draining it. "You weren't carrying anything, and you hardly look the sort to have a diamond-crusted pocket watch," he added after he'd swallowed. There, that surely had covered his lapse.

A small smile played briefly over Sebastian's mouth, there and gone. "Exactly. They would have been poor thieves indeed to have followed me halfway across town for nothing more than a plain watch and a few coins. I think someone found out I was asking questions, and they were waiting there in order to warn me off."

"I see." Ves didn't like the implications of this, not at all. "You think Mr. O'Neil didn't leave of his own free will, and that whoever made him disappear doesn't want anyone looking too closely into the circumstances of his departure."

Sebastian nodded. "My friends don't believe me—though they might, once they find out I've been followed." He hesitated. "You believe me, don't you?"

Unfortunately, Ves did. The question was, had Fagerlie had the man removed in order to free up the position for Ves, or had that merely been a happy coincidence?

If Fagerlie was involved and Sebastian found out, he would assume Ves had been in on the plot as well. Worse—it would mean Ves might not get the map drawn in time, or Fagerlie might be forced to flee, or any of a dozen other scenarios that all had the same result: the curse on himself and Noct wouldn't be broken.

Ves couldn't let that happen. He couldn't let down his brother. He might be able to eke out a pale existence such as he had in Boston—no friends, but a job, a place in society, and some contact with other people, however superficial. He'd always be afraid of discovery, but he could do it.

Noct couldn't. The curse was far worse for him. If Ves failed, Noct would be doomed to spend his entire life hidden away, with only Ves and the constant terror of discovery as his companions.

It was possible Fagerlie had nothing to do with any of this. That O'Neil's disappearance had, in fact, been an unplanned opportunity that Fagerlie had seized upon. The strange note left for him this morning seemed to support that theory, at least.

"I believe you," Ves said, leaning in and lowering his voice. Sebastian leaned in as well, close enough Ves caught his scent, of vanilla and old books, mingled with the beer on his breath. "Whoever left the note on my desk has access to the bindery. Do you think another librarian might be behind O'Neil's disappearance?"

Sebastian bit his lower lip, teeth white against the soft pink curve. "It could just be someone unhappy that Mr. Quinn hired an outsider, I suppose. Did you make a complaint?"

"On the first morning of my employment?" Ves arched a brow. "I wadded it up and threw it in the trash. Besides, I thought I knew who it was from."

"Me." Sebastian winced. "Would you recognize the handwriting again?"

"It was typed."

"Blast."

Ves considered for a moment, then said, "*If* the same person arranged for O'Neil to disappear, then it must be someone in the library. Or on the janitorial staff, I suppose. At any rate, we should keep our suspicions to ourselves for the moment. We don't want to tip anyone off prematurely."

"We?" Sebastian asked, his eyes brightening behind the glass lenses. "You mean to help me find Kelly?"

Kelly. Ves wondered if there had been something more than friendship between them, then pushed aside the thought. That was none of his business. "I do. I rather feel as though I owe it to the man, since I wouldn't be here in other circumstances." Plus it would let him reassure himself Fagerlie wasn't involved.

Sebastian nodded. "Thank you, Vesper. I can't tell you how nice it is to have someone finally believe me."

"I'll take a careful look through the bindery tomorrow, just in case Mr. O'Neil left some clue behind there," Ves said.

"An excellent idea." Sebastian finished his own beer. "Another round?"

It startled Ves that he actually wanted to stay. But he was already risking too much by agreeing to spend more time with Sebastian while they looked into O'Neil's disappearance. "I should return to my room."

Disappointment flickered across Sebastian's face, replaced quickly by a smile. "Of course." He put out his hand, and Ves took it automatically. "I'll see you in the morning."

Sebastian seemed inclined to let his palm linger. Ves savored the warmth of the touch for a moment, before withdrawing. "Tomorrow," he agreed, and thrust his hands into his pockets, as though he might somehow preserve Sebastian's heat from the cool air outside.

CHAPTER 8

*W*hen Sebastian woke the next morning, he felt lighter than he had in months.

To say last night had taken an unexpected turn would be an understatement. Though the terror of being chased revisited him in dreams, his rescue at Ves's hands had proved to be an unlooked-for turning point.

And how embarrassing *that* had been. Of all the people to run into, Vesper Rune would have been at the very bottom of Sebastian's list. And yet, he hadn't hesitated to come to Sebastian's defense. He hadn't even asked why the men were after Sebastian, or if they were armed, before confronting them.

A part of Sebastian felt mortified to have cowered in the lane while Ves faced the men down. Thankfully, Ves hadn't needed Sebastian's help. Quite the opposite—alone, he'd cut an imposing figure, his muscular physique and heavy-lidded glower more than enough to give the men pause. If Sebastian had been with him, he might have rather undermined the effect.

Even better—Ves believed that Kelly's disappearance could have been due to foul play. He meant to help. Sebastian was no longer alone in his investigation, and that by itself lifted a weight from his shoulders.

Though the note Ves had received was troubling. Sebastian doubted it had any connection with Kelly's disappearance, though he couldn't entirely rule it out. But to think someone in the library had gone from wary distrust of outsiders, to pure prejudice, was disheartening. Sebastian would keep a close eye out, and if any more harassment occurred, he'd take a complaint to Mr. Quinn himself.

As Sebastian settled in to his own duties—sorting through a box of documents donated from the Abbott estate, due to the lack of any heirs to receive them—he couldn't help but recall how Ves had looked at him while they spoke. The way his eyes had lingered hungrily on Sebastian's lips.

Sebastian grinned to himself. He'd seen that look before, more than once. Vesper's interest in him wasn't purely that of a colleague. Given the stiff way the man held himself, how he'd blushed and glanced away, before gradually letting his eyes wander back, Ves might be reluctant to admit his attraction even to himself.

No matter. Sebastian would be more than happy to help with that, given the opportunity. He very much wanted to feel the strength of those arms wrapped around him, to run his own hands over Ves's muscular shoulders. To feel his weight press Sebastian into the softness of a bed…

A knock at the door broke Sebastian from his fantasy. He started guiltily and called, "Come in!"

Arthur stepped inside, and his grim expression killed any lingering arousal. So did the way he shut the door behind him, as if to make sure no one overheard their conversation. "Sebastian. How are you this morning?"

Sebastian waved away the pleasantry. "What's wrong?"

"You recall I suggested Mr. O'Neil might have fled because he stole a book?"

Sebastian's heart sank. "Yes, but…"

"I started an inventory of my own collection." Arthur sighed. "It turns out a rare unsuppressed copy of Flamsteed's *Historia Coelestis Britannica* has gone missing. It's a catalog of stars, but unlike most copies it includes some of the Royal Astronomer's thoughts on more… esoteric matters. Including on his apprentice, Edmund Halley."

"But the curses," Sebastian objected. "How could he have stolen anything? Surely he couldn't have made it past them easily. Are you certain it hasn't been signed out by one of the staff?"

"I checked the card; there's no record of it being removed from the library. So either it's been misplaced in some fashion—not impossible —or O'Neil stole it."

"Couldn't it have disappeared some time ago?" Sebastian asked hopefully.

Arthur shook his head, a pitying look on his face. "I'm afraid both the card and my own memory confirm Dr. Bell took it to one of the reading rooms—and returned it to my care—a little over a week before O'Neil left." Arthur put a hand on Sebastian's shoulder. "I know you don't want to believe Mr. O'Neil could do such a thing, but it would be an awfully big coincidence otherwise, wouldn't it?"

Arthur was right; Sebastian didn't want to believe it. He'd befriended the man. If his judgment in character had been poor, his mother's had been even worse, since she'd been the one to train Kelly. Wouldn't she have seen some hint in all the time they spent together in the bindery?

Of course, if Sebastian had just done as she wanted, none of this would have happened in the first place.

"We need to tell Mr. Quinn," Sebastian said heavily.

Arthur gave him a lopsided smile. "It's kind of you to say 'we,' but that isn't the duty of an archivist. The theft was from my collection; I should be the one to report it."

"But it was my speculation that led to the inventory." Sebastian stood up and clapped Arthur on the shoulder. "Let's go."

Ves's sleep of the night before had been troubled. When he'd finally managed to sleep at all, that is, having spent hours berating himself for being so foolish as to agree to help Sebastian.

The smart thing to do would be to put O'Neil's disappearance out of his mind. Maybe Fagerlie had disposed of the man—what then? It wasn't as though Ves was stupid enough to believe his employer wanted a floor plan of the museum library for the sake of scholarship. Fagerlie was a sorcerer; the Ladysmith had the finest collection of occult tomes in America. It wasn't difficult to deduce why he'd want access.

Theft was one thing. But murder…

"You cannot be weak," his mother had said on a long-ago spring morning. Despite the warm air, drapes hung over every window, blocking the view of the interior should anyone happen past. No one had ever casually trespassed on their remote homestead so far as Ves knew, but Mother had been paranoid about taking chances.

Her eyes gleamed in the dim light of the kerosene lantern. *"Do you understand me, Vesper? You were created for one thing and one thing only: to kill the enemies of our masters. Are you going to fail them? Are you going to fail me?"*

He swallowed, desperate to please her. *"I understand,"* he said, even though the thought of killing anything made him sick. But if he argued, she'd punish him.

Sometimes, she punished him even when he gave her the answers she wanted. So he simply stood in silence, ramrod straight, waiting for her to decide. He'd been able to hold the pose for hours, ever since he was old enough to walk.

"I'm not sure you do," she said at last. *"Fetch me the cane. And wake up Nocturn—I want him to see this."*

Ves sighed as he settled behind the desk that had belonged to his predecessor. Maybe he was weak, in mind if not in body. He hadn't precisely fooled himself into believing Fagerlie wouldn't do anything criminal with the map. He'd just ignored that part, preferring to focus on his dreams of escape. The curse would be lifted, he and Noct would be on a train headed west no later than the twentieth of May. No need to worry about the consequences of his actions, because he wouldn't be around to see them.

Would Sebastian be disappointed when he realized what Ves had done?

What a stupid thought. He'd had one drink with the man. They weren't even friends.

Sebastian could look after himself. Noct needed Ves. There was no question as to where his duty lay.

A soft knock at the door startled him out of his thoughts. "Come inside," he called.

Sebastian stuck his head in. "Do you have a moment?"

He'd just finished reassembling the signatures of the diary and put them in the book press, intending to work on the cover next. "Of course."

Sebastian shut the door and leaned one hip against the table with the book press on it. "Arthur Fairchild—have you met him yet? Anyway, he found a book missing from his collection. He's certain Kelly took it."

The dejected sound in his voice pricked Ves uncomfortably. "How can he be sure Mr. O'Neil is the thief?"

"I'm not certain how anyone not a librarian could get around the curses."

"Right. The curses," Ves said. Gods of the wood, these people were a superstitious lot.

Sebastian frowned. "You can't tell me the Boston Public Library doesn't use curses to prevent theft."

"They do not."

"How on earth do they keep the books secure, then?" Sebastian asked, sounding honestly baffled.

Ves blinked. "Um, a combination of watchful eyes in the reading room, limited access to parts of the stacks, and security guards."

Sebastian shook his head in wonder. "That sounds both inefficient and ineffective."

Ves let the matter drop. "What did he steal?"

"An unsuppressed copy of *Historia Coelestis Britannica* by John Flamsteed, the Royal Astronomer. Edmund Halley was his apprentice."

The book would be valuable on its own, and likely even more valuable than usual now with Halley's Comet in the sky. But could it have held some shred of knowledge, some esoteric fact, that Fagerlie would find useful or even necessary? Could it even have something to do with the ritual Fagerlie intended to use to cure himself and Noct?

Hopefully not, since the book appeared to have vanished along with O'Neil. Then again, the fact Fagerlie wanted a map of the library suggested he might want a great deal more than a single book.

"That doesn't explain the threatening note I received," Ves said slowly. "Though I suppose that could be unrelated." Perhaps some sensitive soul had unconsciously sensed that Ves was a thing of destruction and despair, and anonymously expressed their instinctive dislike. "We can search the bindery, if you like. See if we can find some clue as to what has happened to O'Neil. I've already looked through the desk—any personal items he might have left behind are gone, but if you're willing, feel free to conduct a more thorough search in case I missed something. I'll look through the various cabinets and make certain they only contain the supplies they're meant to. Oh, and I should check the backlog, in case the book was sent here for repair and there was no note made of it."

Sebastian looked down at him, eyes wide behind his silver spectacles. "I don't mean to keep you from your own work, but thank you."

Ves's throat tightened. He wondered suddenly what would have happened if he were a normal man. Human. Unafraid.

"You're welcome," he said, his voice huskier than he'd meant it to be.

Sebastian's lips stretched into a slow smile. Now that he'd dropped his chilly demeanor, stopped treating Ves as an intruder, he was even more of a temptation than before.

No. He couldn't let these thoughts get the best of him, not when there was no hope of having anything more. Ves turned away quickly and went to the nearest cabinet.

It wasn't long before Sebastian said, "I believe I've found something."

Surprised, Ves left off his own search and joined Sebastian at the desk. The archivist had emptied and removed the drawers, and now he drew Ves's attention to the empty space where one had been. "Look—a tiny spring." He pushed it in with a pen nib, and a small click sounded.

Sebastian smiled triumphantly as what had appeared to be a decorative column separating the pigeon holes shifted slightly. He tugged on it, and it slid out; the column was in fact the front of a concealed document drawer.

"How did you know to look for a hidden drawer?" Ves asked.

"I didn't, exactly." Sebastian flushed slightly. "Puzzle boxes and the like are something of a hobby of mine, so I just thought I'd take a quick look and see if there were any hidden compartments."

"Well done," Ves said. "What's inside?"

Sebastian turned up the drawer. An envelope with something heavy inside tumbled out, along with a sheet of paper yellowed with age.

Ves picked up the paper first. On it, a bold hand had written:

"To whomever comes after me: I charge you to continue our sacred work. To stand against necromancy and things from the Outside, and bind them so they cannot exert their will on our world."

Below were four signatures:

Nathaniel R. Ladysmith, December 13, 1859
Thomas Halliwell, February 10, 1864
Rebecca Rath, October 31, 1882
Kelly O'Neil, January 28, 1905

Ves's fingertips tingled faintly. He'd seen signatures in blood enough times to recognize it now. "Rebecca Rath—that's your mother, isn't it?"

Sebastian's face had gone pale with shock. "I...yes. And Thomas Halliwell was my great uncle—my maternal grandmother's brother."

"But what does any of this mean?" Ves was no sorcerer, but he would have bet his last dollar that there was some sort of magic at work here. If he placed his own signature below the others, he'd be taking the most solemn of oaths.

What the devil was going on in this place?

He'd scoffed when his seatmate on the train had warned him against coming to Widdershins. But its museum was a maze, and its library a labyrinth. The head librarian kept a skull on his desk and a bloodstained book on his wall, and threw knucklebones to decide who to hire. Bats performed pest control. The librarians were convinced curses kept their books safe from theft.

And now it seemed those who worked in the bindery had been signing some sort of blood oath to bind more than just books.

"It's the sort of thing one might find in a secret society, though one with a very limited membership." Sebastian pushed his glasses up on his forehead and squinted. "I'd have to take a closer look, but on first inspection the paper appears to have been made prior to the 1860s. We have a few—sadly few—documents signed by Mr. Ladysmith, so I would have to compare them to confirm the authenticity, though at first glance it seems to match. But Kelly's and my mother's signatures are real."

"I bow to your expertise, archivist," Ves said. "I think it's safe to assume Thomas Halliwell's is authentic as well, then."

"He trained my mother, just as she meant to train me." Sebastian's lips flattened into a tight line. "The only time she ever raised her voice to me was when I told her I didn't mean to take her place someday."

"It seems this was more than just a job to her."

"It was a sacred trust," Sebastian agreed. "One wrapped up in secrecy. She must have felt she couldn't tell me the truth about the position, at least not until I agreed to become her apprentice."

The sorrow in Sebastian's eyes cut unexpectedly. "Would have you acted differently, if you had known?" Ves asked.

Sebastian sighed. "I don't know, to be honest. I truly don't." He glanced at the oath. "Do you mean to sign it?"

"I try to avoid signing my name in blood whenever possible," Ves said dryly. "Don't you?"

"I mean generally, yes. But you're going to have to if you're hired on a permanent basis. I'm sure it was the same at the library in Boston."

"It absolutely was not."

"Really?" Sebastian asked, in apparent sincerity. "How odd." He picked up the envelope, turned it over—and all the color drained from his face.

"Sebastian?" Ves sat forward, concerned. "What's wrong?" When Sebastian didn't reply, he reached for the envelope.

Mr. Sebastian Rath was scrawled across the front in the same handwriting as O'Neil's signature.

CHAPTER 9

*T*he next day, Sebastian sat in his office, wondering what
to do.

It was Saturday, normally a half-day of work at the museum, but
he was unable to keep his mind on business. The envelope had proved
to contain a key—but absolutely no clue as to what the key opened.

He took it from his pocket and stared at it again. It was completely
innocuous, not very different from the key to Bonnie's door on his
own key ring. It hadn't unlocked anything in the bindery; there were
no locks of the correct size even. It was the right size for a house key,
but what house could it unlock?

So many secrets. Kelly's secrets; his mother's secrets; apparently his
great-uncle's secrets.

If he'd agreed to be her successor, she would have told him about
the oath. About what it meant, and why Nathaniel Ladysmith, of all
people, had signed it.

Or if he'd pulled her from the fire that day. Forced himself through
the searing flames and carried her out, burned but alive.

Sick of his own thoughts, he put the key back in his pocket and
went to the bindery. Ves called for him to enter at his knock, and
when he stepped inside, he was greeted with a smile.

God, what a smile, one that lit Ves's handsome face from within. Sebastian considered locking the door behind him, falling to his knees, and showing Ves just what he could do with his mouth.

But he didn't want to frighten Ves off. Best to take it slow for once in his life. Which wasn't something Sebastian was used to doing. Most of the time, when he went to the bathhouses or the bars that catered to a certain type of clientele, it was merely the matter of exchanging a few looks and words, before retreating to a private room.

That wasn't the approach he wanted to take with Ves, though, even if it might have worked. The more he got to know the new binder, the more he liked him. Not to mention they worked together. This wasn't a matter of a single fuck, then going their own ways.

"The diary is ready," Ves said, picking up a book and handing it to Sebastian.

What had been a moldy wreck was now a lovely volume, bound in red morocco leather, *The Diary of Glen Parry* neatly stamped in gilt letters on the spine. Sebastian opened it carefully, to find the pages in vastly better condition than they had been: mildew removed, tears repaired, and grime washed away.

"Excellent work," he said, and meant it.

"I passed your test, then?"

Heat crept up Sebastian's cheeks. "I'm sorry."

"Don't be. I've come to understand the position I occupy has personal significance for you." Ves hesitated. "If it was you who left the note, I would understand."

Now Sebastian felt even more of a wretch. "I wasn't as kind to you at first as I could have been. Please accept my apology. But it wasn't me behind the note."

"Apology accepted." Ves crossed his arms. "Have you thought more about what the key might unlock? And why O'Neil left it for you to find?"

"I've thought of nothing but," he confessed. "But I honestly don't know. I suppose it could be the key to his apartment, but if so, there's nothing left to find. Everything was removed the day Kelly departed."

A sympathetic look crossed Ves's face. "So you believe he did steal the Flamsteed, intending to take advantage of the mania for the comet to get an inflated price?"

"I don't know. I never would have believed it, but…maybe I've just been fooling myself this entire time."

"Possibly. It would explain why he didn't ask for references—if Mr. Quinn knew where he was looking for employment, it would be easy to chase him down after the theft was eventually discovered." Ves chewed on his lower lip, then seemed to come to a decision. "Why don't we return to his apartment building and talk to the landlady. See if we can get our hands on his mail."

"If she's even there."

"If she isn't, we'll break in."

Sebastian blinked in shock. "Break into her apartment? But—that's illegal!"

"I'm quite aware." Ves shrugged uncomfortably. "I thought, with your mania for puzzles, you might have branched out into lock picking. And it isn't as though we mean to steal anything from her, except for letters that belong to O'Neil in the first place."

"I did play with locks as a child, though it's been a while," Sebastian admitted. He wasn't at all certain this was the right thing to do… but they'd run out of any other options. Either he followed this last final path hoping for a clue, or he decided Kelly was a thief and gave up trying to figure out what door the key might open.

"All right," he said. "This afternoon, do you think?"

"Too many people going in and out on a Saturday afternoon," Ves pointed out. "I'd say early tomorrow, when people are at church. Unless you'd prefer to go to church yourself."

"Bonnie goes, but my attendance is haphazard at best. I think you have the right idea. Meet me in front of the museum tomorrow morning?" He held out his hand.

Ves shook it. "I'll see you then."

Neither of them pulled their hands back. "Thank you," Sebastian said, tightening his grip slightly. "Truly. You don't owe me anything, and yet you've helped me every step of the way."

The color rose in Ves's cheeks. "I'm as curious as you to discover what happened to my predecessor."

"Then I am grateful for your curiosity." Sebastian reluctantly let go. "I'll see you first thing tomorrow."

Ves lingered in the bindery after working hours, with the excuse of needing to catch up on the work that had been neglected while there was no one to do it. Which was true as far as it went, but his actual intentions were far less scrupulous.

The more he got to know Sebastian, the worse he felt about his plan to betray the library to Fagerlie. But it wasn't as though he and Noct were going to get another chance. The museum was surely insured against theft, and Sebastian would get over his disappointment eventually.

It was already Saturday, and the comet would pass between the earth and the sun late Wednesday. He'd spent every spare moment he could find working on his map, but his involvement with Sebastian had cut into his time. Still, he could make significant progress today, especially if he remained until after nightfall.

Once everyone else was gone, Ves quietly entered the stacks, armed with his paper and pencil, and began to draw again. The doors to the bat room stood open, though the sun was still high enough to keep them somnolent.

As he sketched the maze, he slowly penetrated deeper into the heart of the library. The rooms made little more sense laid out on paper than they did when walking through them, but he could tell they wrapped around some central column. No doubt it supported part of the museum roof, though he didn't honestly know enough about architecture to be certain.

The hours passed by, the silence at first broken only by the rustle of his clothing and the scratch of his pencil. The light coming through the random shafts faded, and a dark shape flitted past.

Ves paused and looked up. The bats had emerged from their slumber, and they swooped and dove, an occasional chitter reaching him just on the edge of hearing. As he watched them, something in him uncoiled. This was the closest he'd gotten to nature of any sort in so long; even in this artificial setting the tiny beasts were a balm to his heart. Perhaps having bats in the library wasn't as insane an idea as he'd thought.

He went about his work, and the bats went about theirs. The dinner hour came and went, but he ignored his grumbling stomach.

As he'd hoped, he was able to work steadily and without interruption, and soon he had both the first and second levels completely mapped out.

By now, the darkness was near-absolute. There was no need to turn on the electric lights, and Ves had no desire to attract the attention of a curious security guard. The only illumination came from the moon, filtering down through shafts to the lower levels. When he started back toward the ramp that would take him to the lowest floor, the only sounds were the whirring of the bats and his own steps.

"Binder," whispered a voice in his ear.

All the hair on Ves's neck rose. This was the same voice he'd heard while sketching during lunch on Thursday. Then, he'd assumed it was some trick of the acoustics.

But he was the only one here, now, unless someone was sneaking about without light, hiding in such a fashion even his night-piercing eyes couldn't make them out.

It seemed unlikely, to say the least. He firmed his stance, scanning the darkness around him. "Who's there?" he called. "Show yourself!"

"Binder." The voice was more of a growl of hatred now.

The voice definitely belonged to a some*thing* as opposed to a some*one*. The skin on his back twitched and prickled. He was no sorcerer, but he wasn't entirely human, either. "Be you flesh or spirit, in the name of the Black Goat and her thousand young, I command you to reveal yourself."

The growl grew louder and angrier, sound turning into words: "Get out!"

A book flew off the shelves and struck Ves in the shoulder. He snarled and spun, his field of vision widening and sharpening as his eyes shifted form. "Reveal yourself, creature of the air! I call upon the Lord of the Wood, All-Mother, the—"

The words cut off as a heavy tome with an iron clasp smashed into the side of his head. "Get out!" the thing screamed. "*Get out*, GET OUT, *GET OUT!*"

With every escalating shriek, invisible forces hurled another book at him. He evaded most of them, but even as he dodged and ducked, a breeze began to ruffle his hair.

So deep within the building, there was no logical reason for there to be a breeze. But summoning wind was a favorite trick of sorcerers.

Whatever force had turned itself against him, he clearly had no ability to stop it. Ves stuffed his sketches inside his vest and ran toward the entrance of the library. The wind continued to rise, and books launched themselves at him as he ran. His heart pounded and his back ached. He took a wrong turning, swore at himself and doubled back. The wind tore his hair now, and the great stacks of wood and iron groaned and creaked. He had to get out before whatever was attacking him wrought true destruction.

The sense of something racing up behind him strengthened. Malevolent hatred beat against his back, and the scars there seemed to awaken to fresh pain. Whatever it was, it wanted him dead.

He burst into the reading area and sprinted across it without pause. For a terrible moment, he imagined the door to the library would be locked, and he'd be trapped inside.

The door swung open before he could even touch it. Ves staggered to a halt in the hall outside—only to have the door slam definitively shut at his back.

Ves put his back to the wall and regarded the library entrance. He wasn't winded—it would take a great deal more to tax his stamina— but he was both confused and concerned. He shut his eyes, composing himself, so that if any security guard came to see what the commotion was about, he'd appear human.

"*Binder,*" the voice had said, as though the word were a curse.

A bodiless something that apparently hated bookbinders was hiding in the library. And the last binder had left under circumstances that were questionable, to say the least.

Had *this* been what the note was warning him of? Did someone else working in the library know about the voice and tried to frighten Ves away before history repeated itself?

Ves touched the paper hastily stuffed into his vest. He'd made good progress. Even if he confined himself to working hours, he'd surely be able to complete the final part of the map by Wednesday afternoon.

He'd finish the map, take it to Fagerlie, and leave. Then the spirit in the library would be someone else's problem.

CHAPTER 10

*V*es sat on the trolley beside Sebastian, trying not to brush against his companion as the car jostled over crisscrossing tracks. He was painfully aware of Sebastian's warmth, and the memory of the touch of his hand yesterday kept returning.

He shouldn't be here. Every moment he spent with Sebastian made him feel easier in the man's presence. Which in turn heightened the possibility of discovery. If he was found out before he'd finished the map, all of his hopes for himself and Noct would be dashed, probably forever.

Yet he couldn't seem to stay away.

He'd spent the early hours of the morning trying to decide whether he should tell Sebastian about the thing in the library. Its anger toward him as a binder certainly seemed to tie in with Kelly's disappearance, stolen books notwithstanding. But would Sebastian believe him—and even if he did, would that belief help, or just get Sebastian into danger?

Sebastian believed in curses and blood oaths, both of which could be real. But that didn't mean he knew anything about true magic. People believed all sorts of things, after all. One of Ves's fellow workers in the Boston Public Library bindery had soundly berated another man for daring to whistle inside, claiming it would invite in the devil.

The fact that a third man had slipped and broken his arm three weeks later was considered incontrovertible proof that he was right.

If Sebastian believed him, but then fell back on some folk custom to try and banish whatever lurked in the library, it would either have no effect...or, worst case, succeed in drawing its attention.

Today was Sunday. Ves would be gone by Thursday morning. He wouldn't be around to protect Sebastian.

Sebastian nudged Ves with his elbow. "You seem lost in thought."

Ves turned to him, then wished he hadn't. They were far too close, Sebastian still leaning into him, their arms pressed together. He smelled so good, of books and vanilla and musk, and Ves had the mad urge to press his face into Sebastian's hair and breathe deep.

Which was insane, of course. Still, he couldn't quite bring himself to draw back from the warmth of the other man's arm. "I'm just thinking back to some of the things I picked up in the rare book trade," he lied.

Sebastian frowned and drew back. "I didn't know you'd done such work."

Blast. "Mr. Quinn is aware," Ves said hastily. "I know the reputation the trade has among librarians, and it is deserved. But I don't condone stealing from the public on behalf of the rich." He smiled thinly. "Or even of stealing from institutions which serve the public good, such as the Ladysmith."

Sebastian relaxed slightly. "Then I'm even more glad I asked for your assistance, if you have some knowledge that might help in the matter."

"If I have to call upon any connections I formed in the trade to track down the missing book, I shall. Hopefully it won't come to that."

"Are these people dangerous?" Sebastian asked. "What if the two men who followed me are connected to the theft in some fashion?"

"While not impossible, it is unlikely," Ves assured him. "These are people who stick to the shadows and avoid confrontation whenever they can."

After growing up on Grandfather's tales, the rare book trade had seemed so tame. Stories of theft and betrayal were passed on in whispers, as though they were somehow shocking. But Ves had never met a man among them who'd cut the throat of a friend to get his hands on an incomplete volume. None of them had performed the rites on the hill to call up forces from beyond the earthly realm, or broken the minds of informants until they went screaming to the madhouse.

Amateurs, Grandfather would have called them.

He'd taken especial pride in his copy of the *Liber Ivonis,* pieced together from no less than three incomplete copies, one only a fragment of five crumbling pages. It had taken Grandfather almost forty years to find those three copies, or so he claimed, and he'd done murder to get each one.

In comparison, Ves's time in the rare book trade had been downright peaceful, working among dilettantes whose greatest aspirations were to make money and stay out of jail. Men who scoured public libraries for a first copy of Poe's *Tamerlane*, rather than attempting to destroy the world.

"Speaking of the men who followed me," Sebastian said, peering pensively out the window. "Our stop is next. What if they're still surveilling the apartment, waiting for me to return?"

"We'll go at least one stop farther than we need to, in case they're watching for the trolley. But it's more likely their lookout is at the apartment building itself." Ves considered. "We could…hmm. In the extreme, we could rent a cart and horse, and return after dark pretending to deliver a package. You could hide inside a large crate…"

He trailed off, realizing Sebastian was looking at him oddly. It was a trick he'd used to smuggle Noct in and out of apartments in the past, but Sebastian would become suspicious if he realized Ves could easily tote around a crate with a full-grown man inside.

"That may not be practical," he added.

"Probably not," Sebastian agreed with a grin. "There's a fire escape around back, in the alley. It's not visible from the front of the building, but I made note of it while I was there."

His grin faded as he spoke, and for a moment he looked haunted. Ves wondered at it…but he was already too entangled to risk further involvement in Sebastian's life. "Then we'll take it to the roof, then enter the building and take the stairs down from there. We'll exit the same way, if we can."

They rode the trolley to the second stop, then climbed out. Near the stop, a man in a ridiculously tall hat had set up an open case packed with glass bottles. "Protect yourself from the poisonous gases of the comet's tail!" he shouted, gesticulating at his wares. "One pill an hour until the comet passes will guarantee your safety! Only five cents a bottle to save yourself and your family!"

Sebastian shook his head. "People do let their imaginations run away from them."

"Yes."

Something about his tone seemed to catch Sebastian's attention. "You don't believe the comet will wipe out all life on earth, do you?"

"No. Of course not." Ves felt his shoulders grow tense. "My mother and grandfather thought the world was going to end. They spent their whole lives preparing for it."

He locked his teeth together. He shouldn't have given away even that much of the truth.

"Oh," Sebastian said, startled. "Were they in some sort of cult?"

Why had he been so foolish as to say anything? "Yes. I ran away when I was seventeen." Ves gestured vaguely to the world around them. "As you can see, nothing came of their prophecies. So no, I don't put much store in the comet heralding doomsday."

They walked the rest of the way in companionable silence. Sebastian led them in a circuitous route, so they approached the apartments via the alley running between the backs of two rows of buildings. Lines of laundry flapped overhead, and a group of children ran past, chasing a hoop.

The black iron of the fire escape hung against the fresh brick of the apartments. Sebastian stopped with a curse at the sight. "Damn it. The ladder is up. I should have realized it would be."

Ves eyed the bottom level of the fire escape, the ladder drawn up and secured to its railing. It was a good ten feet off the ground—in other words, nothing for him.

"I'll take care of it," he said. "You go and stand watch at the end of the alley."

"How are you going to get up there?" Sebastian asked with a frown.

Ves shrugged, his face closed off once again. "I'll find something to stand on and jump."

It would take quite a jump...but Sebastian didn't have any better ideas at the moment. "I'll help you look for a crate or a rock."

Ves shook his head. "I'll take care of it. You go stand lookout. I don't want to have to explain what we're doing back here to the police."

"All right." Sebastian reluctantly turned away and headed a short distance down the alley. The rear entrance to a restaurant was propped open, and men unloaded boxes of vegetables from the back of a wagon. Steam billowed out, accompanied by a burst of Mandarin, followed by laughter.

How long had the apartment building been watched? Kelly had disappeared two months ago. Surely the men hadn't been following every single person to go in and out of the place.

They hadn't followed him until his second visit. Had Mrs. Pickman been paid to send word if someone came around asking questions about Kelly? He hated to think it of the woman, but he couldn't rule out the possibility.

A clang of iron-on-iron came from behind him. He hurried back, past the flapping maze of laundry. The fire escape was down, and Ves stood on the lowest platform, buttoning his coat, as if he'd removed it for the exercise.

Sebastian looked around, but didn't see any obvious crate or barrel stacked so Ves could have reached the ladder. The man must be an Olympian, to have jumped high enough to hoist himself up.

"Impressive," Sebastian said as he scrambled up the ladder.

Ves didn't smile at the compliment, only held a finger up to his lips. "We don't want to alert anyone inside, assuming anyone is at home this time of day," he said in a low voice.

They managed to reach the roof without encountering any residents. A few blankets lay up there, along with a mattress. Either someone had been sleeping up here to escape the heat, or been using the roof for romantic rendezvous. Or both.

Sebastian tried the door, and it opened easily under his hand.

Inside, the stairwell led down through the center of the building. Voices and the notes of a badly tuned piano escaped from some of the apartments, but they met no one else on the stair.

When they reached the landlady's apartment, Sebastian knocked in the faint hope she might actually be in for once. It went unanswered.

"Now it's your turn to stand guard," he said.

He'd spent yesterday afternoon re-familiarizing himself with the picking of simple locks, including the one on Bonnie's front door. The children had watched in fascination, but he'd refused to show them how to do it themselves, for fear of their mother's wrath. The inexpensive lock on the landlady's door presented no great challenge, and he had it open within seconds.

"After you," he told Ves with a bow.

They slipped inside, Sebastian locking the door behind them out of habit. Only a little light made its way through the drapes, even on a sunny day like today. The air had grown stuffy in the warmth, with the sort of dead feeling air gets when no one has breathed it in, or moved through it, for several days. The landlady must have gone on a trip, which explained why she never seemed to be home.

The sitting room apparently doubled as the landlady's office, judging by the ledgers on the shelf above a rolltop desk. The desk was open and unlocked, the current ledger keeping track of who had and hadn't paid the month's rent neatly centered. To either side were piles of correspondence.

Ves took the left-hand pile, and Sebastian the right. After a moment, Ves said, "Here."

He passed Sebastian a small stack of letters, held together with a rubber band. Sebastian tucked them into the inner pocket of his coat. "That was easy. We should—"

His words were cut off by someone fumbling at the door.

CHAPTER 11

"Door's locked," a rough male voice said. Not the landlady returning from her trip, then. "They ain't in there."

"That librarian keeps coming back for a reason. We might as well check it out. It's a simple lock. Just give me a few seconds," said another.

Sebastian froze, eyes wide as he stared at the door, like a rabbit confronted with a hawk. Ves cursed silently and grabbed his elbow. He jumped, and Ves put a finger to his lips, hushing him.

They needed to get out. Hopefully, one of the other rooms would have a convenient window they could climb through. Ves crossed the room, moving unhurriedly so as not to cause too much noise. The farthest chamber from the door proved to be the bedroom. There was a window they could hopefully ease open, and—

"There," said the second man with satisfaction, and the hinges squeaked as the front door opened.

No time left. They were going to have to run or fight—

Sebastian seized Ves's arm and pulled him to the left, away from the bedroom door and out of sight of the men coming inside. Ves caught a brief glimpse of himself in the mirror as Sebastian swung open the door to a large wardrobe—then climbed in, pulling Ves after him.

The wardrobe was almost entirely empty; the landlady must have taken most of her clothes with her, or else packed them away. Even as footsteps sounded in the sitting room, Sebastian pulled the door nearly shut, leaving only a tiny crack to peer out through.

"What are we looking for?" one of the men asked.

"I dunno. A book, maybe?"

"It'd help if the boss told us anything."

Ves tried to breathe quietly, but not shallowly. He'd need the air if they were discovered. He listened intently to the sound of footsteps, the mutters of the men, the rustle of the papers on the desk being tossed about. Sebastian's fingers were still locked around Ves's arm. In the cramped confines of the wardrobe, their bodies pressed together from thigh to shoulder. Sebastian's heat soaked through their layers of clothing, and Ves suddenly found himself acutely aware of every tiny movement.

Ves didn't touch anyone but his brother, not if he could help it. At some point in his infancy, he must have been held and cuddled, but by the time he was old enough to begin training, that had transmuted to blows and beatings. Only the voice in the woods had offered comfort, and it never appeared to either of them in physical form.

And after they escaped…well, until the curse was lifted, there was no hope for either of them. Noct didn't dare even to be seen, and Ves couldn't risk anything that might lead to discovery.

If Sebastian knew what he was pressed against now, he'd run. Scream. Possibly try to kill Ves, though he didn't seem the violent type. But people changed in the presence of monsters.

Despite knowing better, despite their precarious situation, Ves's skin *ached* for more. So close, he could smell Sebastian's scent, of old books, vanilla, and human warmth. He wanted to press his face into Sebastian's hair, to feel his bare skin, to…

"Nothing," one of the men said in disgust.

"Let's check the other rooms real quick, just to be sure we're not missing something. We lost the librarian, but maybe we don't have to go back to the boss empty-handed."

Blast.

Ves leaned in until his lips were all but pressed against Sebastian's ear. "Follow my lead."

Sebastian shivered but nodded. Ves gathered himself, ready to move the instant it was required.

A man came into the room. Through the cracked door, Ves recognized him as one of the two who had chased Sebastian Thursday evening. The floorboards squeaked as he drew closer. Ves took a deep breath, then let it out. His back ached as the skin tried to stretch, and his eyes burned. It took every ounce of control he'd learned over the long, harsh years to hold himself still as the man stretched a hand toward the wardrobe.

Ves exploded out, all of his weight smashing into the door. It crashed into the man, tumbling him to the floor. Ves didn't waste time kicking him, only grabbed Sebastian and hauled him after as he ran for the front room.

The other man had heard the crash. He was just emerging from the kitchen as they burst out of the bedroom. Without breaking stride, Ves swung his fist as hard as he could into his face.

The man's nose gave way beneath Ves's blow with a satisfying crunch, accompanied by a spray of blood. He reeled back, half-collapsed to the floor, and cleared their way out.

They rushed from the apartment, leaving the door open behind them, and across the small lobby. A woman gathering her mail let out a startled exclamation. Sebastian's foot slipped on the marble tiles; Ves's grip on his wrist kept him from falling. Then they were outside, down the stairs, and onto the sidewalk.

Luck was with them; the trolley had just pulled up at the stop. They hurried aboard, and as the trolley began to roll away, Ves spotted the man from the bedroom running toward it. He was too slow, though, and was soon left behind.

Ves collapsed onto an empty bench, Sebastian beside him. "Are you all right?" Ves asked.

"Yes." Sebastian glanced down. Ves realized he was still holding Sebastian's wrist and snatched his hand back, face burning.

"It sounds as though they haven't been watching the apartment," he said, to cover his embarrassment. "They've been watching you."

"Not a comforting thought." Sebastian peered out the window, as though he feared they might have somehow kept pace with the trolley. "But *why?* I'm just the library's archivist. Who on earth would want to have me followed?"

None of this had sat easy with Ves, but the knowledge that Sebastian had been targeted filled him with a cold fury. If Fagerlie was behind any of this…

Ves ground his teeth. His duty to Noct had always been clear, even before they'd fled their childhood home. His entire purpose, the reason he'd been born, was so that Noct might ascend. And even though they'd both rejected that destiny, circumstances meant he had to support Noct. It was no burden; he was happy to do it. Noct wasn't just his brother, but his best friend.

His only friend, until now.

Sebastian was his friend, too, though. Surely Ves had a duty to him.

At least until Wednesday night. Then Sebastian would be on his own.

Ves stared out the window and tried very hard not to think about that.

"Home sweet home," Sebastian said. "Or, rather, my sister's house, but she's kind enough to let me live with her."

Ves stood uncertainly on the walk outside the house Sebastian had suggested they retreat to, so they could look over O'Neil's mail. It had an eclectic appearance, as if its architect had been unable to settle on a single style. To one side of the entrance, a narrow turret jutted up, while the other side sported broad, shallow bay windows. The main part of the roof was steeply gabled, but one end was unexpectedly interrupted by a sort of half-turret. Balconies jutted out in random spots, each of a different design, and the carriageway might have belonged to another house altogether before being uneasily joined to this one.

"It's something," he said.

Sebastian grinned at him. "Don't worry, it's much more orderly on the inside. You should have seen the house we grew up in. That one looked normal from the outside, but the interior was practically a maze. It originally belonged to my grandmother and great-uncle, so no wonder mother ended up working in the library—it must have felt just like home." He started up the walk. "Come on—Bonnie's probably about to put dinner on the table."

Ves felt rooted to the spot. He'd never *been* in someone's private home before, other than the one he'd grown up in. He'd set foot in boarding houses, of course, but only in the rooms he was looking to rent for Noct and himself. He seldom sat through the communal dinners they offered, preferring to eat in his room, alone with his brother, whom none of the other boarders ever knew existed.

"I don't want to put her to any trouble," he said. "I'll just...we'll take a look at the mail tomorrow, at the library."

"Don't be ridiculous—the more the merrier," Sebastian beckoned to him. "I promise, she'll be glad to meet you. They all will."

"They?" Ves asked in alarm, but by now Sebastian had reached the entryway and opened the door. Not knowing what else to do, Ves followed him.

A huge vase of flowers sat on a table in the front hall, perfuming the air. "Pete's back!" Sebastian exclaimed in obvious pleasure.

"That I am!" called a deep voice from the room ahead of them. Sebastian led the way, and Ves followed, though he wasn't certain if he should.

A grizzled man with a face weathered by the elements stood in the sitting room. In his arms, he cradled an infant who was probably only a few months old. His thick gray beard jutted out over the baby, as though protecting it.

Upon seeing Sebastian, his seamed face split into a grin. "Ah, Sebastian, good to see you. I've just been getting acquainted with the little one, while Bonnie sees to dinner."

"I'm glad to have you safely back," Sebastian said. He turned to

Ves. "This is my sister's husband, Captain Pete Degas of the *Hawthorne*. He's just back from hauling cargo around the world for the last...how long has it been, two years?"

"Aye," the captain agreed.

Sebastian reached for the infant, then turned and held it out to Ves. "And this is Bonnie's youngest, Clara. Clara, this is Vesper Rune, a very nice man from the library."

Ves wasn't sure if he was more shocked by Sebastian describing him as "nice," or by the fact he seemed to be trying to hand the infant to him. Then it occurred to him that, given the baby's age, it couldn't possibly belong to Captain Degas if he'd been at sea for two years.

Degas, however, was beaming at the baby as if she was the most perfect thing he'd ever seen. "Go on, now, don't be afraid to take her. She'll not bite—she's got no teeth to do it with!"

Degas laughed heartily. Ves shot a panicked glance at Sebastian, then slowly reached out to take the baby.

"There you go," Sebastian said. "Support her head—yes, just like that."

Now that they were both unencumbered by the baby, Sebastian and Degas embraced, clapping each other on the back. "Bonnie tells me you're still working at that library," Degas said. "You always were one for books, weren't you? Just like your mam."

Sebastian's expression flickered slightly, but he nodded. "Just like."

Feet thundered on the stairs behind them, and two girls ran in from the front hall, one chasing the other. "Go into the yard if you want to race, girls," Sebastian called, seeming glad for the distraction. "You know better than to run on the stairs. Now come here so I can prove to our guest you're human children and not wild horses."

They obeyed, staring at Ves with open curiosity. "Helen, Jossie, this is Mr. Rune," Sebastian said. "Go tell your mother to set another place for dinner."

They took off at full speed. Sebastian shook his head. "It's chaos around here, I'm afraid," he told Ves. "You'll be driven mad if you stay for long." But the fond note in his voice gave the lie to his words.

Ves wasn't sure how to respond. He'd never spent much time around children. He and Noct had been each other's only companions growing up. Neither had gone to any sort of school, and they'd lived so far out in the woods that only once had adventurous youths stumbled across them.

It was spring when the group of four boys carrying packs and hunting knives came upon them. They'd been playing in the glen at the foot of Caprine Hill, the tallest peak near Dunhollow, cradled and bolstered by the voice of the forest as it sang to them. Adults knew better than to stray anywhere near the area; it had the blackest of reputations in the region, and had even before Grandfather settled there.

Much later, Ves wondered why the boys had come to such a deserted area. Had they thought to prove their courage by climbing Caprine Hill and seeing the standing stones atop it? Perhaps they'd scoffed at the old tales of the thing that walked those woods and its thousand young.

They screamed when they saw Ves and Noct. Two broke and ran. One froze in his tracks. The fourth had a deeper reserve of either courage or madness, because he'd lifted his knife and ran at Noct, howling: "Kill it! Kill it!"

Noct had only been eight years old, and he'd screamed in terror. Ves was ten, but as big as a boy three years his senior. He'd managed to wrestle away the knife before anyone got hurt. All the boys ran, then.

He hadn't wanted to tell Mother. But Noct was in hysterics, and Ves hadn't yet learned to lie to her effectively. When she found out what happened, she'd stalked out into the yard with a knife of her own. There'd been chanting and then the sky grew dark.

"That takes care of them," she said when she came back inside. "They won't be carrying tales of us to outsiders."

Then she'd beat Ves, because he could have just killed the boys himself and spared her the trouble.

Ves swallowed against the knot in his throat and looked down at the infant in his arms. A small frown tugged at her round features, as though something troubled her sleep. Then it smoothed away and she blinked open blue eyes. The shrill voices of the other girls rang from the rear of the house as they tried to shout over each other.

How they'd all scream if they knew. And Sebastian and Degas…

Well. If Ves hadn't believed his mother before when she said outside folk would see Noct and him as things to be put down, he'd gotten proof that day in the glen.

"She likes you," Sebastian said. At his words, the baby began to fret. "And there I go, waking her up."

Ves held her out, and Degas took her back. She tangled one hand in his beard and began to wail in earnest. "There now, girl, what's the trouble?" he asked, bouncing her.

A boy of perhaps eleven, wearing an apron, appeared in the doorway. "Mom said dinner's ready," he said, and gave a quick bob of his head to Ves.

"Thanks, Willie," Sebastian said. He turned to Ves with a grin. "Come on—time to meet the rest of the family."

CHAPTER 12

$\mathcal{D}$inner was a chaotic affair, as it always was in the Rath household. Bonnie had brought out the good silverware, presumably to impress their guest. Willie laid out the dishes of broiled fish, new potatoes, and preserved asparagus, with root beer for the children and wine for the adults to celebrate Pete's return.

"It smells delicious," Ves said, from where he sat beside Bonnie.

"Help yourself," she replied with a smile.

He reached for the silver serving spoon—then dropped it with a gasp, snatching back his fingers as if he'd been burned.

"I-I'm so sorry," he said, cheeks flushing. "Silver gives me a rash, you see."

"Oh, dear, let me get the regular tinned steel for you," Bonnie said, quickly removing his fork, spoon, and knife.

Sebastian leaned across the table. "I'll serve for you," he offered, picking the serving spoon up. "Let me know how much."

"I'm sorry to put you to trouble," Ves said.

Bonnie snorted as she returned with a set of everyday utensils for him. "I have four children, Mr. Rune. Let me assure you, you're no trouble at all."

Once they had tucked in, Bonnie began to pepper Ves with

friendly questions, until Pete laughingly told her to let the man eat. All of the children were naturally curious as well, even little Tommy, who only stared agog at the stranger. To be fair, he stared at Pete, too, since he'd been far too small at Pete's last visit to remember the man.

Sebastian took the opportunity to put aside all the worries that had been building inside him about Kelly, and the stolen book, and the men who had apparently been following him. He listened as eagerly as the young ones while Pete related some of the adventures he'd had on the sea since last he'd seen them. His tales were filled with the wonder of the ocean, the terror of storms, and the beauty of far-off ports. Every character was a splash of color, from the smuggler with a heart of gold, to the dastardly pirates who'd found the *Hawthorne* wasn't the easy quarry they'd hoped for.

A glance at Ves showed him equally enrapt. When Pete finished a particularly exciting story about an encounter with smugglers in Singapore, Ves's expression grew wistful. "I wish I could see such things."

"Come with me, lad, and you will." Pete shot Sebastian a wink. "Dusty old books are for dusty old men like Sebastian—sign on to my crew, and you'll know what it is to be young!"

"You're twice my age, Pete," Sebastian objected.

"I'll come with you!" Willie offered.

Jossie clapped her hands. "I want to come, too!"

The mood instantly sobered. Jossie and Willie were both Pete's natural children, and Sebastian wondered if a love of the sea could be passed down through the blood.

"Ah, Willie, it's a hard life, my boy," Pete said, his tone sobering. "One that takes too many young men to their graves. I'd rather see you and your brother and sisters safe here on land, going to school and getting the book-learning I don't have."

Willie scowled. "But I want to go. I want to work with you."

"We'll talk about it again when you're older," Pete said with a glance at Bonnie.

She nodded. "That's right." She glanced around the table. "Now, who would like some dessert?"

"Actually, Sebastian and I had some things to discuss," Ves said, shooting him a look.

The poor man appeared a bit overwhelmed. "Of course. If you'll excuse us."

Sebastian rose to his feet, and Ves followed him to the back stair, which was nearest at hand. His room was directly off the stair on the second floor. The door stood open, as did the windows, letting in the evening breeze. It combatted the heat rising from the kitchen below, leaving the temperature pleasant.

Ves followed him in, pausing to look around at the boxes and dissected pictures crowding the room. "You weren't joking when you said you like puzzles."

Sebastian shrugged awkwardly. "It's a foolish hobby, I suppose."

"No. I like it. I like how your mind works." Ves flushed slightly. "Thank you for inviting me to dinner."

"Our pleasure." Sebastian sat on the bed, since there was only one chair.

"Your sister is very kind," Ves added. "Captain Degas seems nice as well."

"Bonnie wouldn't have a husband who wasn't." And since Ves couldn't have missed the fact Clara was too young to be Pete's natural child, he added, "She has three of them."

"Three...husbands?"

Sebastian shrugged. "It's a port town. You know the old saying: a wife in every port, a husband on every ship."

"I can't say I've ever heard that, no," Ves said, eyes wide.

"Huh. Perhaps it's a Widdershins saying, then." Sebastian folded his hands around his knee. "It works wonderfully. Her husbands all get the comfort of a home when they're in port, complete with wife and children. Bonnie and the children get the security of having more than a single man to rely on. Everyone is aware of the situation and is happy with it."

"It sounds very civilized," Ves said. "I never really met my progenitor. My father, that is," he corrected quickly. "I knew *of* him, and we often communicated, but never face to face. I grew up in a one-room shack in the woods with my mother and her father." Ves looked around the bedroom almost wistfully. "It was nothing like this."

Sebastian felt something relax inside him. Widdershins was an unconventional place, but still, some looked on Bonnie's way of living with a judging eye. Ordinarily, he wouldn't have brought a newcomer like Ves here.

But Ves had saved him from those ruffians twice now. And Sebastian was startled to realize he *liked* Ves quite a lot. Maybe it should have been Sebastian in the bindery—but that was his fault, not Ves's.

And speaking of the ruffians... "I don't understand why anyone would follow me."

Ves folded his arms over his chest and leaned against the wall beside the closed door. "It must have something to do with O'Neil's disappearance. You're the only one looking into it. Which, in addition to the warning note I received, makes me wonder if the rare book trade is actually involved at all."

"What do you mean?"

"If this was a simple case of book theft, those men wouldn't still be in town. Even if they thought Kelly had hidden the book somewhere, they'd cut their losses and go back to wherever they came from. Or, if they're local toughs, this mysterious boss of theirs would have." He shook his head. "Not to suggest the rare book trade can't get ugly. But those who supply the books rely on drawing as little attention to their activities as possible."

"Then what's going on?"

Ves let his arms fall. "I don't know."

"Perhaps the letters will tell us." Sebastian stripped off his coat, then took them out of the inner pocket and tossed them on the bed. "The writing desk is small—turn on the lamp there beside the bed, and we should have both the space and the light here."

A look of alarm flashed across Ves's features, as though he thought Sebastian meant to seduce him right then and there. Not that Sebastian would have any objections to doing so, but still. "I promise not to ravish you."

Ves's olive skin flushed scarlet. "I-I didn't mean to—that is—you shouldn't say such things."

"Why not?" Sebastian pulled the rubber band off the pack of letters. "Does it offend you that I like men?"

Ves's eyes looked as though they might pop out of his head altogether. "I…you do? I mean, no, of course not. I-It doesn't offend me."

Sebastian smothered a grin. In other circumstances, he might have considered trying to seduce Ves. Even though he never invited lovers back to the house, he might make an exception in this case.

But he hadn't brought Ves here for such pleasantries, alas. He spread out the letters and gestured to him. "You take half, and I'll take half."

Ves settled onto the opposite side of the bed, still blushing. There were only about a dozen pieces of mail, one of which was a Sears & Roebuck catalog that could be immediately set aside. Most of the remaining mail proved to be fliers, bills of various sorts, and three pieces of personal correspondence.

Ves scanned the first. "This seems to be a letter from some member of the family…talking about O'Neil's aunt and her health troubles. It's signed Benny."

"His Uncle Benjamin," Sebastian supplied as he picked up a similar missive. "I think he moved away from Widdershins before Kelly was even born. Some people just don't take to the town, I suppose." He slit open the envelope with the letter opener from his desk. "This is from Benny as well, asking why Kelly hasn't written back."

"And so is this third letter," Ves said. He looked up and met Sebastian's gaze. "It looks to me as though Mr. O'Neil's family didn't know he was leaving town. Did he have any relatives still in Widdershins?"

"No." Sebastian felt his hopes of finding Kelly alive fade. "The fact they haven't heard from him…well, it's not a good sign, is it?"

Ves shook his head slowly. "Again, if he merely meant to steal a book, sell it, and leave town, he surely would have sent some missive telling his relatives that he'd resigned from the Ladysmith and was relocating from Widdershins. But he didn't." He paused. "Unless he meant to use the money and start over somewhere new, with a false identity."

Sebastian tugged at his hair. He didn't want to imagine they'd gone to all of this trouble for nothing. "There must be something here."

Ves picked up a letter, then tossed it down. "A catalog, fliers for businesses, and a series of increasingly urgent demands to pay the electric bill."

Sebastian frowned. "The new tenant of the apartment should be receiving those...wait."

He snatched up one of the bills and pulled it free from the envelope. "Look—the address being billed is different from the mailing address. This bill isn't for the apartment. Kelly must have a second apartment, or even a house."

Their eyes met across the bed. "The key O'Neil left for you," Ves said. "I think I know what it goes to."

Ves sat down on the edge of the bed in his rented room, unsure whether the evening at the Rath house made him want to laugh or cry.

He didn't know how normal families worked. Or at least, normal compared to what he'd grown up with; ones with adults who didn't expect their children to help them end the world.

Possibly everyone had simply been on good behavior in front of a stranger. But somehow, he didn't think so. The children were well-behaved, but not perfect. They'd laughed and talked over one another, and quarreled, and raced about the house. Most astonishingly, none of them had seemed to fear the consequences.

Not to say they hadn't obeyed when one of the adults chided them, but none of them had seemed truly *afraid*. No adult had raised a hand, or screamed invectives at them.

Again, perhaps they'd been putting on a show in front of a guest, and even now the girls were getting the strap for running down the stairs. But given their lack of flinches when Sebastian corrected them, the absence of dread in their eyes for what would come next when Ves made his farewells, he didn't think so.

Their house hadn't been the neatest, but it was warm, welcoming. And the entire Rath clan, including Captain Degas, had been unfailingly kind to one another.

They'd been kind to *him*.

He flopped back on the bed, staring at the ceiling without seeing it. There was the rub. They'd seen him as human and treated him as such. But if they knew the truth…

Would the older boy, Willie, have run at him with a knife, screaming that he had to be killed? Certainly Captain Degas would have reached for any weapon available to defend his unconventional family. And Sebastian…

For a moment, he'd half thought Sebastian was *flirting* with him. Thank the trees, the mirror in Sebastian's room had been angled in such a way so as not to easily betray Ves to him. Though Ves had almost done that himself with the serving spoon.

Silver revealed his monstrous nature, one way or another. Either burning his skin on contact, or by showing far too much in the reflection of silver-backed mirrors.

But Sebastian hadn't noticed. He'd been too focused on Ves himself, and then on the letters.

Beautiful Sebastian, who Ves was plotting to betray in almost precisely the same way as the absent O'Neil might have done. Oh, he didn't mean to steal a book himself—but surely Fagerlie did. What else could there be worth finding in a library?

And then Ves would disappear without a trace, just as O'Neil had. Would Sebastian look for him? Or realize the truth, and curse Ves's name?

Ves pressed his fingers into his eyes. Once he was cured, once Noct was cured, they'd be free to move among normal people without fear of discovery. They'd find other friends, other families. Maybe Noct would start a family of his own. Ves ought to look at tonight as a promise, a preview. Not a betrayal, exposing innocent children to his monstrous self, deceiving their parents and uncle into thinking he was just a normal man, rather than a thing created to destroy.

Gods. He wanted to scream until his lungs bled. He wanted to pick up one of the mirrors turned to the wall and smash it into tiny bits, then grind those into dust. More than anything, he wanted to leave behind this burden of constant hiding, of suppressing the truth, of putting on a mask every morning.

And if he wanted those things, how much more must Noct want them?

Ves let his hands fall to his side. If things had been different...but they weren't.

Tomorrow, he'd go with Sebastian to the address from the electric bill. Find out whatever he could. Either clear his conscience, that O'Neil's disappearance hadn't in fact been engineered by Fagerlie one way or another, or else discover his worst fears were correct.

And if they were...then what?

His first duty had to be to Noct. *Had to.* His brother depended on him. Ves couldn't let him down by backing out.

Even if he was beginning to wish he could.

CHAPTER 13

*V*es left the boarding house before sunrise the next morning, having slept poorly—for the short instances he'd actually been able to sleep. Halley's Comet blazed in the east, and he spotted more than one person with a telescope on their lawn or roof, observing its passage. The first newsboys passed him on bicycles piled high with their wares, and on a whim, he stopped at a corner and bought a paper.

As had become usual, news of the comet filled substantial inches of column space. An astronomer in Arizona repeated assurances that, despite what Monsieur Flammarion claimed, the cyanogen gas in the comet's tail would be too tiny an amount to harm anything when the earth passed through it.

Apparently, not everyone believed him. According to several articles, religious fervor had taken hold across the country, and church services ran continuously day and night in towns from Virginia to Texas. Workers quit their jobs to join revivals, praying for forgiveness and salvation now that the end of days were upon them.

Ves didn't know about any actual prophecies saying the comet would bring on the end of the world—but then, why would anyone have bothered with them, since the worst was meant to have already happened?

It would be a night for potent magic, though. At his guess, any number of cults were already making preparations for calling up whatever might serve their purposes.

Would anyone dance on Caprine Hill Wednesday night? Would fires burn amidst the stones, calling the Black Goat of the Wood forth to spawn yet more of its thousand young?

Once at the museum, Ves took advantage of his early arrival to work on his map of the library. When eight o'clock came around, he retired to the bindery and attacked the backlog of periodicals that needed to be bound together. He carefully cut each installment in a volume free of its original binding, then used a sponge soaked in water to remove any remaining traces of glue. After assembling a volume, he placed it in the book press and began work on the cover.

His mind wandered as his hands worked. Before they'd parted the night before, Sebastian had said something about updating Mr. Quinn as to their inquiry into O'Neil and the missing book. With the head librarian's permission, he'd fetch Ves shortly after lunch, which was one of the reasons he had come in early. Technically it didn't *matter* if he did his job well, since he'd be long gone by the time his trial period ended. But it was a point of pride; if he was to set his hands to the task, then he wanted it done correctly, and as completely as possible.

Shortly before lunch, he put everything in order. His coffee had gone cold while he worked, so he made for the staff room to refresh it.

Two men already sat there; they fell silent when he entered. "You're our new binder and conservator, isn't that right?" one of them asked.

He nodded. "Vesper Rune."

The man smiled broadly. "I'm Arthur Fairchild, and this is Mortimer Waite. Please, call me Arthur."

"And you may call me Mr. Waite," said the other. His suit was new, without a trace of wear on it, and small rubies studded his cufflinks. Most librarians Vesper had met were anything but wealthy, but Mr. Waite and Miss Endicott both seemed to come from money. What on earth were either of them doing working here?

"Don't be rude, Mortimer," Arthur chided. "We're all librarians together, aren't we?"

"Mr. Rune is an outsider," Waite said disapprovingly.

"So is Miss Endicott, and yet you're engaged to be married," Arthur replied.

Waite merely shrugged.

Whatever workplace maneuvering these two sought to engage him in, Ves wanted none of it. He poured fresh coffee and retreated to the bindery, closing the door firmly behind him.

A breeze ruffled one of the journals waiting to be bound. The newspaper he'd bought on the way in blew off the desk, scattering onto the floor.

Ves froze, every muscle tense, the skin along his spine aching. All around him, whispers gathered, echoing from one section of the room, then the other.

"Binder...get out...leave or die..."

The hair on his neck prickled, and he put down his cup. Straightening, he paced around the bindery, listening. But the whispers seemed to come first from one direction, then another.

"What are you?" he challenged. As a youth, he'd heard voices from the wood and the hill on certain days—but those were known, expected. The things they had belonged to didn't haunt buildings. "Are you some creature of the Outside? Some ghost or spirit?"

"Leave or die."

He folded his arms stubbornly over his chest. "No."

A windstorm struck the bindery, scattering papers, flipping open journals, even hurling a pile of books from the table. Ves braced himself, its magic flowing around him. He didn't know what this thing was—but it didn't know what he was, either.

The door opened and Sebastian stepped inside. "Are you—" he began.

A gust slammed the door behind him—and then there were books lifting up, flying at him in the storm.

Ves didn't think, only moved. He flung himself onto Sebastian, knocking him to the floor, and did his best to cover the taller man with his own body. Books slammed into him with bruising force, and the binding awl from his own kit buried itself in the back of his thigh. He gritted his teeth and fought to keep control, to not give himself away.

The wind died away, its fury exhausted. Ves remained in place, waiting for it to start up again, but nothing happened.

He sat up, just a little. Sebastian was under him, blinking in surprise. Ves became suddenly, achingly aware of the other man's body beneath his. Long thighs pressed against his own, and the sight of Sebastian's wind-tumbled hair and flushed cheeks sent a rush of blood to his groin.

He rolled off of Sebastian hastily. The motion bumped the awl in his leg, and the sharp pain killed his ardor. He yanked it free and took out his handkerchief to clean off the blood.

"You're hurt," Sebastian said, sitting up.

"I'm fine." With the thin steel awl out, the flesh would have already closed. One of the few benefits of being a monster.

The bindery was a mess, with scattered paper and thrown books everywhere. As for the ghost, or spirit, or whatever it had been, there was no trace.

"What the *hell* is going on in this library?" Ves wondered aloud.

Sebastian climbed to his feet, then reached down to help Ves up. Instead of releasing his hand, he stared into Ves's eyes. "In this specific case, I have no idea." He took a deep breath, as if bracing himself. "Vesper…there's something you should know."

Sebastian's fingers were warm and soft against his own. "Wh-what?" Ves managed through the tightness in his throat.

"You're going to think me mad, but…" Sebastian's mouth quirked ruefully. "Sorcery—magic—is real."

They went to Marsh's for lunch; Sebastian didn't want to conduct a discussion of magic on an empty stomach. He spent the walk over trying to think how to convince Ves of the truth of the world. As for his part, Ves remained silent, even when they slipped across from one another in a booth near the back of the restaurant. Did he think Sebastian was a lunatic?

When Sebastian had come to fetch Ves to go to lunch, he'd been shocked to step inside and find himself in the middle of a windstorm. Then even more shocked when Ves had knocked him to the ground and proceeded to try and protect Sebastian with his own body.

It warmed him to know that Ves would do that for him. He only wished he'd been able to enjoy the position. He tried to remember the sensation of Ves's weight atop him, but it was drowned out by confusion and fear.

Ah, well. Perhaps he'd get another chance. Assuming he could convince Ves that he wasn't a ranting maniac, at least.

They both ordered coffee and the fish sandwich. While they waited on their food to come, Ves leaned back in the booth. "So. Magic."

How on earth was he to explain this to an outsider? "This will sound as though I should be sent to Danvers, but hear me out. There are things in this world that most people don't know about." Sebastian fixed his gaze intently on Ves, trying to convince him with will alone. "Beings, both earthly and from the Outside, beyond our comprehension. Arcane lines inscribed on the world. Sorcery."

Ves nodded. "I know."

"You—you *know?*" Sebastian gaped at him. "How on earth do you know that?"

Ves's brows lowered. "I'm more concerned about how you know, Sebastian. Are you a sorcerer?"

"Good God, no. Are you?"

"I couldn't cast a spell if my life depended on it." Ves's chin lifted slightly. "So you aren't a sorcerer. Why do you know about the arcane arts, then?"

"At this point, almost everyone in town does," Sebastian said. "Again, this might sound mad, but it's the truth. A cult tried to end the world as we know it in 1902 and bring back those who had once been masters over the earth, before the age of mankind. The battle to stop them took place here, in Widdershins."

The color drained from Ves's face, lending a grayish tinge to his olive skin. "Oh. I...I see."

"I wasn't here for it—long story, I'll tell you later. But suffice it to say, only people who've moved to town after don't know about the arcane."

The waiter reappeared with the sandwiches. Sebastian picked his up, stomach growling, but Ves only stared at his plate blankly.

"What's wrong?" he asked. "Ves? Are you all right?"

Ves's throat worked as he swallowed. "I told you I was raised in a cult. They worshipped nameless gods, collected unspeakable tomes, and sometimes cast spells. All in preparation for the end of the world."

Sebastian almost choked on the bite of fish sandwich he'd taken. "Dear lord," he managed when he could speak again. "I thought you meant they were part of something like the Millerites."

Ves laughed, though there was no humor in it. "Well, they did have their own version of the Great Disappointment in 1902."

"But...you ran away when you were seventeen, right?" Sebastian asked.

"In spring 1902, yes. Apparently I cut it closer than I meant." Ves picked up his sandwich but only continued to stare at it. "I didn't want any part of the grand destiny they tried to create for me. Certainly I didn't want the world to be subjugated to things from the Outside. I didn't bring any of their twisted philosophy with me. The only important thing I took from them was my knowledge on how to bind and conserve books, since the types of tomes they collected were often in dire shape." He bit his lip. "They...weren't like your family."

That sounded bad. "I'm so sorry you went through that, Vesper," he said sincerely.

Ves's startled eyes met his. Then Ves looked away again, blinking rapidly. "I...no one's ever said that to me before. Not that I've ever told anyone."

He sounded so lonely, so sad, that it broke Sebastian's heart. He put down his sandwich, reached across the table, and took Ves's hand. "Then I'm honored you told me."

Ves gazed at their hands for a moment. Then he turned his palm-up, curling his fingers into Sebastian's.

Sebastian's breath caught. Not from lust, but from something he wasn't entirely sure he could put a name to. He only knew that he was deeply glad to be here, with this man. That Ves felt Sebastian was worthy of confiding in.

He'd let down so many people in his life. But he swore at that moment that Ves would never be one of them.

CHAPTER 14

They elected to walk from the restaurant to the address on Kelly's electricity bill. As they strolled, Ves told Sebastian about the various unnerving encounters he'd had in the library, starting with a whisper and escalating to the attack in the bindery that morning.

His head still spun, to think that Sebastian not only knew about the arcane, but apparently almost everyone else in town did as well.

If he'd stayed, if he and Noct had accepted their grand destiny… this was where he would have come to lead an army of cultists and monsters. He would have fought against Mr. Quinn, and Arthur, and Mortimer Waite, and all the rest. Against Rebecca Rath and Kelly O'Neil. Against Sebastian.

Gods of the wood, he'd never been so glad he'd taken Noct and fled.

Mother and Grandfather would surely have come here to welcome back those who had once ruled the earth, and whom they wanted to rule again. This was where they'd died.

He'd had no idea he was setting foot in the town that had seen their defeat. He'd assumed things hadn't gone their way when the world failed to end. As for the cult itself, he'd been unable to find a trace of it when he made cautious, veiled inquiries later. They were gone, wiped from the face of the earth, their grand design unsuccessful.

Cultists who failed didn't usually survive the experience, so it had come as no real surprise. He and Noct had never really spoken about it, never mourned, just quietly gone on and tried not to dwell.

Now he learned that he'd come to the very town where defeat found his only human relatives. What had happened to their bodies? Had they been incinerated by magic, or thrown into a pit?

He'd never know. And it shouldn't have bothered him, not after everything, and yet somehow it did.

"I wish you had mentioned this from the start," Sebastian said, once Ves was done telling him about the spirit.

Ves offered an apologetic shrug. "I didn't think you'd believe me. Or, if you did believe me, you wouldn't really comprehend the truth of the arcane and might put yourself in harm's way by accident."

Sebastian waved a dismissive hand. "No, I understand. The newest employee, babbling about ghostly whispers and books moving on their own, before his trial period is even up…I'm sure you were worried Mr. Quinn would fire you as a drunkard or a madman."

It hadn't even occurred to him, probably because he wasn't going to be in the position much longer anyway. "Er, yes," Ves said quickly. "That too. So I take it this sort of thing isn't a common occurrence in the library?"

"Surprisingly enough, no." Sebastian frowned thoughtfully. "From what you're saying, it sounds as though the spirit, or whatever it is, has a grudge toward the Ladysmith's bookbinder. Do you think it haunted Kelly as well? Or perhaps he was safe, since he'd signed the oath we found in the desk? I wonder if it could be some sort of guardian that thinks you're an outsider meddling where he doesn't belong?"

"I haven't the slightest idea." Ves stepped to one side as a young woman sped past them on a bicycle. "Would Mr. Quinn know?"

"I don't think so," Sebastian said. "I met with him this morning and told him about everything we found. He didn't know about the pact or the blood signatures. I think he was a bit annoyed about that, to be honest. Though not half as annoyed as he'll be when we tell him there's some kind of malevolent force targeting you."

A part of Ves wanted to laugh. He tried to imagine having this conversation with his supervisor at the Boston Public Library and failed utterly. "I'm not worried about myself. But what if it starts attacking other people?"

"Irene is a sorceress. Perhaps she'll know how to stop it."

Ves came to a halt. "A sorceress?" His mother had disdained clothing except as necessary for modesty and the elements, preferring to focus all her time and energy on knowledge and power. Irene, on the other hand, looked as though she'd stepped out of a fashion-plate in a Parisian magazine. It had never occurred to Ves that sorcery didn't mean hiding in the woods in poverty.

"It's not her main area of focus, but her family are all well-versed in the arcane," Sebastian said reassuringly.

"Is everyone in this town something other than they seem to be?" Ves exclaimed. He'd come here thinking Widdershins wouldn't be much different from Boston, only smaller.

His seatmate on the train had tried to warn him, but Ves had been so sure he knew what he was walking into. His mother had spoken derogatorily of everyone outside the cult, calling them sleepers who knew nothing about the real world, who moved through it in a false dream, refusing to open their eyes.

Shame washed through Ves at the realization he'd let that assumption creep into his own thinking. He'd been so certain only he knew the truth, that everyone around him was ignorant.

Sebastian offered him a warm smile. "I'm no more than what I seem," he said. "Just a humble archivist, spending my days processing and cataloging material. So much cataloging."

The sun glinted off his silver-rimmed glasses and brightened his hair. His smile was open, uncomplicated, and Ves had to struggle against the wild urge to kiss him.

"A humble archivist, who will stop at nothing to find out what happened to his friend," Ves said. "I think you underestimate yourself, Mr. Rath."

Sebastian's lips parted slightly, as if in surprise. Then he hooked his arm through Ves's, tugging him along. "As much as I love a compliment, standing here won't bring us any closer to finding out what the devil is going on."

Ves's heart pounded at the arm so casually linked through his own. It was nothing, just a friendly touch, and yet it made him desperately crave more. If he had any sense at all, he'd use the first opportunity to slide his arm free. He couldn't risk Sebastian touching his back; he had to keep distance between them.

Instead, he walked arm-in-arm with Sebastian in companionable silence the rest of the way.

Their destination lay within one of Widdershins's more decrepit neighborhoods. The area stretched between the river and the docks, and had in the past been far grander than it was now. Once-proud roofs sagged, gardens had become thickets of weed and bramble, and paint peeled from the weathered walls. Though Sebastian had lived in Widdershins his entire life, he'd never set foot here.

"I'm almost surprised anyone bothered to run electricity to this neighborhood," Ves remarked, eyeing the tangle of wires overhead. Seagulls perched along the roofs and atop the poles, shrieking at one another.

"The city was determined to have access to it for every house," Sebastian said with a shrug. "Lord knows, they've spent more money on worse things."

He stepped up to the door, then glanced around. A woman was busy hanging washing on the lines flapping overhead, and a small group of children were playing sea monsters and sailors, but no one seemed to be paying them the slightest attention. Taking out the key, he slipped it into the lock.

It turned easily—someone, no doubt Kelly, had taken the time to oil it in the near past. The hinges failed to squeak as well, which surprised him given the exterior of the place.

The door opened onto a small hall. A framed staircase immediately to the left ran up to the second floor, while the open doors revealed parlor, sitting room, and dining room. The air smelled musty, and the boards creaked beneath their feet as they stepped inside.

Sebastian tried a light switch without much hope given the numerous unpaid bills. Nothing happened, but the sunlight coming through the grimy windows would be enough for the moment, without having to resort to the flashlight he'd brought from home.

"I'll look on the second floor," Ves offered.

"All right, but be careful on those stairs."

The steps groaned beneath Ves's weight, but held. Once he was safely up, Sebastian started his own search. Dust coated the bare floor, and damp spotted the walls. His eyes itched, and he sneezed twice.

The sitting room, dining room, and kitchen were bare, save for an enormous cast iron stove which had probably been deemed too heavy to bother moving. But just as Sebastian began to worry there was nothing to find, he stepped into the parlor.

The fireplace still bore the remnants of a fire, long cold. A chair with faded upholstery was drawn up near it, a thick blanket abandoned on it, as if Kelly had merely stepped out for a moment. A desk with ink, fountain pen, and an open notebook stood beneath the window with the best light, a wooden chair accompanying it. Several boxes sat scattered about: on the floor in front of the hearth, beside the comfortable chair, and on the desk.

The floorboards behind him creaked as Ves stepped inside. "There's nothing upstairs."

"This looks like the only room Kelly used." Sebastian's heart knocked against his ribs as an odd feeling of dread swept over him. There was little chance he'd like any answers he found here. Even so, he forced himself to cross to the desk and look at the open notebook. "This is his handwriting."

Ves seemed to sense his hesitation. "Would you like me to go through it? You can inspect the boxes."

"Thank you, but no. I'm the one who knew the man." Sebastian sat down and pulled the open notebook close. Though the writing was recognizable, the script looked rushed, as if Kelly had dashed out the words in a passion.

I need to know more about Halley's Comet. The Books of the Bound were created beneath its last visit in 1835. It must have sorcerous significance to them. But what? Will it quell their power? Or make them stronger? Did the Daylight Comet in January have any influence on them?

I wish Rebecca were still alive.

Should I take Sebastian into my confidence? Or Miss Endicott? Her family knows things, but they also have a history of seizing magical artifacts for their own use. Would they actually help, or would they take them for themselves?

I'll wait. I still have time.

God, I wish I knew which of the books was unaccounted for. Could the fire have destroyed it? But if that was the case, Dromgoole and Ladysmith would have simply burned them, not gone to elaborate lengths to trap them.

Right now, I'd settle for knowing where the one in the library is. And which? Blood, breath, bone, or flesh?

Breath…words? That would make sense. Breath is words. Blood is family. Bone? Flesh?

I have to find the other plans Dromgoole created. But there are so many letters, and I'm so tired.

It doesn't matter. This is the burden I took on when I signed the oath in my own blood. And if I fail…

Rebecca would have told Sebastian where to look in the desk. I'll leave the spare key there for him, just in case.

When he reached the end of the page, Sebastian silently passed the book to Ves. Ves's brows drew down, and his frown deepened more and more as he read. When he was done, he said, "She didn't tell you, though."

Of all the things to trouble him, this should have been the least. And yet it wasn't, and Ves had intuited it immediately.

"I gave up the right to know when I turned my back on the family tradition," he said, and strove to keep his sorrow from his voice. "She was entitled to her secrets. I'm only surprised Kelly assumed she would have told me to start with."

Ves leaned over and put his hand on Sebastian's shoulder, squeezing gently. "Family tradition be damned. There's nothing wrong with you wanting to live your own life. Or do you think I should have done what was expected of me, and helped end the world?"

"That's different," Sebastian objected.

"Only in scope. You wanted to be a librarian and an archivist, not a bookbinder and conservator. It was your life and your choice. You did nothing wrong."

Sebastian's chest ached, and his eyes burned. He blinked rapidly. "I...thank you. It means a great deal to hear that."

Ves offered him a small, commiserating smile and let his hand fall. "I wonder if O'Neil might have taken the *Historia Coelestis Britannica* because of the connection to Halley."

Grateful for the change of subject, Sebastian said, "I'm no expert on astronomy, but Arthur said this particular copy had Flamsteed's thoughts on him. Still, it was just a catalog of stars. It wouldn't have had information on the comet itself."

"Perhaps there was something he discovered which led him to that book," Ves suggested. "He then took it without bothering to note that he was borrowing it, because he meant to bring it back promptly."

"He wasn't stealing it, so the curses let him leave with it," Sebastian murmured. "So this doesn't have anything to do with the rare book trade. You were right." For a moment, he let his relief that Kelly hadn't betrayed the library overwhelm him before realizing the implications. "He didn't run off and sell it. And, judging by this, he didn't just quit abruptly on a whim." He met Ves's gaze. "Do you think he's still alive?"

"I honestly don't know," Ves said. "But I doubt it. I'm sorry."

Sebastian bowed his head and let out a sigh. "Do you think whomever hired those men to follow me believes I know more than I do? That Kelly confided in me?"

"It seems likely." Ves ran a hand through his hair, leaving it mussed. "What do you think about the actual contents of what O'Neil wrote? These Books of the Bound? Nathanial Ladysmith signed the blood oath you found in my desk, so it sounds as though he was in some way involved."

"Whatever they are, Kelly thought one of those volumes was in the library." Sebastian took the notebook from Ves. He flipped back a page, but rather than an explanation, found a list titled *Known Works by Alexander Dromgoole.* "It seems he had developed a fascination with the Ladysmith's architect."

Ves lifted the dusty lid from the box on the desk. "Letters. Addressed to Dromgoole." He went to the larger box on the floor. "This one seems to contain architectural drawings. What do you bet they're by him?"

"Not a bet I'll take," Sebastian said. He lifted the first letter from the stack in the box. Something about the handwriting nagged at him, though he couldn't say what. "It doesn't look as though this one was ever posted. There isn't even a stamp." He inspected it more carefully. "It looks as though someone slit open the envelope, though. Kelly?"

"Maybe." Ves looked up from where he sat on the floor now, sorting through the drawings. "What does it say?"

Sebastian took out the letter and opened it carefully.

December 21, 1860

My darling Alex,

Perhaps I should cease writing letters to you. Some might call the practice morbid, given that you are shut away in that dreadful place in Taunton. Others might say this is my way of denying that the price you paid for our great work is permanent, that your mind will never be your own again.

I have asked myself these things, over and over. It destroys my heart to imagine you in that place. I know the man I loved is gone, but seeing his body in such conditions, screaming and ranting and begging, is too much.

So perhaps this does allow me some denial. If nothing else, I am so used to ordering my thoughts in letters to you, it at least lets me clarify things to myself, even if you will never remark on them.

I miss you so much, my darling. Day and night, you're never far from my thoughts. You haunt me, even though your body still lives.

I want to let you know our work still stands firm. Two Hallowe'ens have passed now, and even when the veil is thinnest, the books remain contained in their separate prisons. By the grace of God, they shall stay that way forever—though of course we both know nothing is truly forever.

So long as our work holds, their malign influence will be contained. Your creations will stand, even though no one else can ever know that four of them conceal and constrain a great evil.

As for myself, I have become a humble bookbinder. The museum president, director, and board all think me mad, or at least eccentric. Why on earth would the man who spent his fortune to construct a museum for his adopted town of Widdershins then go on to do a menial job within its walls? Oh, you should hear the rumors! They would make you laugh until tears.

But this way I can ensure that others will come after me to take up the charge and make certain the Bound Ones remain so. They will walk a lonely path, I fear, but they will walk it in my footsteps.

By God, I miss you, my love. Perhaps, if the fates smile kindly, I will dream of the old days tonight.

Yours forever,

Nathaniel

CHAPTER 15

Sebastian carried a bottle of scotch onto the balcony where Ves awaited him. They'd hired a cart and driver to transport the boxes of material to Sebastian's office in the museum. Before leaving Kelly's secret house, he'd inspected the emptied desk for any hidden drawers, but none had presented themselves, so he felt confident they had everything.

Bonnie insisted on feeding them, and Sebastian had been glad when Ves agreed to stay for dinner a second night in a row. Once they finished, they retreated upstairs to one of the two balconies. The other opened off of Bonnie's room, but this smaller one led off the turret landing and overlooked the street.

Ves sat in one of the wicker chairs, half-hidden in the growing darkness. Sebastian poured them each a drink, then took the chair closest to the other man.

"So," Ves said, "Alexander Dromgoole and Nathaniel R. Ladysmith were...what? Fighting sorcery? Hiding magic books? Both?"

Sebastian took a sip of his scotch, letting its peaty flavor roll across his tongue. "That's what it sounds like. Hopefully we'll learn more, considering there are four boxes of letters to go through. Not to mention the architectural drawings."

"I hope so." Ves drank as well, then winced.

"Not much of a scotch drinker?"

"I haven't had the opportunity."

Sebastian waited for Ves to elaborate, or not as he chose. A part of him burned with curiosity to know more about Ves's past. He couldn't imagine what it must have been like to grow up in the very cult that had attacked Widdershins eight years ago, let alone what it must have cost to leave his family behind. It spoke volumes about Ves's character, that he'd been able to turn his back on everything he'd no doubt been taught growing up and strike out on his own.

Sebastian didn't want to push, though. It was up to Ves whether or not to tell him, and when.

"It does sound as if one of these evil books is hidden in the library somewhere," Ves said.

Sebastian accepted the change of subject. "Indeed. Nathaniel wrote as if he expected the binders following him to know about it. Where and what it is. But Kelly didn't. Did Mother? Or Great-uncle Thomas?"

"Maybe your mother didn't have a chance to tell Mr. O'Neil?" Ves suggested. "Was her death…unexpected?"

Not what Sebastian particularly wanted to talk about. "She perished in a house fire."

"I'm so sorry."

"So am I." Sebastian threw back his drink and poured himself a second. "The house was in full blaze when I came home that day. I tried to go inside, but the heat was too great. The flames were everywhere. Even the firemen couldn't go in." He stared at the depths of the scotch in his glass. "She was still alive. Trapped inside. I heard her…"

"Gods of the wood." Ves put aside his glass and leaned forward, settling both hands on Sebastian's shoulders. "This must all be terribly difficult for you."

Ves's hands were strong, reassuringly so. His scent teased Sebastian's nostrils: bay rum cologne, underlain by something else. Something like black pepper, mingled with a verdant forest.

Sebastian touched one of Ves's hands. "Whatever secrets she had, they died with her."

"Assuming she even knew about the books." Ves gave a final squeeze and sat back, though not all the way. "I assume the fact this spirit is obsessed with the library's bookbinder means it has something to do with these Books of the Bound."

"That seems obvious," Sebastian agreed. "We'll consult with Irene first thing tomorrow. She knows the most about magic and other-worldly beings. Perhaps she's even heard of these books and can point us in the right direction."

That uneasy look touched Ves's face again. Perhaps his upbringing had given him an aversion to sorcerers. "Where do you think the one might be hidden in the library?"

Sebastian chewed at his lip. "If I were going to hide a book in a library full of other volumes, I'd put it inside a false binding and assign it a fake card. I'd give it a title so tedious no one would ever want to open it. *My Brilliant Thoughts on All Subjects Beneath the Sun,* by Mr. J. Smith."

Ves laughed. It was the first time he'd done so in Sebastian's presence, and the sound lifted his heart unexpectedly. "Some benighted fool would probably request it anyway."

"I'd say Dr. Norris from the American History Department, but he'd never admit anyone's thoughts were more brilliant than his own."

Ves chuckled again and tossed back the rest of his scotch, before holding out the glass for a refill. "If I had to work the desk, I'd go stark raving mad."

"I have, and nearly did." Sebastian sobered. "That will be the second thing to do, I suppose. Once I inform Mr. Quinn of what we've found, he'll have every librarian scouring the shelves for this *Book of Breath*, or whatever it proves to be."

Ves watched him over the rim of his glass. "And what will the head librarian do with it?"

"Find somewhere secure to hide it, probably." Sebastian shrugged. That was Mr. Quinn's problem, not his. "And of course we still don't know what became of Kelly."

It seemed more and more likely that the worst had happened, and Kelly was dead. God, why had Sebastian waited so long to look for the man? He should have insisted on a search right away, even if no one else believed anything was wrong.

Yet another person he'd managed to let down.

"The men following you…it's possible they killed him," Ves said. "Please, Sebastian, be careful."

"I have been. I'm keeping an eye out, and making sure not to walk down any roads without plenty of other people in sight." Sebastian offered him a smile. "Perhaps they had second thoughts when they discovered I have so fierce a protector."

Ves's olive complexion had reddened from the drink, and the color of his cheeks deepened at Sebastian's remark. "You said O'Neil sent a letter of resignation. Was it forged?"

"I wouldn't have thought so." Sebastian called it to mind. "I didn't examine the signature, though. And the rest of the letter was typed. I only glimpsed it, when Mr. Quinn sought to reassure me Kelly hadn't simply vanished. Perhaps I should take a closer look. I have some experience comparing signatures, considering people do try to pass off fakes to the museum library."

"I'm cursing myself for throwing away the note left for me," Ves said. "We could compare it to the typewritten resignation letter and see if they came from the same machine."

"You didn't know." God, surely someone in the library hadn't been responsible for Kelly's death.

Ves sighed. "I'm sorry, Sebastian. For all of this."

"That's very kind of you, but none of it is your fault." He hesitated, but the scotch was warm in his blood, and the night air cool on his skin. "At least this mess allowed me to meet you."

Ves turned toward him, brows arched in surprise. And before he could think on it any further, Sebastian leaned forward and kissed him.

Ves kissed him back. His mouth tasted of the scotch they'd drunk, and the kiss itself was untutored, but it fired Sebastian's blood. He traced the seam of Ves's lips with his tongue, then slid it in. Ves moaned in response, and with that encouragement, Sebastian made to shift into his lap.

The touch of Sebastian's thighs against his seemed to shock Ves back to reality. He pulled away, every muscle going rigid. His eyes were wide, chest heaving, and he shook his head in denial. "No. I can't."

A mixture of embarrassment and worry crashed down over Sebastian. He jumped up and took a step back, hands out before him. "I'm so sorry. I thought—"

"Don't apologize." Ves scrambled to his feet and edged around Sebastian, toward the door. "It-it's not you. I just—I can't."

He fled through the door and down the turret steps. A few moments later, he emerged from the front of the house and ran down the street as though being chased by demons.

"Fuck." Sebastian sank down in the chair Ves had vacated, cradling his head in his hands. "Stupid, stupid."

Ves wandered the streets aimlessly, long after full night fell over Widdershins. He could still taste Sebastian on his lips, feel the brush of his thigh through their trousers.

In some other world, the moment could have been perfect. The drink had relaxed him, but not so much that he hadn't ached at Sebastian's nearness the entire time they sat on the balcony. The moment Sebastian kissed him, his skin had felt on fire, his cock straining against his trousers.

In that other world, he would have wrapped his arms around Sebastian, pulled him into his lap, and discovered where things went from there. They might even now be in Sebastian's bed, limbs tangled, skin touching.

But he didn't live in that world. And in this one, he'd been a fool to let down his guard for even a moment.

He imagined the expression of disgust on Sebastian's face if he'd seen him unclothed. Would he have attacked Ves? Or simply run downstairs, shouting for Captain Degas to fetch a weapon?

Ves found himself on the docks, a part of town he'd not been in before. The sea lapped against the quays, and fishing boats bobbed with the gentle movement. Ropes creaked, and the voices of sailors still at work aboard one of the trans-Atlantic cargo ships carried clear over the water.

He kept wandering, past the commercial part of the port, then past the area allotted to smaller, private craft. Eventually, he reached a long pier likely used for fishing. It was deserted now, so he wandered all the way to the end and stood staring out at the restless waves.

He should never have helped Sebastian. Should have kept his distance. If he'd just done that, he'd be quietly finishing the map he owed Fagerlie, instead of getting no work done on it whatsoever today. He'd take it to Fagerlie, have the curse lifted from himself and Noct, and leave town Friday morning.

Instead, he'd gotten involved. Let himself make a friend. The sort of friend who kissed him in the twilight, and who he wanted very badly to kiss back.

But if he hadn't gotten involved, if the men who had followed Sebastian had their way, Sebastian might even now be buried somewhere in a shallow grave beside O'Neil.

Ves sat down, dangling his feet over the water. The waves sparkled in the light of the half-moon. Fins cut through the water farther out, though he couldn't have guessed what sort of creature they might belong to. Dolphin? Orca? Shark? Something else entirely? As he'd told Sebastian, nothing in this town was what it seemed.

He felt a kinship with the creature, whatever it might be. Like fins above the water, only a small part of himself could be glimpsed; the rest remained hidden from sight. It had bothered him before, of course, but never so much as it did now.

Had Fagerlie killed O'Neil to open up the binder's position for Ves to fill? Whether he had or not, Ves couldn't pretend anymore that this was simply about stealing a rare book. Fagerlie had to be after the *Book of Breath,* assuming that was the Book of the Bound in the library. Given he'd been attacked by a spirit that used wind and whispers, it seemed a fair guess.

O'Neil had speculated the comet might exert some sort of influence on the book. And Fagerlie insisted on having the map no later than Wednesday afternoon, mere hours before the comet's tail brushed the earth.

Had he ever meant to free Ves and Noct from the curse?

Why had Ves been so stupid as to leave Noct with Fagerlie? He should have insisted on bringing his brother along on the train, hidden in a crate. But when Fagerlie had offered a ride in a closed carriage from Boston, with a stay in a private home rather than a tiny room in a boarding house, it seemed to make so much sense.

He'd been the perfect fool for Fagerlie to manipulate.

Fagerlie wouldn't simply let Ves back out now. He'd use Noct as a hostage.

He wished he could turn to Sebastian for help. But doing so would mean revealing the truth. Sebastian might know about sorcery, but that didn't mean he'd help a monster. He thought Ves had simply been born into a cult; he didn't realize Ves had been created for no other purpose than to destroy. Didn't understand he was a thing of inhuman darkness.

But if Ves remained silent and did what Fagerlie asked of him, even if he and Noct were allowed to go on their way afterward, what would become of Sebastian? Had the men following him been working for Fagerlie—but what possible motive did Fagerlie have for caring about Sebastian one way or another?

Ves stared at the waves for hours, wondering what to do. The sea whispered against the pier, but it gave him no answer.

CHAPTER 16

*T*his time, Vesper reached the café first. He'd barely had time to order his coffee before Fagerlie slipped into the chair across from him.

"You've finished the map?" Fagerlie asked without preamble.

Of course that was his main concern. Ves had expected it, and yet the abruptness—no, the eagerness—in Fagerlie's voice rubbed him the wrong way. He held up his hand, signaling Fagerlie to hold off, while the waiter returned with the coffee, then fetched another for Fagerlie.

As soon as he was gone, Fagerlie leaned forward. "Well? You have it?"

"No." Ves watched the older man's face closely as he absorbed the answer. "I asked you to meet me because I have questions."

Fagerlie's pale eyes gave nothing away. The man looked oddly washed out, with his silver hair and gray suit, his white skin and blue irises. "Oh? Do tell."

Ves folded his hands in front of him on the table. "The man who was the Ladysmith library's binder and conservator before me. He disappeared under…mysterious circumstances. I don't suppose you know anything about that?"

Fagerlie's eyes widened. "Disappeared? How?"

Ves shrugged. "That doesn't matter. Did you have anything to do with it?"

Fagerlie gave him a long judging look. "Actually, I didn't. I'd been contemplating how to get someone into the library, when I saw the posting in the Boston paper. I took it as a sign. Why would I assume he'd left the post under unusual circumstances?"

"And the men following Sebastian Rath?"

Now Fagerlie was starting to frown in irritation rather than confusion. "That name means nothing to me."

"The library's archivist. Two ruffians have been following him. They aren't in your employ?"

"Don't be absurd." Fagerlie scowled. "I have more important things to worry about than some archivist." The scowl became tinged with suspicion. "And what concern is it of yours? Your sole job is to draw me a map of the library by tomorrow evening. You only have a little over twenty-four hours, and now I find you're wasting time worrying over how you got your position and whatever petty intrigues this archivist is involved in?" He leaned back, mouth almost in a snarl. "I found you and your brother living half lives in Boston. I offered to help you become normal, asking only the most minor of tasks in exchange. I never imagined you'd be too incompetent to do it."

Ves's face flushed. "I'm not incompetent."

"Then do your job." Fagerlie stood up and left without a backward glance.

Ves stared at his empty chair. Should he believe Fagerlie? If the man was trying to fool him, wouldn't he have reacted with anger at the accusation rather than simply dismiss Ves's questions out of hand?

Should Ves have told him he knew what Fagerlie was after? But no —he didn't want the sorcerer to feel cornered, not with Noct as a potential hostage.

Ves buried his face in his hands. By the trees, he wished he had Noct to talk to. Or Sebastian.

Could he tell Sebastian some edited version of the truth? Pretend he had been hired to steal a book?

But then Sebastian would feel betrayed—rightfully—and Ves

would lose all access to the library. He wouldn't have the map to barter for Noct's safety.

If only he'd been born a normal person. But he hadn't, so there was nothing to do but press forward alone.

※

"Will we be seeing Mr. Rune for dinner again tonight?" Bonnie asked over breakfast.

Sebastian bit back a groan. His head pounded—he'd finished off a good part of the bottle of scotch alone in his room last night and was now paying for it.

"I couldn't say," he answered vaguely, then turned to Helen, who sat beside him spooning cereal into her mouth. "What is your class studying for the last few weeks of school?"

She shrugged. "Fractions."

"We're studying the comet!" Willie offered.

"Tell me all about it," Sebastian said.

The change of subject didn't fool Bonnie. When they'd finished eating, she said, "Pete, dear, do you have time to see the children out the door for school?"

"It'd be my pleasure." Pete turned to little Jossie. "Why don't you find your shoes, my girl?"

"I know where they are!"

"Do you now? Where?"

Jossie sighed and slipped off her chair to start the morning hunt for her footwear.

There was a brief swirl of chaos as Willie and Helen helped clear the table, and Tommy toddled off to play with the toy ship Pete had carved for him while at sea. Sebastian tried to take advantage to slip out the door, but Bonnie cornered him in the front hall. "So. Mr. Rune."

"I have to go to work," Sebastian said.

"It's ten minutes before you usually leave."

"I have...a lot of work today."

"Mmhmm." She crossed her arms over her chest. "Do you want to tell me why you changed the subject so quickly at breakfast? And why Mr. Rune left without saying good-bye last night?"

Sebastian had hoped she wouldn't notice. So much for that. "I…um…well, we had a few drinks from the scotch bottle, and…I don't know."

Bonnie rolled her eyes. "And you started thinking with the head that's not on your shoulders?"

"Bonnie!"

"What? I've created five children and enjoyed doing it. I'm not ignorant."

Most of the time, Sebastian was grateful for a family that loved him. This morning, he almost wished Bonnie was a little more stand-offish. "All right, fine. I kissed him. It was stupid."

She cocked her head. "Why?"

"Because he is—he was, anyway—my friend." He sighed. "There's a reason I don't mix pleasure with friendship."

"The reason is because you've got a hole in your skull, but continue."

Sebastian shot her a glare. "No, it's so things won't be awkward later. Ves…I haven't know him long, it's true, but I enjoy his company. I…*like* him. Now I've ruined it by kissing him, *and* I have to see him every day at work."

Bonnie winced at that. "Yes, well, you might have something there. He won't complain to Mr. Quinn, will he?"

"I shouldn't think so. I would never force my attentions on anyone. As soon as he indicated he wasn't interested, I stopped." Sebastian's shoulders slumped. "Even so, he ran out as though I'd set him on fire. There was a…project we were working on together. I'm afraid facing him again will be awkward."

"It probably will," she agreed. "But don't fret. There are more men in the sea. And even more on the land." She paused, brow furrowed in thought. "Actually, I think Pete's first mate—"

"No!" Sebastian held up his hands, backing away from her. "Stop talking. Please."

"Oh, what about the adorable tailor at Dryden and Sons?"

"I'm leaving now," he said, opening the door and backing out of it.

"Or the—"

"I can't hear you, because I'm not here!" he shouted, and shut the door behind him.

Thanks to Bonnie, he was almost late to work. Which was fine: Ves came in early, but Irene never walked in an instant beforehand, even though her family's chauffeur drove her to the museum each morning. Instead, she sauntered in right at eight o'clock, her hair perfect and never wearing the same outfit twice.

Bonnie's attempt at commiseration hadn't helped Sebastian's mood, and he found himself pathetically grateful to have an excuse not to face Ves, at least for a little longer. Yesterday, he would have gone straight to the bindery. Today, here he was hoping not to casually run into a man who might under other circumstances have become a good friend.

Maybe they could just...pretend it hadn't happened. A few years from now, they'd laugh at Sebastian's clumsy attempt at seduction. Joke about what a terrible match they would have made.

Thankfully, Irene swept into the library and relieved Sebastian of the company of his thoughts. She wore an exquisitely tailored ladies' suit accompanied by a chiffon turban-style hat with black and white feathers.

"Irene!" he exclaimed as he approached her. "How is my favorite Endicott today?"

She gave him the look the sentiment deserved. "What do you want, Sebastian?"

He grinned. "Something that will gladden your sorcerous little heart. Have you ever heard of the Books of the Bound?"

"I have not." A gleam came into her eyes. "Tell me all about them."

Ves spent as much time mapping the library's lowest level as he dared. It was both necessary—as Fagerlie had reminded him, the comet's transit would occur tomorrow night—and an excuse to hide from anyone who might be looking for him. Sebastian, for example.

It was cowardly of him, of course. Just as it had been cowardly to flee from the Rath house last night. What must Sebastian think of him?

He couldn't stop remembering that kiss. The softness of Sebastian's lips. The heat of his tongue in Ves's mouth.

The flesh to either side of his spine shivered, even as his cock roused. He had to get himself under control, curse it all.

Eventually, he tucked the crude maps safely away in his vest pocket and made for the staff room. He poured a cup of coffee, nodded good morning to Arthur as they passed in the hallway, and entered the bindery.

He'd barely had the chance to set his coffee down when there came a tremendous crash from the direction of the staff room, accompanied by a cry of pain and surprise.

"What now?" Ves muttered, and rushed back the way he'd come.

A young woman stood in the staff room, cradling one hand with the other, her dress and round-lensed glasses covered with hot coffee. The urn itself lay on the floor.

"Are you all right?" Ves asked.

"I-I think so." Her voice sounded rather shaken for a simple accident, and Ves paused in the act of kneeling to pick up the urn.

"Did you get burned?" He pulled a handkerchief from his pocket. When she didn't take it from him, he dabbed gently at the coffee clinging to one cheek. The skin beneath was reddened, but didn't seem badly injured. "What happened, Miss…?"

"Cohen." She blinked a few times, then recovered enough to take the handkerchief and set about cleaning her glasses. "I was about to pour some coffee, but…I suppose my grip must have slipped, but it felt as though some force struck the urn from my hand."

Damn it. He and Sebastian had believed the library's resident spirit had a problem with bookbinders in particular, but it seemed to be expanding its attacks to others now.

"May I see your hand, Miss Cohen?" he asked, since she still favored it. He'd tended Noct's wounds over the years; the principles were likely the same for those of purely human heritage. "Vesper Rune," he added, realizing he'd failed to introduce himself. "Binder and conservator."

She smiled tremulously and held out her injured hand. "Amelia Cohen, Librarian. I oversee the Paleontological Collection."

"That sounds fascinating," he said honestly, as he inspected her fingers. Her skin was soft and her hand warm, and it felt odd to touch a virtual stranger so intimately. Or at all. "The good news is, nothing seems to be broken. You might wish to take an aspirin and rest the hand. And I'd report this to Mr. Quinn."

She frowned now. "You don't think it was an accident?"

"No. I most certainly don't."

Ves returned to the bindery to find none other than Mortimer Waite tapping his foot impatiently. Waite had set a stack of books perilously near Ves's coffee cup, and turned a pair of vexed eyes on him when he entered.

"There you are," Waite snapped. "I must say, if you keep up this slipshod work ethic, you won't be employed much longer, Rune."

Vesper forced himself to walk past Waite without reacting. The journals from the day before had been pressing overnight, so he removed them and put them on the sewing table, then set about transferring the next volume to the press.

Waite clearly wasn't accustomed to being ignored. "I uncovered some books which need conservation and minor repair while searching for any missing books. Arthur's wild goose chase."

It was nothing of the sort, but Ves didn't mean to enlighten him. He only grunted in acknowledgement.

Waite growled in annoyance. "These books are from my—I mean, the library's—Widdershins Collection. So do be careful. Many of these are one-of-a-kind items, invaluable to our town."

Ves ground his teeth together at the implication. He left his back to Waite and turned the screw on the press. "I assure you I will."

"I lobbied Mr. Quinn for this position to be given to my cousin, Jeffry Waite," Waite said, apparently spurred on by Ves's failure to respond any further to the insult. "In my opinion, it offers too much access to sensitive material for an outsider with no pedigree."

Ves had a pedigree, and for a wild moment he was tempted to share it with Waite and send him away screaming. But that was madness, so he swallowed it down and only said, "Mr. Quinn clearly disagrees."

"With all due respect to the head librarian, the Quinns have only lived in Widdershins since the 1790s," Waite sneered. "An entire century after the Waites helped found the town. But I don't expect an outsider like you to understand."

"I'm sure you're right," Ves agreed placidly. "Now, if you would leave me to work, I'll look at your volumes as soon as I'm able."

"Don't dally," Waite warned.

When the man was finally gone, Ves went to the piles sitting near his coffee. It didn't matter, he told himself as he drained the cup. Whatever happened tomorrow, he'd be gone the day after. Who cared if Waite was an ass; Ves would never have to see him again.

He winced at the bitterness of the coffee. It must have sat too long in the urn, acquiring a metallic taste even the sugar he'd added couldn't conceal. And the sugar hadn't dissolved properly; there were grains in the dregs.

Disgusted, he lowered the cup. Coating the bottom was a layer of white sediment that made his blood run cold.

Rodents were a constant threat to bookshops and libraries, and he'd seen enough rat poison over the years to recognize it now.

Mortimer Waite had just tried to kill him.

CHAPTER 17

*I*n the end, Sebastian avoided telling the same story twice by asking Irene to come with him to Mr. Quinn's office. The head librarian listened attentively while Sebastian laid out everything he and Vesper had uncovered, along with the spirit of breath that had a grudge against Ves. When he was done, Mr. Quinn sat back, thin hands steepled and an odd smile on his face.

"A hidden tome, right here in the library," he said. "In my dreams…but this is reality. What a joyful day."

Irene and Sebastian exchanged a worried look. "It seems like the sort of thing that ought to be contained," he said. "That has been contained in the past? I'll have to look further into the letters, of course."

"Not to mention this spirit is most likely tied to it in some fashion," Irene said. "Perhaps the spirit is what's bound? Both it and the book must be stopped."

"And stop them we shall. Our first duty is to protect the town." Mr. Quinn spread his spider-like fingers. "But in order to do so we must find the book. Hold it in our hands."

"Right," Sebastian said. He glanced at Irene, who merely shrugged.

"Since the spirit appears to be drawn to Mr. Rune, the simplest solution might be to provide him with some sort of ward." Irene tapped her lips with one manicured finger, eyes narrowed in thought. "I'll have to consult with some of the alchemists back at the estate, though."

"Do so, Miss Endicott. In the meantime, Mr. Rath, summon the librarians." Mr. Quinn rose to his feet. "I will address everyone at once."

He led the way out of the maze of back halls. When they emerged behind the desk, it was to find Dr. Norris with a list of books in hand.

"—and I need these right away," he was saying to Arthur, who currently manned the desk. "I have a very important presentation next week."

"The library is closed," Mr. Quinn announced. "Please return the day after tomorrow. Perhaps we shall be open then."

"But I need these!" Norris exclaimed, brandishing the list.

"They'll likely still be here on Thursday."

Norris's face grew red. "You can't close the library! You only exist to help with *our* research."

Mr. Quinn spread his hands as though helpless. "And yet, I am closing it now."

Norris glared. "Dr. Gerritson will hear of this!" he declared, before stomping away.

"Mr. Fairchild, if you'd usher any stragglers from the reading room, I would appreciate it," Mr. Quinn said. "Mr. Rath, ring the bell."

The bell hung in a shadowy recess, accessible only by sliding one of the tall ladders over and climbing to the top. Due to some strange trick of acoustics, the ring of the bell in its recess could be heard even in the farthest recesses of the library.

Sebastian clambered up and rang the bell vigorously. Mr. Quinn swept past, making his way to the room on the second floor where the librarians would know to meet him.

As Sebastian climbed down, he spotted Ves coming toward him, a worried look on his face.

Oh dear. Things were about to become awkward.

"What was that?" Ves asked. "Is the library on fire?"

"Good God, no!" Sebastian exclaimed in horror. "It was a summons. We'll clear the library of any patrons and gather for an emergency meeting in the sword room on the second floor."

Ves frowned. "You have a bell you ring to call emergency meetings?"

"Of course. The Boston Public Library didn't?"

Ves shook his head, bemused. "No."

"Well, that certainly seems an oversight, doesn't it?" From all that Ves had said, the Boston Library sounded like a truly strange place. Sebastian was grateful for the normality of the Ladysmith. "This way."

"Wait." Ves reached for him, then seemed to think better of it. "I...I'd like to apologize. About last night."

Sebastian locked away his own disappointment. "I shouldn't have been so forward, especially with a co-worker."

A look of misery flashed over Ves's face, there and gone so fast Sebastian wouldn't have seen it if he hadn't been staring at him. "I overreacted. I wish...it doesn't matter. I apologize, and I hope we can remain friends."

Relief slid through Sebastian. "I would very much like that. Bonnie asked me to invite you to dinner again."

Ves wavered. "I don't wish to intrude."

"You aren't. She wouldn't ask if she didn't want you there." When Ves didn't answer, he said, "Think about it. Now, let's go, before we're late."

Ves kept a close watch for Mortimer Waite as the librarians gathered.

Anyone else would be lying on the floor of the bindery by now, vomiting and writhing in agony. But Ves was a monster, and thus very hard to kill. Silver nitrate in his cup would have had the desired effect, but enough arsenic to poison half the library left him with only a mildly aching stomach and a foul, metallic taste in his mouth.

Waite had no way to know Mr. Quinn would call an emergency

meeting. He must have planned on returning after enough time had passed for Ves to be incapacitated and removing the incriminating cup.

It had been stupid, turning his back on a man he knew didn't like him. Though Waite probably had plenty of time to put the rat poison in the cup while Ves was distracted by the commotion in the staff room.

That the spirit struck when it did, lashing out against a seemingly random librarian, was surely no coincidence. Waite must know about the Books of the Bound, might even be in league with the spirit.

It was all beginning to make sense. Waite had killed O'Neil, possibly in the same manner he'd tried to murder Ves. He'd put forth his cousin for the bookbinding position, which would have let them search the bindery at their leisure for any clues O'Neil had left behind. When Mr. Quinn hired Ves instead, Waite first left the note warning him away, and when that didn't work, decided to remove him the same way he'd removed O'Neil.

And of course, when Sebastian refused to give up looking for O'Neil, Waite hired two men to follow and intimidate him. Clearly the Waites were considered an important family and had plenty of money; Mortimer could probably act with impunity knowing the police would never dare accuse him even if the men were caught.

He needed to warn Sebastian...but how? He couldn't easily explain away drinking coffee laced with arsenic, yet showing no ill effects. Nor could he waste precious time pretending to be sick. Roughly thirty-six hours from now, the comet's tail would envelope the earth.

He was running out of time.

Ves resisted the urge to bury his face in his hands, but only because it would have caused Sebastian to ask what was wrong. He was being torn in so many different directions: Sebastian, the library, Noct, Fagerlie, his own desire for a normal life...

This was supposed to have been simple. He wasn't meant to make life and death decisions, just draw a map and leave.

Making decisions had never been part of his training. He'd been meant to follow orders like a good soldier, not think for himself. Nocturn was the one who would be tasked with ruling over a city of horror and slaves once the age of humanity came to an end.

"Why is Mortimer glaring at you?" Sebastian asked.

Ves cursed his distraction. He'd hoped to catch the look on the man's face when he saw Ves was still alive, but he'd been too deep inside his own head to notice when Waite walked in. Now he sat on the other side of the room, beside Irene and seemingly bored. "I didn't see. You say he was glaring?"

"A bit."

Before Ves could ask anything further, Mr. Quinn entered the room. Silence instantly fell, all attention focused on the head librarian. They seemed to Ves like soldiers waiting for commands.

"There is a dangerous magical book hidden in our library," Mr. Quinn said, beaming as if announcing a special treat. "The nature of its magic is unclear, as is its location. Has anyone noticed any of the books behaving in an unusual manner recently?"

One of the younger men raised his hand. "*The Confession of Ovid Gilman* spoke to me while I was dusting the other day."

"It speaks to everyone, Mr. White. Ovid Gilman murdered thirteen people and requested to have his confession bound in his own skin after he hanged. It is impossible to shut him up on the subject of his crimes. I asked for *unusual* occurrences."

Ves looked around to gage if Mr. Quinn was joking. He didn't appear to be.

When no one else spoke up, the head librarian folded his hands in front of him. "Then we will scour the shelves—every volume must be examined against the catalog and its contents assured to match both cover and card. It will not be an easy task, but we must be thorough. I will personally handle all restricted tomes." He scanned the determined faces turned toward him. "Naturally, if you find any book in need of conservation, make a note of it. Mr. Fairchild will compile them into a list for Mr. Rune's attention, once there is time. Are there any questions?"

There were not. Mr. Quinn went on, "There is also another matter I must bring to your attention." He gave an abbreviated summary of Ves's encounters with the spirit, then said, "If you hear or feel anything out of the ordinary, report it directly to me *immediately*. Miss Endicott will be consulting on how best to protect ourselves from this entity, but in the meantime be on your guard. Vigilance!"

Mr. Quinn finished by assigning sections of the library to various librarians and sub-librarians. They nodded firmly when given their tasks and departed instantly to begin work, with no grumbling about the immense task before them.

"Don't worry," Sebastian murmured to Ves. "If the book is here, we'll find it."

"They certainly seem…eager to get to work," Ves said carefully.

"They believe in the library's mission," Sebastian replied, pride warming his voice. "To preserve knowledge and assist in research, to defend the town against arcane threats."

"You do realize how mad that sounds, don't you?" Ves asked.

Sebastian frowned. "No. It's a necessity. We serve Widdershins, in whatever way is required of us."

"Mr. Rath, Mr. Rune." With the rest of the librarians sent on their ways, Mr. Quinn turned to them. "Your task is to delve through these letters and drawings Mr. O'Neil collected."

"I'd like to authenticate Mr. Ladysmith's handwriting," Sebastian said.

"Naturally." Mr. Quinn tilted his head. "Do you need any assistance, other than Mr. Rune?"

Sebastian glanced uncertainly at Ves. "If you don't wish to work together…"

This would give Ves the chance he needed to keep an eye on Sebastian. Make sure he was safe from Waite. "Of course I do."

The happiness in Sebastian's smile called forth an ache of longing in his chest. "Then no, Mr. Quinn. Vesper is all I need."

On the way to Sebastian's office, they stopped first at the Widdershins Collection overseen by Mortimer. The collection housed important documents, including those concerning the museum's founding. One of these, the official declaration granting the funds for the museum's construction, bore Nathanial R. Ladysmith's signature. Mortimer wasn't there, but Sebastian knew where the documents he was looking for were kept, and removed them himself.

Ves's presence warmed Sebastian, and he found himself in a far better mood than he'd expected. It seemed they'd be able to put the awkwardness of last night behind them and move forward as friends. Indeed, as they headed for Sebastian's office, Ves struck up a conversation.

"How well do you know Mr. Waite?" he asked.

"Mortimer? Well enough, I suppose." Sebastian glanced down at Ves curiously. "Better since his engagement to Irene."

Ves looked faintly alarmed. "He's engaged to Miss Endicott?"

Sebastian shrugged. "I don't really see it myself, but they seem content enough, and it makes their families happy. The Waites are one of the old families, you see."

"I don't, actually." Ves stuck his hands in his pockets. "People keep saying that, but no one explains what it actually *means*."

"Oh!" It shouldn't have been so easy to forget Ves was an outsider. "A handful of families founded Widdershins in 1693. They were all acolytes of Theron Blackbyrne, who turned out to be a necromancer. For future reference, the old family names are Marsh, Lester, Whyborne, and Waite. There used to be the Abbots, but their line died out. All of them grew to prominence one way or another—I'm sure you recognize the Whyborne name from the railroad company. Most of the families have had only a few children with each generation, but there are a *lot* of Waites, so not everyone you meet with that name will necessarily have any money or social standing."

"But Mortimer does."

Sebastian nodded. "Indeed. One of his cousins is the current heir to the bulk of the family fortune, and Mortimer is well provided for."

Ves's expression gave nothing away. "But what is he like as a person?"

They reached Sebastian's office. The space was far more cramped than Sebastian would have liked. Thanks to the Ladysmith's strange architecture, the walls formed a rhomboid shape. The boxes of letters covered part of the floor, and Kelly's notebook was locked in the desk. Shelves lined the walls, mostly filled with the various references he needed to assess books, letters, maps, or anything else the library might acquire.

He gestured Ves to take one of the two chairs, while he settled himself behind his desk. "Why do you ask?"

Ves hesitated. "He came to the bindery this morning with some books that needed conservation work done to them. He mentioned he'd wanted the bookbinder job for a cousin and was disgruntled I had it. The encounter caused me to wonder if he might have been the one to leave me the note. Or if he knew about the Books of the Bound and wanted his cousin in the position, since it seems to have some significance. I suspect he might be the one behind O'Neil's disappearance, the threatening note to me, and the men following you."

Sebastian bit his lip. He wanted to dismiss the idea out of hand... but the old families had earned their reputation for ruthlessness. "He did know of my concern for Kelly, yes. As did Irene and Arthur. As for the Books...they do sound like the sort of lore the old families might have passed down over the years. After murdering Kelly—or having him murdered, more likely—he could have wanted a cousin to be the next binder to get access to the bindery and anything Kelly might have hidden there."

"And he's having you followed, because he thinks you know something. Which you do." Ves's expression was grave. "Sebastian, you have to be careful. And make sure this room is secured at all times."

God. The theory certainly explained a great deal. Still, it was difficult to think ill of his fellow librarian. And could Irene have truly misjudged his character so badly?

Then again, from what he knew of the Endicotts, they could be awfully ruthless themselves. She might miss some warning signs others would see, assuming they indicated only the level of cut-throat ambition she was accustomed to.

"I don't know," he said at last. "Certainly we can't go accusing him without proof." Another thought occurred to him. "Although if you're right, you could be in danger as well."

Ves smiled faintly. "I'm tougher than I look."

"I'm sure you are, but..." Sebastian trailed off before he could stay something stupid. *I don't want anything bad to happen to you. It would break my heart if you were hurt.* "Just be careful, all right? I'm worried about you."

Ves looked surprised by the sentiment, as though he'd never had someone show concern over his well-being. "I...yes." A light flush crept up his cheeks. "Thank you, Sebastian."

CHAPTER 18

Sebastian wasn't at all surprised when the signatures matched. The letter he examined had indeed been written by Nathaniel Ladysmith.

Nathaniel Ladysmith, speaking of his love for the architect who had designed his museum. No wonder its eccentricities had been allowed to stand. He'd built it exactly as Dromgoole had wanted, as a testament to his lover.

In the meantime, Ves had turned his attention to Kelly's notebook and was taking notes on the contents. While he worked on that, Sebastian set himself to putting the collection O'Neil had left behind into some order. Chronological seemed the best way to start, but the boxes were in a wild jumble.

"I wonder where he found it?" Sebastian mused as he worked. "This collection of letters, I mean."

"I might be able to answer." Ves sat back, blinking as though his eyes had gone dry. "This isn't just a notebook about his investigation. It appears to have been his commonplace book, and he used it to jot down his thoughts on all sorts of subjects. There's a great deal about margin width, naturally."

"Naturally," Sebastian laughed.

Ves shot him an affronted look. "Margin width, especially in rebinding, is of utmost importance. A handsome width is easier on the eyes and allows for future rebinding should that become necessary. *And* it preserves the spine, as the reader isn't obligated to practically tear the book in half to read the words closest to the gutter."

Sebastian held up one hand. "I stand corrected. I cannot understand why there aren't more odes to excellent binding practices amongst the annals of great literature."

"Keep on like that, and I shall throw a book at your head," Ves threatened, but with a smile.

God, but he had a lovely smile. His brown eyes lightened, and it seemed as if some of the care lifted from him, at least for a moment.

Time to stop thinking like that. "So other than proper margins, what did Kelly have to say?" Sebastian asked.

Ves's smile slipped away, as quickly as it had come. "He mentions your mother quite a bit at first."

Surely someday the pain would be less. "I imagine he does."

"He wishes he knew more about the nature of the Books of the Bound." Ves flipped back in the notebook and cleared his throat, before reading:

If only Rebecca had more time to find the Bound Book she was looking for. Or if she'd confided in me where she suspected it might be hidden. But she wasn't certain, and wanted to wait...I suppose the lesson here is not to wait on anything. You never know when time will run out.

Ves ran his broad, blunt fingers across the page of his own notes. "The books have something to do with Nathanial Ladysmith—we already knew that, obviously. Some of the notes O'Neil made about the letters suggest Ladysmith was also concerned with the books breaking free of their traps?"

Sebastian shook his head. "I have no idea what that could mean."

"O'Neil wrote here that he wondered if you did. If Rebecca had confided something to you that she hadn't to him."

"No," Sebastian said heavily. "Though…God, now that I think of it, Kelly and I spent a great deal of time together about a year, year-and-a-half ago. He'd invite me out for drinks or dinner, or come round to the house. The conversation often turned to Mother, of course." He examined memories suddenly turned suspicious. "I think…he might have been trying to ascertain what I knew, without asking outright. After a time, we grew more distant—I thought he was just busy, but perhaps he'd realized I wasn't as useful as he'd hoped I would be."

The thought cut keenly. He'd imagined Kelly his friend, but perhaps he'd just been a potential source of information, dropped when he could supply no more.

"Then that was foolish of him." Ves's eyes were unexpectedly gentle. "He should have been glad to call you a friend, no matter the circumstance."

Sebastian met his gaze, intending to say something light. But the words deserted him. Rust and gold threaded through Ves's eyes, giving them an almost orange cast when the light struck them just right. In his unguarded moments, he seemed so alone, so sad, and Sebastian wanted nothing more than to hold him close.

But he'd already tried that and been rebuffed.

He looked away and cleared his throat awkwardly. "The letters?"

"Oh. Um, yes." Ves referred to his notes. "It seems that O'Neil combed through the archives whenever he had a chance, looking for anything on either Ladysmith or Dromgoole. He says something about 'Dromgoole's lost works?'"

Sebastian shrugged. "I don't know anything about that. The museum was Dromgoole's only piece of public architecture, but otherwise, I confess myself ignorant when it comes to the man's career. I'll have to check the archives myself."

"That would probably be wise. At any rate, he didn't seem to turn up much, but he speculated that there might be some lost storerooms in the museum where Ladysmith hid things."

Sebastian's lips parted in shock. "Are you saying the collection was already here?"

"Not in the library, of course. And he had to find the original plans for the museum, since there weren't any on record. Apparently, he located them in the hands of the descendants of the man who had been in charge of records and deeds at city hall when the museum was built. Why the fellow absconded with them, rather than file them as required, even his family didn't know. They'd kept them as a curiosity." Ves turned and stared at the box of drawings. "They're likely in there."

"Likely, yes." Sebastian swallowed. "And Kelly used them to find a lost storeroom?"

"It sounds as though there is more than one room that appears on the plans, but has no door into it in modern times. Kelly concealed himself until late at night in a different storeroom, then snuck into the room beside the hidden one. He chiseled his way through the wall, then used the clutter in the first room to hide the hole." Ves looked up. "Does that seem likely? Surely someone would have noticed."

"The museum has sixty years of accumulated artifacts and specimens from every part of the globe," Sebastian said. "I've never been to the storerooms myself, but surely most of them aren't routinely accessed. I imagine such damage might go unnoticed for years, or even decades, until some researcher needed to examine an obscure species of frog, or taxidermied bird skins, or underwhelming fossil fish."

"Oh." Ves looked somewhat taken aback. "I suppose the library is more organized than I thought."

"You'd be surprised."

A shadow materialized in the doorway, and Sebastian jumped. But it was only Irene. "Have you found anything, gentlemen?"

"A bit," Sebastian said. "Nothing especially helpful, but we're working toward it. I authenticated the letters and am trying to sort them into order by date. You?"

"Not a bloody thing," she said with a scowl. "I tried a spell or two in the bindery that I thought might compel the entity to reveal itself, but no luck. At any rate, it's five o'clock, and the rest of us are getting ready to leave for the night. I intend to look into the family's records, or the ones we have left, anyway, and see if I can find any mention of these Books of the Bound. Unfortunately, our library was destroyed along with our estate in Cornwall, but we've managed to rebuild a small part in the intervening years."

Ves stood up, glancing at the box of architectural drawings. "We should leave as well."

"Agreed." Sebastian rose to his feet as well. "I'll find you in the morning, Irene." He watched her depart, then turned to Ves. "Have you thought any more about dinner? Bonnie would love you to come."

Ves wavered. "I…I have something to attend to, I'm afraid."

"Stop in for a short while, after?" Sebastian suggested hopefully. "I'm not—that is, just for talk."

Ves glanced away. "Perhaps."

The man had things to do, Sebastian reminded himself. They'd repaired their budding friendship, but that didn't mean Ves wanted to spend every evening together.

"You're always welcome," he only said. And tried not to feel sad when Ves nodded curtly and made for the door.

Ves stopped at Marsh's rather than eating at the boarding house. He needed some time alone with his thoughts.

The evening rush of customers came in just behind him, most of them clerks or office workers, mixed in with a few skilled laborers. No doubt those who toiled in the fish cannery or on the docks had their own places to retreat to. A murmur of voices soon filled the air, but none of the tables seemed inclined to pay attention to any of their fellow diners, for which Ves was grateful.

Mortimer Waite had tried to poison him. And he couldn't tell Sebastian, which meant trying to find some *other* proof.

Except he didn't have time. The earth would begin its pass through the comet's tail shortly before midnight tomorrow.

And Ves now had the means of giving Fagerlie exactly what he wanted. He didn't even need to finish his map.

He could go back to the museum library as soon as he was finished eating dinner. See the bats, break into Sebastian's office, and steal the architectural drawings of the Ladysmith. He'd be reunited with Noct by dawn.

It was still possible—not likely, but possible—that Fagerlie meant to keep his half of the bargain. He'd free the brothers of the curse that warped their blood, then head about his own business while they caught the first train out of Widdershins.

But that would leave Sebastian at the mercy of a murderer, someone who had already had him followed. It would leave the town —maybe the world—at the mercy of whatever the *Book of Breath* could do in the hands of a man like Fagerlie.

It sounded as though Ladysmith and Dromgoole had gone to great lengths to bind and trap the books. Which suggested either the two men had been caught up in some sort of folie à deux, or the books presented an urgent danger.

The bitter truth was, no matter what Ves decided, he would lose Sebastian. But if Fagerlie did indeed keep to his word, at least Noct would have a life to look forward to. They'd both be free at last.

Yet how could he head off into a new life while Sebastian remained in danger?

Ves resisted the urge to bury his face in his hands, though only because he didn't wish to draw attention to himself. Gods, he hated this. Why couldn't he have been born to normal parents? He'd never asked to make these kinds of decisions.

He'd been created to destroy. Not to be a friend, certainly not to be a lover. He wasn't supposed to be around normal people. No wonder he didn't know what to do now.

He had to talk to Noct. This was too big for him alone. He'd sent letters to Fagerlie here in Widdershins; he knew the address of his rented house. He'd go tomorrow and demand to speak to his brother. And if Fagerlie refused…

Then they'd both find out what Ves was truly capable of.

CHAPTER 19

"Has Mr. Rune forgiven you yet?" Bonnie asked after dinner that night, while she and Sebastian washed up. The children were reading or playing quietly, and Pete was in the sitting room, rocking little Clara.

Sebastian concentrated on drying the dish she handed him. "Of course. No one can resist my charm."

She snorted. "Of course. Then where is he?"

It was strange that the dinner table had felt emptier, somehow, without Ves. The children and Pete had all asked after him and expressed disappointment when Sebastian explained his friend had other obligations. Apparently, Bonnie hadn't believed the excuse.

"He said he had business of his own." Sebastian put the plate into the drying rack and accepted the next. "He's a handsome young man in a new town. He probably has a lot of more interesting things to do than spend the evening with children and old folk like you."

"Watch yourself!" she exclaimed, flinging suds at him. "You're eleven months older than me!"

"And yet I stay young through clean living and piety."

This time she dug her elbow into his ribs. "Right. Just like that Dorian Gray fellow in the book."

"I did know a painter once…"

"Besides," she cut him off, "I know when you're changing the subject. Fine. Have it your way."

They finished the dishes, and Willie came in with a question about mathematics. Since he was hopeless when it came to numbers, Sebastian made his escape to the sitting room. Tommy sprawled on the rug, playing with his toy ship along with Jossie. Helen perched in a chair, practicing her cross stitch. Pete dozed in his chair, Clara securely tucked against his chest, her tiny hand fisted in his beard.

Just as Sebastian went to sit down himself, there came a knock at the door. His heart leapt—had Ves decided to take him up on a visit after all?

"I'll get it," he said as Pete blinked awake. He hastened into the small entry room and swung open the front door in greeting. "Vesper —" he began, then stopped.

The two ruffians who had chased him now stood on the stoop. One pointed the black bore of a gun directly at his face.

Uncertain what to do now that he'd made his decision to visit Noct in the morning, Ves wandered idly in the direction of the boarding house. He passed the small café where he'd met Fagerlie. The smell of roasting coffee and cinnamon floated into the street. It was filled with an evening crowd that seemed to mainly consist of students from the town's university, arguing politics and philosophy over steaming cups.

He couldn't imagine what their lives must be like. What it would feel like to be so normal. To not have their every moment in public tinged with the dread of discovery.

His evenings with the Rath family had been the closest he'd ever known to that sort of normality. But he'd only had even that because of deception.

Sebastian had asked him to come over to talk, even if he didn't want dinner. After last night, Ves doubted Sebastian would try to kiss him again, but that still didn't make it safe to go. If Ves had any sense at all, he'd close his heart, harden his will, and concentrate on nothing other than keeping Noct safe.

But he hadn't been meant to have sense, had he? He'd been born to clear the way, to be a soldier. To follow orders, and sometimes to command—but only when directed by those above him. Noct was meant to be the clever one, the sorcerer, the one who would do the real work of ruling once most of the human race had been killed or subjugated.

Ves left the café behind and turned his steps toward the Rath house. He wouldn't stay long, but maybe even a brief conversation with Sebastian would settle his nerves, or calm his mind, or…

The door stood wide open.

Ves froze, every sense on alert. Perhaps an open door shouldn't be so alarming, but from what little he'd seen, folks in Widdershins regularly locked their doors after dark. Of course, one of the children might have forgotten to shut it in a moment of excitement. Helen or Willie would appear any instant to close it…

No. He brushed aside the urge to rationalize. He knew when something wasn't right, and this very much was one of those times.

Moving as stealthily as possible, he slipped through the hedge and into the yard. The windows on the lower floor were open to catch the breeze, and as he drifted nearer, he could hear raised voices from within.

"You've caused too much trouble, librarian," a man said. "And now that your friend isn't around to protect you, it's time for you to pay."

The men shoved Sebastian in front of them, into the sitting room, the gun trained on his head. Helen let out a short scream and dropped her cross-stitch to the floor. Tommy and Jossie froze, and Pete started up —but he had little Clara in his arms.

"Don't you fucking move," said the gunman. "Or else I'll spread your brains across the floor, too."

Pete stopped, turning his body to shield Clara.

"What's going on—" Bonnie called as she stepped into the room from the direction of the kitchen, Willie behind her.

Sebastian wanted to scream at her to run—but that would likely only end up getting her shot. His heart pounded so hard he felt light-headed, and he kept his hands up in surrender.

"What do you want?" he asked, and his voice trembled in fear. If they hurt Bonnie or Pete, or heaven forbid one of the children...

"Whatever it is, just tell us," Bonnie said in a reasonable voice. "My jewelry is in a box upstairs. We don't have much cash, but—"

"Shut it," snarled the gunman. He ground the bore of the weapon painfully into Sebastian's head. "Well, librarian, I'll bet you're surprised to see us here."

"T-Technically I'm an archivist," Sebastian stammered.

"How fancy," the other sneered. His nose was badly swollen, and listed to one side. Ves must have broken it in the scuffle at the apartment. "You've been poking your nose where it doesn't belong, *archivist.*"

Bonnie shot him a look of horror. Sebastian swallowed and tried to steady his nerves. "Perhaps I have, but my family is innocent. Let's just leave. I'll go with you quietly."

"Oh, no." The man shook his head. "It's too late for that. You're a dead man, but we need to know what you figured out. And what you might have told your family. No loose ends."

Oh God.

The gunman gave Sebastian a rough shove. He staggered in the direction of the open window, barely catching himself on Clara's cradle before he hit the ground.

"I don't know anything," Sebastian protested. "I swear. I was just looking for Kelly—Mr. O'Neil. He, ah, owes me money."

"If you're going to lie, do a better job at it," the gunman said. He moved to stand over Sebastian, the weapon held firmly but not pointing at anyone in particular.

"Exactly." His companion strolled across the room as well, a smirk on his face.

"Now listen here," Pete said.

The gunman swung to point the weapon at Pete and Clara. "Shut up. You think I'd hesitate to shoot a baby?"

"No!" Sebastian shouted. He lunged up from the floor, no plan in mind, only to draw fire away from Clara.

A tentacle as thick as his arm whipped through the open window, seized the gunman's wrist, and wrenched it back.

❧

Sebastian gaped. The gunman spun toward the window, shouting in anger and pain. He pulled the trigger, but the bullet lodged in the ceiling.

Then Ves was in the window and climbing through. But not Ves as Sebastian knew him.

His eyes had gone a strange orange-gold color, the pupils rectangular rather than round. Goat eyes, some stupid part of Sebastian's brain babbled. Ves's coat was gone, and his vest and shirt hung half-torn off. From his back emerged eight black tentacles, four to either side of his spine. Two helped heave him through the window, and a third was still wrapped around the gunman's wrist.

"Fuck—it's one of the Dark Young!" the other man shouted, and drew a wicked silver blade from his coat pocket.

"No!" Sebastian cried, at the same time Peter ordered: "Run, children!"

But it was Bonnie who acted. She grabbed up the scented candle, the one she'd left unburned in deference to him, and lobbed it at the man's head.

The candle caught the ruffian in the temple—not hard enough to hurt him, but hard enough to distract.

Ves surged across the room. The gunman screamed as his wrist snapped, and the weapon fell to the floor. At the same instant, two tentacles whipped toward the man Bonnie had hit. One snaked around his throat, the other around his waist, and heaved him straight into the brickwork of the fireplace. His skull connected with a wet crack, and he went limp in Ves's grip.

The other man was still shrieking. Ves hurled him into the wall.

He collided with a much less final sound and crumpled into a moaning ball against the baseboard.

Everything went still and silent. Ves stared down at the dead man with his strange goat eyes, an expression of horror on his face. The tentacles hung around him like some sort of dark nimbus, poised and ready.

Sebastian's mind spun. What *was* Ves? Not one of the kindred of the sea, not with those eyes. *"One of the Dark Young,"* the intruder had said, seconds before Ves killed him right there in the sitting room. Thank God the children had run when Bonnie told them to.

"Ves?" Sebastian said, unsure what to do.

Ves's head whipped up. His gaze met Sebastian's, and he swallowed heavily. "I'm sorry," he said.

Then he was gone, back out the window, leaving only the swaying curtains in his wake.

CHAPTER 20

"It was a monster, I tell you!" the gunman shouted. "A monster!"

His yells turned into a cry of pain as the police officer cuffed his hands behind him, heedless of his broken wrist.

"Is that so," the officer said, clearly uninterested. "What do you expect, breaking into people's houses and threatening them with a gun?"

The policeman hauled him away. A detective watched them, then turned to Sebastian, who sat on the couch beside Pete. Bonnie had taken all the children up to her bedroom, attempting to calm them.

The body had already been removed. All that remained of the night's terror was a splotch of blood and hair on the brickwork of the hearth.

"Sounds like a case of self-defense if I've ever heard one," said the detective. He'd introduced himself, but Sebastian was too rattled to remember his name. "Good thing you managed to get the jump on him and break his wrist. Too bad the other fellow tripped over his own feet and hit his head on the hearth, but what can you do?"

They'd said no such thing to the detective. They hadn't needed to;

the moment the gunman had started raving about monsters, the police had filed the incident under "L" for *Look the other way*. Sebastian had no doubt the medical examiner would find whatever the detective told him to find.

As for the criminal himself, no judge or jury outside of Widdershins was going to believe he was attacked by a monster. And even if they did, the bullet hole in the ceiling and the testimony of the Rath clan was proof enough he'd broken into their house and threatened them with a gun. They'd say his motive was robbery and that would hopefully be the end of it.

God. They might have died tonight, if Ves hadn't saved them.

"Thank you, Detective Boyd," said Pete, who'd apparently been paying more attention than Sebastian. "I've spent most of my life at sea, survived hurricanes and pirates, but I've never been so afraid as when that lunatic was pointing a weapon at my children."

The detective nodded gravely, then tipped his hat to them. "Good night, captain, librarian. You should have a quiet night, unless you've reason to think otherwise." He paused, but when they didn't contradict him, he said, "Call us if you need to."

Bonnie came down just as Boyd left. "Everyone is asleep except for Helen," she said. "She apparently wants to, quote 'grow up to be like Mr. Rune.'"

Sebastian took off his glasses and rubbed at his face, a half-hysterical laugh bubbling beneath the surface. "That doesn't seem very likely."

"What is he, Sebastian?" Pete asked, his grizzled face creasing into a frown. "The bastard he killed called him 'one of the Dark Young.' What does that mean?"

"I don't know." The world was comfortably blurry without the lenses between himself and it. "I didn't know. I thought he was human."

Bonnie gave a dismissive wave. "What does it matter? What *I* want to know is, what have you been up to, Sebastian? Trouble came looking for you here and put my children in danger. I won't have that."

"I didn't think they would come for me here." Stupid, in retrospect. "I'm sorry. I'll tell you everything I can. It's…it has something to do with the library's bookbinders. With Mother."

Bonnie's eyes widened. "I see." She took a deep breath. "Where is Mr. Rune?"

"I don't know."

I'm sorry, he'd said. And left. Run.

"Probably he didn't want to explain things to the police," Pete said sagely. "And I'm sure the police are grateful for it."

"I don't think that was it at all." Sebastian put his glasses back on. "I think he was afraid. Of us."

Compassion replaced concern on Bonnie's face. "I forgot he's an outsider. Where would he have gone? Find him, Sebastian, and see if you can convince him to come back with you. I'd feel a great deal safer with him in the house. No offense, my love," she added to Pete.

"I was taken by surprise," Pete protested. "Don't you worry, Bonnie-Bell. I'll be up all night, keeping watch with a stout club. Anyone so much as sets foot on the property, they'll have me to deal with."

Their words floated past Sebastian. Ves had been so hard to read, alternating between stand-offish and…well, he had definitely been returning Sebastian's kiss on the balcony last night before he pulled away.

"It…it's not you. I just—I can't."

He'd been raised by cultists. Swore by the trees and gods, plural.

"I never knew my progenitor."

Whatever had formed the paternal half of his heritage, it might be earthly, but it was definitely not human.

He must have spent every moment since running away from home in hiding. Concealing half of himself. Sebastian's heart ached at the thought; he could barely imagine such isolation. How would it be to live like that, with no one knowing your true self?

And yet, Ves had exposed himself to save them. To save Sebastian for the third time, considering he'd intervened with the same two ruffians twice before, the first not so very far away…

Ah.

Sebastian started for the door. "I think I know where Vesper might be." The memory of the horror on Ves's face struck him forcefully. "Bonnie, if you'd be so kind to clean the bricks before I return with him, I'd appreciate it."

Ves sat concealed in one of the old trees outside his boarding house, waiting for the last light to go out.

He couldn't risk capture. No hue and cry had yet gone up after him, but that was surely just a matter of time. He had to gather his few possessions, and he didn't dare be seen. His coat still lay in the Raths' front yard, and the back of his shirt and vest were shredded where his tentacles had burst forth. If he encountered anyone else in the boarding house, they'd wonder what had happened to him. Ask questions he couldn't afford to answer.

Assuming they didn't just notice the dark knobs along either side of his spine, the inescapable evidence of his retracted tentacles.

Even now, he didn't know what he'd have done differently. The same men from their other two encounters had found where Sebastian lived—maybe had known all along, if it was indeed Mortimer Waite behind it. They'd been armed, and hurting Sebastian, and threatening innocents, and what choice had Ves had, save to act as fast and brutally as he could?

He'd killed a man. And maybe the fellow had brought it on himself, threatening children, but he was still dead at Ves's hand. Or, rather, tentacles.

The gorge rose in Ves's throat, and he shut his eyes until the feeling passed. He'd been trained since childhood to commit wholesale slaughter, but he'd never killed a man before. His victims had all been straw dummies, or rough shapes of wood, to simulate ripping off legs and arms and heads. He'd knocked weapons out of his grandfather's hand, hefted Noct into the air, flung small boulders at targets across fields, but he never *hurt* anyone while doing it.

But tonight, that destructive power had been unleashed, even if only for a single minute, maybe two. Just that brief time was long enough to leave blood on the Rath hearth.

He wished he'd never come here. Except if he hadn't, there would probably still be blood on the floor at the Rath residence, only it would have belonged to the Rath family instead of their attackers.

No use imagining that horror. The past was done, fixed. The only thing that mattered was what he'd do next.

He couldn't go back to the library. His half-formed plan of stealing Dromgoole's original architectural drawings and trading them for Noct was ended before it had begun. In Boston, he might have walked back in and pretended Sebastian was a lunatic, but Mr. Quinn seemed as though he would certainly believe Ves was a monstrous thing. Miss Endicott knew sorcery; she'd understand such hybrid creatures as himself were possible. And of course, Waite must suspect something, since he hadn't dropped dead of poison.

His best bet was to finish his half-done sketch of the library layout, tell Fagerlie it was complete, and pray he actually intended to turn Ves and Noct fully human. Perhaps they'd get away before Fagerlie realized he'd made up half the floor plan. He could send a telegram from the next stop on the railroad warning Mr. Quinn someone had designs on his precious library.

Whatever happened, he'd never see Sebastian again. The knowledge sat in his chest like a stone. If everything had been different, if Ves had only been fully human…

The light in his room came on.

Ves froze, staring in shock at the boarding house window that belonged to his room. He glimpsed the landlady—what was she doing in there?

Then Sebastian's face appeared in the window, and all the air left Ves's lungs.

Sebastian peered out the window that Ves had left open to let the breeze in. He frowned into the darkness, then leaned closer.

Surely he couldn't spot Ves. Sebastian's eyesight was merely human; he couldn't see in the dark the way Ves and Noct could.

Why was he even here? Surely he hadn't come to kill Ves.

But Ves had held the baby, smiled at the children, and been in the same house as Sebastian's sister. He'd trespassed, crossed every boundary. Sebastian had every motive to want him dead.

The archivist spoke with the landlady for a few seconds, then smiled, appearing to thank her. A moment later the light went out.

Ves stayed frozen in the tree. All he had to do was remain still, and the danger would pass. Sebastian would never spot him. He'd leave, and Ves would take the risk and enter the house, get his things, and...

Oh gods, he didn't want to run. He'd known all this was only temporary, but leaving hurt more than he'd ever imagined it would.

A shadow slipped around the side of the house into the backyard. After a moment, it turned on a pocket flashlight and aimed it at the tree. "Ves?" Sebastian called. "Vesper? Are you there?"

Ves's heart stuttered. Sebastian didn't sound murderous, but...

But he wouldn't hide here like a coward. To hell with it. He was so damned tired of *hiding.*

"Have you come to kill me?" Ves asked, and surprised himself with how calm he sounded.

Sebastian's eyes widened. *"Kill you?"* he asked, as though shocked. Then he took a deep breath. "God, no. Of course not."

Anger snapped through Ves's veins. Sebastian spoke as though Ves was being absurd, as though the thought had never crossed his mind. "Really?" he asked. "Why not?"

And climbed down from the tree.

Not using his arms, or his feet, though in truth they would have made it easier. He lowered himself branch to branch, the flashlight tracking his movement, clearly outlining his black tentacles, his orange goat eyes. He'd give Sebastian no excuse, no way of writing off what he'd seen earlier as a trick of the light.

"I am a thing of destruction," he said, refusing to show himself any mercy. "I was born to sow ruin wherever I go. Why wouldn't you want to see me ended?"

Sebastian's lips parted slightly, and he swallowed. "The same reasons I don't ordinarily go around murdering people?"

Ves's feet touched the ground. "I'm not a person, though, am I?"

He flung out the challenge, waiting for a flinch. Instead, Sebastian lost his slightly dazed expression and frowned. "The devil you aren't! Who told you otherwise?" The hand not holding the flashlight curled into a fist. "Damn it, Ves, I'm sorry. I won't pretend to imagine what you've been through, but I'm not your enemy. You don't have to run, or lurk in trees, or…or anything."

It was a trap. It had to be. The one constant certainty of Ves's life had been that anyone outside of the family, the cult, would kill him or Noct on sight. He'd learned his lesson the day the boys came to the glen below Caprine Hill.

"Don't lie to me," he grated out. "I know you're horrified. Disgusted. I pretended to be ordinary. I held your baby niece, ate dinner with your family. You want me banished, if not destroyed."

"I think I've made it clear what I want to do with you," Sebastian said with a rueful smile. "Vesper…I've seen more than you imagine. And the truth is, people come in all shapes, all heritages. Monsters are more often than not one-hundred percent human, and they don't even have the excuse of following their nature."

This wasn't happening. He'd fallen asleep in the tree, was dreaming this other world where he didn't have to flee for his life. Where Sebastian was looking at him with eyes not filled with disgust or hatred.

"I lied to you," he said, because he no longer knew how this conversation was supposed to go.

"You didn't have to, but I understand why you did." Sebastian took a step forward, hand held out. "Bonnie wants you to come back with me tonight. Says she'll feel safer if you're there. And, before you can ask why, because…Christ, Ves, you *saved our lives.*"

Ves swallowed heavily. "I killed a man," he whispered.

"I'm sorry," Sebastian replied, not moving. "God, Ves, I'm sorry it came to that, but if it helps, you did what you had to. And I'm so glad you did."

Ves stretched out his hand and clasped Sebastian's. And then they were somehow, impossibly, in an embrace. He retracted his tentacles and let Sebastian hold him, as he buried his face in Sebastian's neck and tried not to weep.

✿

They walked back home in silence, but Ves allowed Sebastian to hold his hand the entire way, which Sebastian considered a victory.

Ves had looked so utterly wretched when Sebastian found him in the tree. And thank God he'd tried to put himself in Ves's shoes and imagine where he might be hiding until everyone had gone to bed.

It had been worse than he'd feared. Ves thought Sebastian meant to *kill* him, which…well, someone had put the thought in Ves's head, and outside of Widdershins it might have even been true. But that wasn't fair, either. It wasn't outsider versus lifelong denizen: some people understood the concept of family, of blood or not, and some didn't. Surely there were people in Boston who would have embraced Ves for saving their family, and those in Widdershins who wouldn't.

"Why are all the mirrors taken down in your rooms?" he asked, quietly enough that Ves could pretend he hadn't heard.

Ves tipped his head back. "Mirrors are backed in silver. They show my eyes the way they truly are. Every glimpse is a reminder that I'm not human."

He'd resumed his human guise, everything pulled in, eyes brown and round-pupiled. "Does it hurt?" Sebastian asked. "Keeping everything drawn in, I mean. Hidden."

"Sometimes." Ves shrugged broad shoulders. "I'm used to it."

"You don't have to hide within our walls," Sebastian said. "Seriously. Helen told Bonnie she wants to grow up to be like you."

Ves's laugh was the bitterest Sebastian had ever heard. "This is no blessing, nothing to aspire to. It's a curse, and I just…I just want to be rid of it."

He'd looked magnificent, climbing down from the tree: his muscular body half exposed by his torn clothes, his eyes blazing defiance—and who really cared if they looked like goat eyes? The tentacles were strong enough to support his entire body easily, and though

Sebastian had never thought himself as having an interest in inhuman anatomy, the fact they were a part of Vesper made them...intriguing.

Which, he'd just keep to himself, because saying so would be completely inappropriate. "You can tell me, if you want. But you don't have to."

Ves let out a long sigh. "I didn't ask for this. I was born for a purpose, but no one ever asked me if I wanted to fulfill that purpose."

Sebastian squeezed his fingers gently. Prompting.

"I told you my mother and grandfather were in a cult," Ves said. "They worshipped many things, including the Black Goat of the Woods with a Thousand Young."

One of the Dark Young. That at least made sense now.

"Your father?" Sebastian guessed.

"No. I mean, yes, but not exactly? It's not a ram, or a ewe. Or a goat, for that matter." Ves shrugged. "It's creation—pure, chaotic creation. Or so I understand; I've never seen it for myself." He paused, then shook his head. "It spoke to me, though. Whispered through the blooming trees and fertile earth, the hungry calls of baby birds and the dying sighs of prey. It comforted me, made me feel less alone because I was a part of this web of creation. I...I miss it, sometimes."

God. Poor Ves. "And are the other Young like you?"

Ves's lips tightened. "Yes. No. Again: *chaotic* creation. Some are nearly human; some are absolutely not human at all. Once again, so I'm told. I've only actually met one other of my kind."

They stopped on the sidewalk outside the house. "Now I have a question for you," Ves said. "I understand you're grateful I saved you. But why would you want me around your family, now that you know what I am?"

He was looking for an excuse to run, Sebastian sensed. To bolt into the night and never look back. All Sebastian needed to do was confirm his worst fears.

"What you *are* is a good person," he said carefully. "You stood up for me even after I'd been an utter prick to you. You believed me when no one else did. You helped me, even when there was nothing for you to gain by doing so. I'd rather have you around my family than, say, Dr. Norris from the American History Department."

An unexpected bark of laughter came from Ves. Encouraged, Sebastian added, "Count yourself lucky if you never have to work with the man. I don't know how he became the head of a department. Knew the right people at the time, I expect, and has never done anything so egregious as to be kicked out. Trust me, I'd never have *him* over for dinner, not that he'd waste his precious time on a lowly archivist."

Ves shook his head. "I don't understand you," he confessed softly.

"There's not much to understand. I'm a simple fellow." Sebastian tugged gently on his hand. "Come inside. Bonnie will be glad to see you."

Keeping in mind what Pete had said, Sebastian made sure to knock before trying the door. "It's me," he called. "I have Vesper with me."

The door flew open. Bonnie was still up, Clara in one arm, while Pete sat in the entry room with a stout cudgel in his lap. "There you are," she said. "Are you quite all right, Mr. Rune? Those ruffians didn't hurt you?"

Ves looked utterly adrift. "I…yes? That is, I'm fine."

"Thank heavens." She bustled toward the stairs. "The children are staying in my room for the rest of the night, so Sebastian can sleep in Willie's bed, and you can take Sebastian's room. We have an attic room as well, but it hasn't been used in years, so I'm afraid it's not ready for company." She paused on the first step. "Unless you'd prefer to stand watch?"

"I told you, I have it," Pete groused. "They caught me unprepared before, that's all."

Ves held himself very still, something bordering on panic in his eyes. Sebastian put a hand to his elbow and steered him toward the stairs. "Yes, thank you, but I think Ves has had enough excitement for one evening. I'll get him settled."

"But—" Bonnie started.

Sebastian caught her eye. "Mr. Rune doesn't need people talking at him right now."

Bonnie took the hint and hurried up the stairs ahead of them, before vanishing in the direction of her room without another word.

They stopped outside of Sebastian's room. He wished he'd taken the time to tidy it more. "I'll be there," he said, pointing to the door of the boys' room. "I can leave you alone for the rest of the night, or I'll come back in a few minutes, once you've had the chance to settle yourself, and check on you."

For a moment, Ves looked as though he truly didn't know which he wanted himself. Then he glanced at Sebastian and, in a voice that made him shiver, said, "Come back, if you will."

CHAPTER 21

*V*es sat on the edge of the bed, staring into nothing.

He didn't understand how any of this had happened. The Raths, Captain Degas...no one behaved as though he was a monster. He kept waiting for the other shoe to drop, but so far, it simply hadn't.

He remembered again the man from the train, who had warned him not to come to Widdershins. At the time, he'd thought it nonsense. But maybe the man had been right, in a way. Maybe it wasn't a town for normal folk.

But it might be a town for monsters.

He closed his eyes. He still didn't know what to do about Fagerlie, or Noct, or any of it. But at least things weren't as bad as they'd seemed only a short while ago. He didn't have to run, not tonight.

He could sit here on the edge of Sebastian Rath's bed and wait.

He'd removed the tatters of his shirt and vest, but left his trousers on. The bathroom was conveniently located next to Sebastian's room, and Ves had splashed water on his face, used his finger to scrub dentifrice across his teeth, and slunk back to the bedroom. A few minutes later, he heard someone else slip into the bathroom. Sebastian, perhaps, or Bonnie.

When the footsteps approached his door, he knew it wasn't Bonnie.

"Come in," he said in response to the soft knock.

Sebastian stuck his head inside. "Would you like to talk?" he asked, keeping his voice low. "Or would you prefer I leave you alone to sleep?"

Gods. He should tell Sebastian to leave now. Not make things any more complicated.

"What would you like?" he asked.

"That doesn't matter."

"It does. Very much," Ves protested.

"This isn't a test, Ves," Sebastian said with startling gentleness. "I'm fine with either of the two options I offered. You've had a difficult time, and I want to do what's best for you. That's all."

A part of Ves wanted to laugh. *He'd* had a difficult time, when Sebastian was the one who'd had a gun held to his head.

Another part wanted to cry, though he wasn't certain why. "It's just…a lot," he said at last. "I've spent my entire life living under this curse, believing that no one could ever know. That if anyone saw me, they'd try to kill me for being a monster." Like the children in the glen, but he didn't say that part aloud.

"I'm sorry." Sebastian shut the door, then sat beside him on the bed, the mattress dipping under his slighter weight. "I can't imagine how isolating that must have felt. But it's all right. You're safe here."

A terrible, dark knot seemed to unravel inside of Ves's chest. He leaned forward and buried his face in his hands, while a flood of commingled emotions rose in him. Grief and anger, and a powerful relief.

Sebastian didn't try to interrupt, only stayed with him quietly. When Ves finally sat back, wiping at his wet face, Sebastian put a hand to his bare shoulder.

The touch sent a pleasant shiver through him. His skin pebbled, and embarrassment flashed through him as his nipples drew up into tight peaks. Perhaps Sebastian wouldn't notice.

"Are you cold?" He'd noticed.

"No." The word came out husky, and Ves cursed himself.

Sebastian nodded, then said, "Would you like me to leave?"

"No."

"Would you like me to touch you?"

Ves closed his eyes. "Yes."

Sebastian very gently ran his hand across Ves's shoulders, brushing the ends of his soft hair. The muscles beneath his fingers were tense, and Ves's breath hitched. He continued down, tracing the path of Ves's spine, keeping the touch non-sexual and using the opportunity to get a truly good look at Ves's back.

The scars there startled him more than the two patches of dark skin running down either side of the spine. It looked as though someone had whipped Ves, and more than once given some of the scars crossed over one another.

He ignored them for the moment and turned his attention to the dark skin whose texture looked smoother than the rest of Ves's back. The only other sign of the tentacles was four fleshy knobs on each strip, three larger and the lowest pair smaller. How did that even work? Where did they go?

"You can relax if you want to," Sebastian said. "I don't mind."

Quite the opposite, though he didn't want to say that aloud and sound as if he had some sort of sexual fetish. It was more that if he'd thought Ves attractive before, seeing him coming down from the tree had taken Sebastian's breath away. In that moment, Ves had looked…whole. Complete, though Sebastian hadn't even realized before that something was missing.

For a moment, he thought Ves would refuse. Then he sighed, and something seemed to go out of him.

The tentacles uncoiled in a single, smooth motion that somehow looked as natural as a man stretching out his arms. They appeared black in color at first, but then the light caught a patch of skin, and Sebastian realized they in fact had a beautiful blue-gold iridescence to them.

"May I touch?" he asked. "Only if you're comfortable with it."

Ves swallowed audibly. "Go ahead."

The skin was dry and firm. He'd expected it to feel rubbery, but instead the tentacle was startlingly muscular. He ran his hand along its length, and the tip coiled around his fingers. He had the wild desire to bring it to his lips for a kiss, just as he might a lover's hand, but that would surely be pushing too far.

"You're beautiful," he said. "I hope you don't mind my saying that."

Ves turned to him, strange eyes wide. His lips parted, but he didn't seem to know what to say. The moment hung between them, the air thick with promise. Sebastian waited, hope mingled with understanding.

Then Ves leaned forward and brushed his lips across Sebastian's in a question.

Sebastian kissed him back, unable to hold in the moan of eagerness that slipped out. Ves tasted of warmth and desire, and the scent of green leaves and deep forests rose from his skin, mingled with a tinge of black pepper. He wrapped his arms around Ves's shoulders, fingers brushing against the extra appendages as he did so.

Ves's arms went around him, pulling him in tight. Their kiss took on the flavor of desperation, as though they were both drowning and this their only hope of air. The two lower tentacles slipped around Sebastian's waist, tugging him in closer—

"Oh!" Ves jumped back, letting go of Sebastian entirely. "I-I'm sorry."

"Nothing to be sorry for," Sebastian assured him, the words ragged with lust. "You're just *very* good at giving hugs."

Ves stared at him…then started to laugh. "You're mad. Absolutely insane."

"I've been called worse things." Sebastian leaned in, pressing his forehead against Ves's. "Would you like me to make love to you?"

Ves's breath caught. "Y-Yes. Gods of the wood, please."

Sebastian nipped at Ves's lower lip, then pushed him back on the bed. He flung one leg over Ves's hip, straddling him. The hard length of his erection pushed at Sebastian's through the cloth separating them.

Sebastian rocked back and forth, and Ves gasped and grabbed his hips. "Not—not yet."

It would definitely be a shame not to remove some of the layers between them first. Sebastian slid off and reached for the buttons on his own vest. Ves watched with hungry eyes, and ordinarily Sebastian might have made a show of it. But his hands were shaking with need, and the look of raw hunger on Ves's face set his body ablaze. Every inch of skin ached to be pressed against Ves's, and he could feel his pulse in his cock.

He tossed aside every shred of clothing, not caring at the moment what ended up creased on the floor and what didn't. Ves stared at his prick, and his tongue ran over his lips in a way that almost made Sebastian spend on the spot.

"May I take your clothing off?" Sebastian asked hoarsely.

Ves nodded. Sebastian ran his hands down Ves's chest, then over his belly, before leaning in to kiss the trail of dark hair leading down past the edge of his trousers. A whimper of need was Sebastian's reward, and he smiled against his lover's skin.

He sat back and began to work on the trouser buttons, taking advantage of the act to brush his hand across the straining prick beneath. He peeled them off, along with the drawers beneath, exposing Ves to his sight.

"Mmm," he said, licking his lips. "Beautiful."

Ves laughed again, as though he wasn't entirely certain whether Sebastian meant it. But he did. He longed to wrap his lips around the hard length of prick in front of him, then beg Ves to make thorough use of him. But tonight wasn't about what he wanted.

"What do you wish me to do?" he asked.

Ves blinked orange-gold eyes. "I d-don't know. I've never...no one could know about my true nature, which meant never being intimate with anyone before. What do you like?"

"Many things," Sebastian purred, and grinned at the flush spreading across Ves's neck. "But most of all, I like you." He stretched out on his side beside Ves, not quite touching. "This isn't a test, sweetheart. There's no answer that will disappoint me. Though I've some suggestions, if you want them."

Ves nodded mutely. Sebastian grinned at him. "We can lie here like this. We can cuddle. I can suck your prick. You can fuck me. I can show you how good rubbing cocks can feel."

Ves nodded again. "Yes. That last one. Please."

"My pleasure," Sebastian murmured, and straddled Ves's hips again.

Ves gasped. "I won't last."

"Mmm, that's fine. I'm not going anywhere." Sebastian braced one hand on Ves's shoulder and used the other to loosely hold their pricks together. Ves let out a startled sound of pleasure that sent a thrill of delight through Sebastian. His hands lifted, as though he meant to hold onto Sebastian's arms, but then hesitated.

"You can hold onto me," Sebastian encouraged. "Use whatever arms you'd like. I promise I'll tell you if I don't care for something."

Ves's eyes were wild, the rectangular pupils dilated nearly round with lust. Sebastian met his gaze as he began to move. Precome slicked his fingers, and he put it to good use, smearing it across their skin until they slid easily together. Something curled around the back of one thigh, then the other—the two small, lower tentacles, no doubt. Their firm grip sent a rush through him; he'd always loved being held tightly, and there was no denying it felt good now.

"Yes," he groaned. "Yes, Vesper, you're amazing, you feel amazing, you—"

Ves cried out sharply, hips thrusting up beneath Sebastian. Hot spend coated Sebastian's fingers.

He sat back, wrapping his slick fingers around his prick alone, and pumped it vigorously. Within a few strokes, the pleasure crested, and he groaned again as he spilled onto Ves's chest.

Their breathing slowed gradually. Sebastian offered Ves a warm smile, received a shy one in return. He licked Ves's seed off his fingers. The flavor wasn't quite like that of the other men he'd sucked; less bitter but more earthy, with a faint tang that reminded him of chewing on green stems of grass. "Mmm. You taste good. I can't wait to wrap my lips around your prick and have you come in my mouth."

Ves blinked, then laughed softly. "I...thank you?"

Sebastian went to the washstand and returned with a cloth to clean up the mess they'd made of Ves's torso. "You're very welcome." He paused. "Would you like me to stay?"

Uncertainty crossed Ves's face. "Is that safe? Your sister might suspect…"

Sebastian chuckled. "She already knows I kissed you the other day." At Ves's shock, he shrugged. "We've always been close. Not to suggest we didn't try to kill one another as children on a regular basis, but even then, if anyone else so much as looked at one of us wrong, the other would come to their defense. And at the moment, I think she rather likes you more than me anyway, since I'm the one who brought the trouble to her door."

"That isn't fair," Ves protested.

"But it is understandable. So, shall I stay, or would you prefer to sleep alone?"

Sebastian's heart ached at the vulnerability that showed on Ves's face. "Stay, please."

"As you wish," he said, and kissed Ves again.

"May I ask you something?" Sebastian said quietly. His face was clear to Ves in the dimness, though Ves couldn't guess how much he could see in turn, without his glasses or the ability to see in the dark.

Ves's mind spun, emotions a tumult. Sebastian, handsome Sebastian, had touched him. Skin to skin. Had made him come, then spent himself all over Ves's belly. Looked at him with lust instead of revulsion.

His whole world had changed in just a few hours.

"Yes. Of course," he said.

Sebastian ran a hand over his chest. "You said your family belonged to a cult."

"And that's responsible for my condition," Ves confirmed.

"I wouldn't call it a 'condition,'" Sebastian protested. "You make it sound like you're pregnant, or have tuberculosis."

"That would be a no on both of those," he said wryly. "I've never been sick a day in my life. And though some of the Young are blessed with multiple organs of generation, I am not among their number."

Sebastian nodded absently, as though all of this was perfectly normal. Either he had remarkable aplomb, or living in Widdershins had inured him to oddness. "You said earlier that you were born for a purpose. It's fine if you don't wish to speak of it—just tell me to be quiet."

"You're curious."

Sebastian propped himself up on one elbow. "Of course I want to know more about you. I like you." He offered a crooked smile. "I don't generally invite men back to my room."

"Oh." The words set a warm glow in Ves's chest. "I like you, too."

"I'd hope so. I'm a very likable fellow."

Ves laughed. "And humble."

"That, too. A quality becoming of a librarian."

"But you're technically an archivist," Ves pointed out.

"Damn. You're right." Sebastian dropped a casual kiss on Ves's mouth. "I was a librarian before I finished my degree at Widdershins University, though. History, before you can ask. A good subject for an archivist to know."

"That makes sense." Ves tugged lightly on Sebastian and was strangely gratified when the man immediately snuggled into him. "I don't know a great deal about history. Well, not any of the traditional things one is expected to know. You can't imagine how confused I was when someone first mentioned George Washington to me. When I asked who that was, he looked at me as though I were mad."

"I'd never considered that," Sebastian said. "I imagine there are many subjects left uncovered by cult education."

"You could say so." Ves turned his face into Sebastian's hair, breathed deep. "As for my purpose…I was meant to usher in the end of the world."

"Oh," Sebastian said softly. "You were meant to come here in 1902? To Widdershins?"

"They never told me any details—no whens and wheres. But I was supposed to lead an army of cultists, rain destruction and death down on our enemies, and help bring a close to the age of humankind."

Sebastian shook his head slowly. "I can't imagine you doing that."

Ves snorted. "Neither could I. Which was a bit of a problem, since that was my one and only reason for existing."

"I can see where that would be an issue, yes."

Ves ran his hand along Sebastian's upper arm. "My mother named me Vesper—evening—because I was going to bring the day of humanity to a close. Of course, that meant she and my grandfather had very high expectations of me. I started 'training' by the time I was five years old. I marched, did every sort of physical workout. Practiced killing on straw dummies." He swallowed. "I memorized long sections of text, learned whatever language was required to read the books on our shelf. Any education past that wasn't of importance."

"That sounds very limiting," Sebastian said quietly.

"I suppose. At the time, I was just concentrating on survival."

Sebastian lifted his head, brows drawn down. "What do you mean?"

"As you noticed, I'm fairly unsuited to destroying the world," Ves said with a crooked smile that fooled neither of them. "But honestly, even if I had been, I don't think I could have ever satisfied Mother's exacting standards. The smallest failing or infraction earned a beating. I had to march around the yard for up to twelve hours straight, or stay awake for days at a time, because *you'll have to do it when you're leading an army to victory.'* And if I failed, I'd be punished. Harshly."

"The scars on your back…"

"Yes."

Sebastian kissed him tenderly. "I'm so sorry."

No one had ever said that to him, about what he'd endured as a child. Tears welled in his eyes, and he blinked them back. "It wasn't as bad as it might have been. I'm tough. Physically, I mean. She had to coat the whip in silver dust so it would actually hurt me. I'm also resistant to magic. It isn't that spells can't work on me, but not…directly. That is, if you throw kerosene on me and then set it on fire with a spell, I'll be in trouble. If you try to cast the spell directly at me, not much will happen."

"Useful."

"Except it means I also can't *cast* spells. Mother was *very* disappointed at that." He sighed. "Honestly, my time with the books was the best time of the day. Grandfather was more of a scholar, and he was the one to teach me how to repair and rebind. I owe my career to him, I suppose."

Sebastian's hand trailed across his chest again, a comforting touch. "It sounds as though you were close."

"In a way." Vesper considered for a long moment, trying to untangle the briar patch of emotion. "He was more patient than Mother, although perhaps that's only because I was actually good at what he had to teach me. My time with him was a reprieve of a sorts, though of course he never hesitated to remind me the reason we had the books in the first place."

"Did he never try to rein in his daughter's cruelty?"

If only. Ves shook his head. "He was ruthless in his own way. He'd relate tales of the blood he'd spilled to obtain the books as we worked on them. The lives he'd taken because it was convenient for him, because it served his own ambition. At the time, it didn't seem so horrible, though. I loved him. I loved Mother, for that matter. But they were both true believers in the task their masters had set for them."

"The destruction of humanity?"

"I know it sounds mad." Ves stared at the ceiling. "But I think…I think life had ill-used them both in their separate ways. They were living in a one-room shack in the middle of the woods, after all. To go from that to being dominant over the remnants of humanity, to have thousands of slaves at their command, to finally receive the splendor they thought was their due…you can see how they might have gotten caught up in that dream. Done anything to see it come true."

"But you didn't."

"As I said, I am utterly unsuitable to ending the world." Ves sighed. "I abhor violence. I hit a man who tried to rob me in Boston, and of course I punched the fellow when we were escaping the apartment the other day, but otherwise I've never been in an actual fight. Not until tonight." He swallowed. "And I managed to kill a man in it. As I said, I was made to destroy."

"No." Sebastian lifted his head, staring intently into Ves's eyes.

Apparently he could make out at least that much in the moonlight. "What were you to do—carefully stand back and consider how to disarm men who threatened *a baby?* If you'd hesitated, Clara and Pete might have died instead." He kissed Ves. "You're a good man."

A good man who was still withholding a portion of the truth. But only until tomorrow.

He had to talk to Noct first. He couldn't make a momentous decision that directly affected the rest of Noct's life without his input.

But afterward, he'd come clean to Sebastian. He owed the man that much, and more.

He didn't reply, only pulled Sebastian closer. Sebastian soon fell asleep, but Ves stared at the ceiling, counting away the hours until dawn.

CHAPTER 22

*V*es opened his eyes and found himself in Sebastian's room. In Sebastian's bed, with only sheets against his naked skin.

Well, not just sheets. There was a warm body pressed into his frontside.

Gods, it hadn't been just a wild dream after all.

It didn't seem possible. *None* of it did. He should have been fleeing a pitchfork-wielding mob, or at least looking for somewhere to hide until he could get to Noct.

But it was real. Bonnie Rath had invited him into her home, knowing what he was. And Sebastian…

Sebastian had taken such care with him. As though Ves was someone worth it.

For the first seventeen years of his life, he'd been nothing but a tool to the adults in his life. Or, if not a tool, then an iron ingot his mother meant to shape into something useful by any means necessary. His worth was based on passing her tests, learning her lessons, becoming the soldier who would command an army and help bring back those who had once ruled over the earth.

A means to an end; that was all he'd ever been.

Except to the voice in the forest; the song of the Black Goat of the

Woods. It was a thing of primal creation; simple existence was goal enough. And then Noct had been conceived, and Vesper had sensed the bond, the connection, between them even before his brother left the womb. Sometimes he wished there had been other Dark Young stalking the woods around Caprine Hill, but at least he'd had the voice of the forest, which demanded nothing from him, and Noct who loved him.

After they fled, he'd carefully maintained a distance between himself and everyone else he encountered. He was polite, of course, but he never socialized. Never engaged in small talk. Never gave anyone a reason to care about him.

He'd wrapped himself around Sebastian during the night. Sebastian was hugging one of Ves's tentacles in his sleep, like a child with a toy. Unable to keep from worrying what Sebastian would think when he awoke, he tried to ease it free.

But Sebastian tightened his arms and murmured something. Then he yawned, before pressing back against Ves. "Good morning."

The early light might as well have been bright as midday to Ves. It shaped Sebastian's sleepy features and shaded his hazel eyes to gray. His golden hair was wildly tousled, and Ves had the sudden urge to sweep it back out of his face.

"Good morning," he replied.

Sebastian made a sound of contentment and proceeded to wiggle his backside against Ves's morning stand. "What a lovely position to wake up in. You could bugger me like this, if you want."

All the blood in his body seemed to rush into Ves's cock. For a moment, he couldn't think past need and the mental image of Sebastian writhing while Ves thrust into him.

He groaned and forced himself to roll away. "I truly want to, but everyone else is up and moving about."

"Bonnie will have seen I'm not in the boys' bedroom. She won't come knocking, trust me."

That meant everyone would know what they'd done last night. Well, not everyone, but Bonnie and Captain Degas. The thought of facing them this morning, after having spent himself moaning against Sebastian's cock last night, brought a rush of heat to his face.

"We have work," he said.

Sebastian sighed. "Oh, very well. I suppose we ought to try and find out who those men last night were working for. If it's Mortimer... I hate to think it, but we need to know."

"Oh. Ah, there's something I forgot to tell you last night. Waite tried to poison me yesterday."

Sebastian sat bolt upright in the bed. "What?"

Vesper explained what had happened. "Given the timing with Miss Cohen's experience in the staff room, I assume that was meant as a distraction while Waite came in and poisoned the cup. He and the spirit must be working together. And then I gulped down coffee from an unguarded cup like a fool."

All of the color had drained from Sebastian's face. "You might have died," he said, voice shaking on the final word.

"Oh! Please, don't worry." Ves wrapped whatever limbs he could around Sebastian, trying to comfort him. "I'm fine. As I mentioned last night, it takes a great deal to hurt me. I wasn't injured."

"But you'd be dead in other circumstances." Some of the color came back to Sebastian's cheeks, though not a great deal. "And then we were attacked here last night...my God. We have to warn Mr. Quinn about Mortimer."

Ves took his hand, curling their fingers together, dark olive and pale cream. "I'll go to the police station and see if I can talk to the gunman." The survivor, but he pushed that thought away. "You're of more use at the library at the moment than I am, so you go ahead in to work. Just stay away from Waite until I get back, all right?"

"I suppose." Sebastian freed himself to roll over and pick up his silver-rimmed glasses. "Say you'll come back here with me tonight."

The question warmed Ves from the inside out. Sebastian knew him, knew he wasn't entirely human, but still wanted him. It was a gift he'd never imagined being given.

"Gladly," he said, and hoped he wasn't lying.

He retracted his tentacles and ordered himself as well as he was able, with vest and shirt ripped down the back. "Your coat was in the yard—it's probably downstairs," Sebastian said. "That will at least cover the damage while you go to your apartment after breakfast."

Apparently, he was staying for breakfast.

Sebastian didn't seem even slightly embarrassed as he led the way down the stairs. The rest of the Rath clan was crowded around the table in the dining room.

As soon as they stepped in, Helen shouted: "It's Mr. Rune!" She started to jump up, but her mother said, "Sit down, Helen, and let the man eat."

"Good morning," Captain Degas said, saluting Ves with his coffee cup. He looked exhausted; no doubt he'd kept his promise to watch the house all night. "It's good to see you up and about, Mr. Rune."

The three-year-old, Tommy, toddled over and promptly attached himself to Ves's leg.

Miss Rath sighed. "Just bring him over to me, Mr. Rune. Or may I call you Vesper?"

Ves felt his face heat again. "Yes, please do."

"Bonnie, then." She smiled at him, and he was struck by the resemblance to her brother. "Sebastian, make yourself useful and refresh the coffee, will you?"

Though he'd enjoyed previous meals with the Raths, they'd always been taken under a shadow. The certainty that they'd be revolted by his presence in their lives, if they knew the truth about his nature, his curse.

Now they knew, and yet still here he sat, eating scrambled eggs and toast, and drinking coffee. It was such an ordinary scene, such a normal moment, that it was in turns disorienting and wonderful.

"They'll kill you," Mother had said, when he'd asked why he couldn't go to school like the children in books did. She'd grabbed one tentacle, yanked on it hard enough to make his eyes water. *"That's why. The first glimpse they got of one of these, or your eyes, they'd beat you to death. How do you think that would feel, Vesper? Having your bones broken while they kicked you. Your scalp peeled back from your skull by one of their boots, your nose smashed in."*

"I could hide," he tried, because he'd been young enough to still be stupid.

"All day?" She shook her head in disgust. *"Maybe someday. But what about your brother? What's he supposed to do? Just stay here while you*

prance about with idiots and sleepers? Or are you going to hide him under your coat so he can go to school with you?"

The fear alone would probably have been enough to dissuade him in the end. But her reminder that Noct couldn't even try was enough to convince him never to ask again. Because it wouldn't be fair.

And now here he was, enjoying breakfast almost as though he were a normal person, while Noct was with a man who might mean to betray them both.

"Are you all right?" Sebastian asked in a low voice.

Ves blinked back to the here-and-now. Sebastian watched him with concern, but no one else seemed to have noticed his momentary lapse. "Yes. I'm fine. Just thinking I shouldn't linger, if I'm to stop by my apartment and get changed before going to the police station and asking about the gunman." As he spoke the words aloud, a new concern occurred to him. "Do you think they'll actually let me in to talk to him? I'm just some random person, as far as the police are concerned."

Sebastian nodded. "Tell the officer on duty that you work in the Ladysmith's library. Then offer a bribe. Two dollars should do it. Do you have it? If not, I can make up the shortfall."

"No, no, I have it." It was a bit depressing to think the police were so easily bribed, but that at least was probably no different here than anywhere else. "But why would he care about the fact I work in the library?"

"We've had an alliance in the past," Sebastian said, as though that made any sense whatsoever.

"All right," Ves said, instead of asking a question he suspected had no quick answer. He rose to his feet and nodded at the rest of the table. "I'll see you at the museum, Sebastian."

Sebastian felt as though a weight fell over him when he stepped through the doors of the library. For most of his life, this had been a place of refuge: of quiet and order.

Mortimer Waite had tried to murder Ves, right here in the

precincts of the library. Thank God Ves wasn't entirely human. Otherwise, he would have died in agony on the bindery floor.

Of all the things he'd imagined to face in his life, betrayal by another librarian had never been one of them. A part of him almost resented the entire situation, for no better reason than he should have been floating on a cloud of happiness this morning. He not only had a new lover, but someone he cared about, whom his family had met and liked as well. He ought to be planning a romantic picnic on the cliffs overlooking the sea, or daydreaming about being face-down in the pillows while Ves took him. Instead, he had to worry about an evil book and the traitor in their midst.

"Sebastian!" Arthur called.

Sebastian stopped and turned, surprised. He'd reached the hallway outside of his office, and Arthur hurried up from behind him.

"Goodness, you are in your own head this morning," Arthur said with a fond smile. "I called after you twice."

"Sorry. It was a long night."

Arthur arched a brow. "Oh? Do go on?"

"A gentleman never kisses and tells," Sebastian replied primly.

"And since when are you a gentleman?" Arthur asked. "I noticed you've been spending time with our new binder...?"

Sebastian grinned. His old friend sometimes knew him a bit too well. "I can neither confirm nor deny your observation."

"So I thought. Where is dear Vesper this morning? He's usually here with the sun."

"Is he?" Sebastian supposed he shouldn't have been surprised that Ves was a hard worker. "He had some things to attend to of his own, but I'm sure he'll be along soon. We're working together on a project, actually."

"Is there anything I can help with until he arrives?" Arthur gestured at the locked door of Sebastian's office. "If you need an assistant—"

"No, but thank you." Hopefully Ves would return soon with answers. "I have all the help I need."

CHAPTER 23

*B*ack at the apartment, Ves changed into clothes that hadn't been torn apart and set aside his shirt and vest from yesterday in hopes of mending them.

As a child, he'd mostly wandered the hills shirtless, skin darkened by the sun. There had been no thought to hiding then; the remoteness of the shack ensured few came there. Before the boys who'd attacked them, he'd never glimpsed more than a lone hunter here and there, easily evaded.

Of course, fellow members of the cult sometimes visited. But there had been no need to conceal anything in front of them; quite the opposite. Mother had shown him off like a prize. Her little soldier, who was going to help remake the world into something terrible.

As he descended the stairs, the landlady emerged from the parlor. "A man was here looking for you last night."

"I know. He found me."

She hovered in the doorway, and he suspected she wanted to ask about the mirrors, but was too polite to bring up the subject herself.

He'd let himself look in the bathroom mirror of the Rath house this morning, just for a moment. Searching for whatever it was Sebastian saw in him, or maybe just hoping it wasn't quite as bad as he remembered.

It had been. Terrible goat eyes, and shifting tentacles: he was still a monster.

A monster who'd had sex, though.

He left the landlady, her curiosity unsatisfied, and walked to the nearest trolley stop. Someone had left their newspaper behind, and he picked it up. The headlines were naturally concerned with the arrival of Halley's Comet that night. A diagram showed the positions of sun, earth, and comet, and how they would change from hour to hour until the earth intersected with the trail left behind by the visitor.

Another article, further down, was far more troubling. Police in Oklahoma had rescued a sixteen year old girl from cultists who intended to sacrifice her during the traverse through the comet's tail to "redeem the sins of the world."

Thank the trees she'd been saved…but how many others would not be rescued? How many madmen would destroy lives out of either misplaced religious fervor, or in sorcerous rituals fueled by blood and terror?

Would fires dance atop Caprine Hill tonight? Would there be half brothers and sisters born nine months hence? What sort of sacrifices might occur there, in the place that he'd once called home?

The trolley took him to downtown Widdershins, and he walked the remaining few blocks to the police station. The officer on duty behind the desk glanced up disinterestedly. "Can I help you?"

"A man was brought in last night. He and his partner threatened the Rath family. His partner didn't make it." Ves kept his voice as level as possible.

He'd never wanted to kill anyone. But in that moment, it had felt right to wrap his tentacles around the man, to do *anything* to keep him from hurting Sebastian, or little Clara, or the rest.

"Just a minute." The officer checked a book, presumably one that listed currently incarcerated criminals, then looked up at Vesper. "Bob Underell?"

"I don't know his name."

The officer's eyes narrowed. "So you're not his lawyer."

"No. I work with Sebastian Rath at the Ladysmith's library." Recalling Sebastian's advice, he removed two dollars from his wallet and placed it to one side with studied casualness. "I'd like to speak to Mr. Underell for a few moments."

The dollars vanished with alacrity. "Right this way, then."

Ves followed the officer to the back of the building, where there were three small cells. Two were unoccupied, but the third held the gunman from the night before.

Underell's eyes widened when he saw Vesper, and he scrambled to his feet, flattening himself against the wall as far as he could get from the door. "No—don't let him near me! He's a monster! He killed Jim!"

"Uh huh," the officer said. Ves honestly couldn't tell if he didn't believe Underell or just didn't care. "Fascinating story." He turned to Ves. "He's in one piece now, and he needs to be when you leave, understand?"

"I have no intention of harming Mr. Underell," Ves assured him.

The officer nodded and left, shutting the door behind him.

They were alone.

Ves stepped up to the bars. "I've come to ask you some questions."

A thin sheen of sweat coated Underell's face. "I-I don't know anything."

"Of course you do." Ves wrapped his hands around the iron and narrowed his eyes. "You and your compatriot followed Sebastian Rath from the apartment house where Mr. O'Neil lived. I'm guessing you were also the ones who removed O'Neil's belongings from his rooms." He lowered his voice and locked his gaze with Underell. "The ones who killed him."

"I-I need to talk with my lawyer. I ain't saying anything—"

"Do you really think I'm here to build a case for the prosecution?" Ves gave him the nastiest smile he could muster. "You know what I am."

Underell swallowed convulsively. "Please don't...*Iä, Iä, the Goat with a Thousand Young.*"

How many times had he heard that chant? Hell, how many had he spoken it himself, hands raised to the weathered stones atop Caprine Hill? The firelight had flickered on his mother's face, her eyes turned to the wood with a look of joy he never saw at any other time. Voices responded on the wind, the whisper of the trees that watched their every move with some sense other than sight.

No matter where he went, he couldn't escape his wretched past. "Do you worship the All-Mother, Lord of the Trees?"

Thankfully, Underell shook his head. "I-I give her respect. I don't want to cross her. Or you."

At least there was that. "And I'd prefer not to be crossed. Tell me who you work for, and I'll walk out of here right now. Leave you be."

Underell licked his lips uncertainly. No doubt weighing which he feared more in the moment: those he worked for, who might punish him later, or the monster in front of him right now. "We didn't kill the first binder, I swear. I don't know what happened to him. And we—I —don't know the name of the man who hired us."

Ves didn't want to destroy his clothing again, but he let his eyes go orange. "Don't lie to me."

"I wouldn't! I swear!" Underell's terror seemed genuine. "Please, you have to believe me! We do some work on occasion for the barman at The Silver Key. Nothing too serious, just knock the heads of people who owe him money. He contacted us, said he had a regular looking for some trustworthy men who could clean out an apartment and keep their mouths shut about it. It was easy money."

"What's the barman's name?"

"Renie Milton." Underell swallowed convulsively. "We did the job and got paid. Then last week, Renie contacts us again. The same boss wants us to follow one of the librarians. Find out what he knows about the guy whose stuff we made disappear. Who he's talking with, what he might be looking for. So we do. Renie was the go-between the whole time."

"And last night?"

"I don't know what Rath did, but he stuck his nose where it didn't belong. We were supposed to get rid of him and any witnesses. 'No loose ends,' that was what the boss wanted."

A low growl escaped Ves. Underell took a nervous step back. "So you waited until Sebastian was home and his guard down, and ambushed him there. In a house with *children* in it."

Underell raised his hands in a plea for mercy. "Please—I've done what you asked! I'll do more—whatever you want! Do you want sacrifices for the All-Mother? I can get them!"

Disgust washed through Ves. He blinked his eyes back to human and stepped away from the bars. "You can't give me what I want," he said. "But if I ever see you on the streets of Widdershins again, you'll regret it."

After Arthur left to help the other librarians continue the search for the *Book of Breath*, Sebastian turned his attention to Kelly's commonplace book. He found the point where Vesper had left off yesterday.

Vesper. Hopefully he'd be able to learn something from the prisoner. With any luck, his presence alone would intimidate the man into revealing everything.

Sebastian's heart ached at the familiar sight of Kelly's hand, and he wondered if his mother had kept a similar book. If so, it must have been lost in the fire, along with so much else.

If only he'd followed her wishes, perhaps all this could have been avoided.

Or maybe he'd be the one gone missing instead.

After about ten minutes combing through the book, finding nothing but day-to-day notes, Sebastian came to a solid wall of text. His pulse grew faster, and he leaned in, peering at Kelly's cramped writing through his glasses.

I think I understand, if not all of it, at least where it began. It took months of sorting through Ladysmith and Dromgoole's correspondence, some of which was written using code words, rather than daring to put the truth to paper without some veil to cover it from curious eyes. There are details I need to revisit, which I hope will reveal where the various Books of the Bound are concealed.

So. The beginning. Or what seems to be the beginning, though I cannot in truth say for certain, any more than one who looks upon a spider's completed web can say which strand served as the starting point.

In 1830, a man named Gregorio Hollowell died in Ipswich. He was subsequently suspected to be a vampire, and his body exhumed, the heart removed and burned. This act had a profound effect on his four surviving siblings. Together they turned their intellects to learning the arts of necromancy, though it is unclear what they hoped to achieve by this.

They came to Widdershins around 1833, probably intending to use the arcane maelstrom beneath the city to fuel their magics. Emeline, Filomena, Thaddeus, and Quincy Hollowell.

I haven't yet found anything to explain what happened next, only that the four died, or perhaps were murdered. Under the flaming tail of Halley's Comet in 1835, their bodies were taken apart and made into four books: breath, blood, bone, and flesh. Their spirits were bound to the books, and apparently could grant great power to any sorcerer who laid hands on them.

I don't know how Ladysmith and Dromgoole came across them— hopefully it's hidden somewhere in their letters. But they decided the books were too dangerous to be on the loose.

From what I can tell, the Books of the Bound were still able to exert some sort of influence on the minds of those around them. They needed an extra layer of protection. Dromgoole was to assist with this, along with unnamed others. But how? The only thing certain is that Dromgoole's mind broke as he finished the Ladysmith's library.

So long as the protections remain in place, there's no need to worry. But Rebecca was worried. I wish she'd told me everything.

"So do I," Sebastian murmured.

The next few pages were annotations, along with lists of architectural features common to Dromgoole's known works. Had Kelly been trying to identify other buildings he'd designed?

He turned a page, and found only a single line, written so large it took up most of the sheet.

God help us all. One of the books is free. And I don't know in whose hands it resides.

CHAPTER 24

Thirty-four Cranch Way backed up to the river that flowed through the heart of Widdershins. The nearby fish canning factory loomed against the sky, its stink permeating the area. The neighborhood had likely been a pleasant one long ago, but now it had sunk into decrepitude. Roofs sagged, and many of the houses seemed deserted. An entire block was nothing but burned-out ruins, wildflowers growing amidst ashes, brick chimneys slowly crumbling to join the rest of the long-vanished residences.

The house Fagerlie had rented was one of the better ones, for all that. Though the roofline wasn't straight, it at least didn't look about to collapse. A coat of paint had been put on the door within the last twenty years, and the lawn hadn't succumbed to wilderness. Even so, the place looked forbidding, with curtains drawn over the windows despite the fair spring day.

Ves stood and watched it for several minutes. Noct was probably behind those curtains. Unable to come outside except under cover of darkness. Was Ves about to condemn him to a lifetime spent hiding in attics, behind shutters?

That's why he was here—to talk to Noct. To let him know all was not well and Fagerlie had darker motives than they'd guessed. To warn him they weren't going to be freed from the curse of their blood tonight after all.

Gods of the wood, he hated this. It would have been so easy to just steal the architectural drawings and bring them here. Hand them over and hope for the best. But he couldn't do that to Sebastian, or Bonnie, or the librarians.

He took a deep breath and walked to the door. It swung open before he reached the stoop, revealing Fagerlie on the other side.

"Vesper," he said. "I hope you aren't wasting my time again. Do you have the map I requested?"

Ves stepped up to the door and stopped. "I want to see Nocturn."

"You'll see him in a few hours," Fagerlie said impatiently. "The comet will make its transit between earth and sun tonight! Then, only a short time later, the earth will pass through its tail. If I am to help you, I *must* have the map in my hand by sunset."

Ves's heart hurt, the death of hope painful. "Did you ever mean to help us at all?" he asked. "Or was I just a useful fool?"

Fagerlie scowled. "What are you talking about, boy? If you're here to impugn my character again—"

"You're after the *Book of Breath*."

Fagerlie's expression went from outrage to surprise—then closed off entirely. "Not outside."

It was probably stupid to go into the house...but Noct was in there, and Ves had to talk to him.

Though the exterior of the house had been left alone, Fagerlie had renovated at least some of the interior to make his stay more pleasant. Thick rugs covered the old wooden floors, and the furniture all appeared new.

"Drink?" Fagerlie asked, going to a sideboard in the small parlor.

"I just want to see my brother."

"One moment, first." Amber liquid splashed into a cut crystal glass. "What do you know about the *Book of Breath?*"

"The library's previous binder was looking for it, before he disappeared." Ves paused—he didn't think Fagerlie was implicated, but... "Did you have something to do with that?"

"No." Fagerlie's pale blue eyes met his. "I told you, it was a stroke of luck, that you could take over as the Binder."

"You say it like a title."

"It is." Fagerlie went to one of the chairs near the sole open window and sat down, then gestured for Ves to join him. "Please. Make yourself comfortable. Let us discuss this like civilized people."

Ves hesitated. But when Fagerlie arched a gray brow, he crossed the room and sat. "Talk. Tell me why I should trust you."

"Have you ever heard of the School of Night?"

Ves strained his memory. It sounded familiar...

Right. Shakespeare. *Love's Labours Lost.* He'd bought a second-hand copy of the collected plays, and he and Noct had amused themselves by acting out the parts on long evenings. *"Black is the badge of hell / The hue of dungeons and the school of night,"* Ves quoted.

"Exactly." Fagerlie crossed his legs at the knee, as though preparing to deliver a long lecture. "The School was founded during the reign of Queen Elizabeth, but on the ruins of an even older organization dedicated to the scholarly pursuit of the magical arts. The Wizard Earl, Henry Percy, was a member, as were Sir Walter Raleigh, George Chapman, and others. Christopher Marlowe as well, before he was murdered by a rival cult."

He shook his head sadly, as though mourning a recent loss. "Of course, the School has changed over the years, but its purpose holds. To collect and study magical artifacts in a systematic fashion. To create a science out of sorcery, one might say."

"And you're a member of this organization."

"It is my great honor to hold the title of Professor within the School, yes." Fagerlie smoothed the leg of his expensive trousers. "We wish to study the Books of the Bound. To discover their secrets and add them to our hidden library."

Ves had heard similar lofty statements from his mother and grandfather over the years. He knew a thin veneer of rationalization draped over the naked desire for power when he heard it. "So why recruit me to help you? Surely you could have found someone else to make your map."

"To have two of the Dark Young as allies is no small matter,"

Fagerlie protested. "Few of your half-siblings ever venture into cities. Sorcerers have combed the wilds for years seeking them out, only to wind up strangled by one of the Young they mistook for a strange tree, or a rabbit, or one of another thousand forms. But more importantly, you have the training to be a Binder. And yes, I speak that as a title again. Or did you imagine binding books made from the skin, blood, and flesh of necromancers was an ordinary task?"

Ves gripped the armrests of his chair. "And when were you going to tell me about this?"

"Once I had the map." Fagerlie smiled faintly. "You didn't expect me to just put all of my cards on the table at once, did you?"

It was like growing up in the cult all over again. Everything was whispers and secrets and hoarded knowledge, and Ves's job was to do, not to know. "What is it you want me to do, exactly?"

"Get me my map. As the comet's tail draws nearer, we'll go to the museum library, which should be empty so late at night. Then, once we have the book in hand, you will Bind it to me." He ran a hand over his short silver hair. "I had thread woven from my hair. Emeline—the Hollowell sibling bound into the *Book of Breath*—will likely try to prevent you from binding her." He smiled. "And that is why you're so special, Ves. As you're resistant to sorcery, she'll have little ability to harm you, unlike a human Binder. And then, when her power is mine, I will use it to free you and Noct of your accursed blood, and you can go on your way."

Ves didn't believe that for a minute. But saying so would do him no good at the moment, so he merely asked, "And the comet? What's special about that?"

"The books were made the last time the comet and the earth danced together. We believe—though we cannot be sure—that this second pass will awaken them to even greater power, while weakening the traps around them." He looked thoughtful. "Which could make finding the others easier. The destruction they're certain to cause will hopefully lead us to them. But that is a task for another day."

Gods of the wood. "I see."

"But enough. Time grows short." Fagerlie rose to his feet. "Let's pay your brother a visit."

The attic room held in the heat of the day, but at least it wasn't yet summer's unbearable stuffiness. Fagerlie had provided a bookcase filled with various popular titles and a stack of magazines, plus a bed that was far more comfortable than anything they'd grown up with. Still, Ves's heart contracted to see Noct's accommodations. His brother had been living up here, in relative squalor, while he'd been in and out of the Rath family home: enjoying dinner and conversation, feeling acceptance. More than acceptance, in Sebastian's case.

Noct sat on the floor, propped against the bed, a book in his lone human hand when they entered. He glanced up—and a look of joy transformed his features when he saw Ves.

"You've done it?" he asked, eagerness shining from his eyes. Unlike Ves, he couldn't disguise them as human. Noct's goat eyes were an eerie, pale blue, a startling contrast against his olive skin and black hair. Stunted horns arched amidst the dark curls, and tentacles thrashed beneath the rough smock he wore to conceal most of his form.

The thought of letting down his little brother was like swallowing glass. He'd had such hopes…but now they were dust.

Fagerlie hovered by the doorway. Ves crossed the room and sat by Noct. They hugged, and Ves breathed deeply of Noct's scent: deep forests and musk.

"Not yet," he said. "It's a little more complicated than I thought it would be."

Noct pulled back, not far, just enough to see Ves's face. "Is everything all right?"

Ves took a deep breath. "Everything is fine. I think Mr. Fagerlie will be pleased with the results."

It wasn't a code, exactly. More a certain way of saying things they'd developed since early childhood. Growing up with their volatile mother had taught them that speaking openly of many things would result only in punishment. But there were still ways to communicate, even in front of hostile ears.

"I've been working hard," Ves said, and every word whispered of old scars. "And I just wanted you to know I'm focused completely on our goal. I'll clear the way for you, brother."

Noct's eyes widened almost imperceptibly. "I understand." Some of the many tentacles slipped from beneath his smock and gripped Ves's forearm. "I can always count on you to do the right thing in the end."

"How has your stay with Mr. Fagerlie been?"

Noct smiled. Not his real smile, but a tight, false one. "Very interesting. I've been reading a new novel: *Lord Loveland Discovers America*. Have you read it, Mr. Fagerlie?"

Fagerlie stirred. "I prefer the classics of literature."

"It's about an Englishman looking to marry an American heiress," Noct said. "Normally I prefer stories about soldiers, but I'm certain about this one. I read all the way to chapter three by yesterday morning, and five by nightfall."

Vesper nodded his understanding. "It sounds captivating. You'll have to tell me more when I return tonight."

"Speaking of which," Fagerlie said, not bothering to hide his impatience, "shouldn't you be going, Vesper? You don't have a great deal of time left."

Ves nodded. "Yes."

He followed Fagerlie back to the front door. Once he was out of sight of the house, he stopped and sagged against a lamppost.

"I just wanted you to know I'm focused completely on our goal. I'll clear the way for you, brother," he'd told Noct. Something he might have said when they were meant to bring on the apocalypse, to please their mother and grandfather. But it was nothing they'd ever wanted, so Noct would have taken it to mean something was wrong with their goal.

"I can always count on you to do the right thing in the end," meant "I trust you; we won't go through with it."

"Normally I prefer stories about soldiers, but I'm certain about this one. I read all the way to chapter three by yesterday morning, and five by nightfall." Fagerlie had some sort of guards or ruffians in his employ. Noct had identified at least three present during the day and five at night. Having to rely only on the muffled sounds of footsteps and voices drifting up from below, Noct likely couldn't be sure whether

there was any overlap between the three and the five, or if they were looking at eight minions in total.

"It sounds captivating. You'll have to tell me more when I return tonight." "You're a captive now. I'll rescue you tonight."

Ves tilted his head back and stared at the sky. All their hopes and dreams, everything that had seemed so close, were now ripped away. There would be no release from the curse of their blood, no train to San Francisco where they would begin new lives.

He'd failed Noct. And why not? He'd failed and disappointed everyone else in his family. How could he ever have thought this would end differently?

Heartsick, Ves headed in the direction of the museum. He had a confession to make.

Ves entered the bindery and removed his crude map of the library from the drawer. He stared at it for a long moment, then closed his eyes.

He needed help. Noct needed help.

Sebastian would be angry. Of course he would. But with luck, he'd understand why Ves had acted as he had. Surely Sebastian would have done the same for Bonnie.

He found Sebastian in his office, bent over O'Neil's commonplace book, a worried frown on his face. "What's wrong?" he asked, leaning against the doorframe.

Sebastian glanced up. "One of the books is apparently no longer hidden. Someone out there has it."

Ves's heart sank. "That's not good news." Doubly so, given what Fagerlie had said about the books' power waxing tonight.

"I know." Sebastian took off his glasses and rubbed his eyes tiredly. "But I suppose that's a problem for another time. Were you able to talk to the prisoner?"

"Bob Underell. Yes." Ves frowned. "Unfortunately, he didn't know who had employed him. Let's go to Mr. Quinn's office, and I'll tell you both everything."

"Good idea." Sebastian rose to his feet and crossed the room. He glanced out into the hall, and finding it unoccupied, pressed a kiss to Ves's lips.

"I can't stop thinking about last night," he murmured. "I want to do it all again, and more."

Gods, please, please let Sebastian not be too angry when he found out. "So do I." His throat felt dry. "I like you, Sebastian. A great deal."

Sebastian's smile brightened his hazel eyes. "I'm rather fond of you, as well."

When they reached Mr. Quinn's office, the head librarian was seated behind his desk. A fountain pen held in his long, spidery fingers flew across a page of fine paper; though hurried, his script was precise.

He looked up as they entered and set the pen aside. "Mr. Rune, Mr. Rath. What do you have to report?"

Ves swallowed thickly. "I…I have something to confess, which doesn't reflect well on my character. I beg you, hear me out before passing judgement."

Sebastian frowned. "Ves?"

"Just listen."

Ves held nothing back. He revealed his goat eyes to Mr. Quinn, told them both of Noct's existence and his inability to pass for human. About Fagerlie and his offer, and Ves's own deception. About the map, and his visit to Noct today, and their decision.

He fixed his gaze on the skull on Mr. Quinn's desk as he spoke. It stared back at him, the fleshless mouth seeming to grin and the empty sockets to leer. Only when he was finished did he gather the courage to look at Sebastian.

His expression of shock and growing anger cut Ves to the quick. "I'm sorry," Ves said, and pulled out the nearly complete map. "Here. Take it, just so you know for certain I'm not giving it to Fagerlie."

Sebastian struck the map from his hand. The stack of papers fluttered onto the floor. Ves didn't flinch externally—he'd been hit too many times in his childhood for that—but his soul felt like it was curling into a ball.

"How dare you say you're sorry," Sebastian grated out. "You knew I was worried about Kelly. You pretended to help—"

"I didn't pretend," Ves protested weakly.

Sebastian spoke over him. "And the whole time, you were creating this map of yours, planning to hand it over without question to a sorcerer whose motives you didn't at first know—"

"I thought he meant to steal a rare book!"

"That doesn't make it better!"

"Mr. Rune," the head librarian cut in, "you have disappointed me." He looked down at the drawer containing the knucklebones he'd used the day he hired Ves. "So have you, Erasmus, but I shall deal with you later." His cold, silvery eyes found Ves's face again. "I see no reason to continue your trial period of employment."

Ves's heart beat faster. "You're firing me? Of course you are. But Fagerlie—that is, I thought we might come up with a plan to stop him and rescue my brother."

"My duty is to Widdershins, to this library, and to those in it." Mr. Quinn's cool voice turned frigid. "If Mr. Fagerlie chooses to try our defenses tonight, I assure you, we won't require *your* help to stop him." He rose to his full height. "Now go."

Ves turned desperately to Sebastian. "I know I've no right to ask for your help—"

"That's right," Sebastian cut him off. "You don't. Now do as Mr. Quinn said, and get out."

CHAPTER 25

*V*es stopped only long enough to gather his personal bookbinding kit from the bindery, before wandering away from the museum, no clear destination in mind. Gods, he was a fool. How could he have possibly expected forgiveness after the lies he'd told?

A small, bitter part of him whispered that he should never have confessed. Left the librarians to fend for themselves. His duty was to Noct, not to them. He ought to have stolen the architectural drawings when he had the chance, given them to Fagerlie, then rescued Noct while Fagerlie and his henchmen were at the library.

This was what came from caring about other people. For trying to help. He'd been so stupid, handing over his heart to Sebastian, and now he was paying for it. He felt as though someone had stuffed barbed wire into his chest, leaving it to scrape his insides raw with every breath.

Well, no more of that. From now on, it was just him and Noct against the world.

Assuming he could get Noct out alive. If Fagerlie killed him as no longer useful…

"Vesper?"

Startled, he looked up and saw Bonnie standing outside a department store, little Clara in a baby carriage in front of her and Tommy toddling along beside. Of course he'd run into her, out of all the people in Widdershins.

She'd accepted him. Let him be near her children. And for a moment, he'd thought everything he'd wanted might finally be in reach.

He'd just been lying to himself, though.

"Hello, Bonnie," he said dully.

She watched him with a slight frown. "I imagined you would be at work now."

"I was fired."

Her eyes widened. "What? Why?"

"It's a long story."

"And what did Sebastian have to say? Does he know?"

The barbs in his chest gouged into him. "He knows. I don't think...I don't think we're friends any longer."

Her eyes softened. "I see. Well then. Why don't you come home with me, and you can tell me about it."

He shook his head. "I can't. Sebastian—"

"Isn't here, and I can make up my own mind." She arched a brow at him. "Quite frankly, you look as though you could use a friend, and if Sebastian won't be it, then I will."

"You don't know what I've done."

"And I won't unless you tell me." She gestured impatiently. "Come on, Vesper. You can push the carriage."

"How dare you accuse me!" Mortimer's voice reached Sebastian even through the closed door of his office. "I am a *Waite!* Get your hands off of me, you ruffians! I have no idea how that rat poison got in my desk!"

"I'm sure you don't," said one of the museum's security guards. His almost bored tone suggested he didn't believe Mortimer any more than

Sebastian did. "You've been asked to leave the premises. Come along quietly, and there'll be no fuss."

The commotion died down, so presumably Mortimer complied. Rat poison found in his desk…that was certainly damning.

Irene would be incandescent with fury to discover her fiancé was an attempted murderer, and a bad one at that. Mortimer would be fortunate if the police took him in before Irene could reach him.

What a mess. One librarian a murderous traitor, and their book-binder a liar who'd meant to hand over a map of the labyrinth to this School of Night.

Maybe Sebastian should have been suspicious from the moment Ves admitted he was raised in a cult. How could he possibly be trust-worthy after such an upbringing?

But no—that wasn't fair. So many people overcame terrible child-hoods without becoming treacherous liars who played on the emotions of others.

Ves had done it all for his brother. What might Sebastian have done for Bonnie, if their places had been reversed?

He took his glasses off and buried his face in his hands. Exhaustion slowed his brain; he hadn't slept much last night. The memory of the various reasons why that had been sent another wave of bitterness through him.

Enough. Self-pity would get him nowhere.

He dropped his hands and put his glasses back on. He'd just begun to put the letters into some sort of order. He picked one from around the time of the museum's completion—like the previous letter, this one had never been mailed.

Nathaniel R. Ladysmith
Widdershins, MA

July 3, 1859

Alex,

I don't know why I'm writing this. The staff at the asylum say you have to be restrained, to keep from hurting yourself or those around you. You are in no fit state to read a letter.

I suppose I'm putting pen to paper in anticipation of your recovery. I have to hope that someday we'll be together again. These things that haunt you will loosen their grip on your mind once the final brick is put in place in the library, and Emeline Hollowell trapped completely, where she can no longer taint the sanity of those around her book.

Why did I let you talk me into binding the books to you? The strain of mastering them all was too much for your mind. Why did I listen to you; why didn't I share the burden and bind them to myself instead?

I'll spend the rest of my life despising myself for putting you through this, even if it was at your insistence. I can only pray for your recovery and hope our time together is not at its end.

With all of my love and affection,

Nathaniel

Sebastian's throat felt tight. Alexander Dromgoole had died in the madhouse. Ladysmith's hopes had been for naught; they'd never seen one another again.

God. Poor Nathaniel.

Perhaps Sebastian had let his temper get the better of him when it came to Ves. He was angry and betrayed, but Vesper had confessed in the end. He'd exposed things about himself to Mr. Quinn and Sebastian both that he'd likely never shown to anyone else, and done it to save the library from Fagerlie.

Was Sebastian about to throw away a relationship he'd spend the rest of his life regretting having lost?

He forced his eyes back to the letter. Ves had said Fagerlie meant to have the *Book of Breath* bound to him using his hair as thread. It sounded as though Dromgoole had done the same, only with all four books, and it had driven him mad.

Ladysmith clearly hoped the end of construction on the library would free Dromgoole somehow. "...Once the final brick is put in place in the library, and Emeline Hollowell trapped completely..." he read aloud.

No. It couldn't be.

He put down the letter and began to rifle through the pile of architectural drawings. Dromgoole hadn't restricted himself to any particular type of building, it seemed. There were churches, houses, even a tomb. Finally, near the bottom of the pile, he found page after page detailing the layout of the museum.

Sebastian spread them out across his desk, then onto the floor when the desk proved too small. The set seemed very thorough. There was the overall site plan, then elevations, sections, and floor plans encompassing both entire floors and specific sections. A disproportionately large part of the stack seemed dedicated to the library—although, as the labyrinth was the most complicated single part of the museum, that made sense.

He studied the plans intently. There had been a small renovation on the second floor, after the battle between the world-ending cult and the librarians resulted in damage to one wall during the Dark Days. Otherwise nothing had changed that he could see.

He flipped through to the elevations and sections. There was something about them that nagged at him. Maybe it was simply that they reminded him of the puzzle boxes he enjoyed putting together. Indeed, the library could have been a puzzle box writ large; it appeared the various rooms and sections left a hollow at the center. Or, rather, a single thick column which no doubt supported the roof.

Didn't it?

He sorted hastily back through the other plans. Nothing else in the museum looked remotely like this.

The renovation. The alteration was slight. But if this had been a puzzle box with something inside, the pieces would no longer have fit together correctly. The pattern disrupted.

Or, more accurately, if he was right and the library itself was a trap for the necromancer bound to the *Book of Breath,* there was a crack where she might get out.

Sebastian gathered the plans into his arms and bolted for the head librarian's office.

Bonnie made them both tea, then listened patiently while Ves related to her everything he'd told Mr. Quinn and Sebastian earlier. At this point, keeping secrets hardly seemed to matter, after all. She listened attentively, rocking Clara's cradle with her foot and sipping tea. Tommy busied himself on the floor, rolling a toy horse and carriage back and forth, back and forth.

"I just wanted a normal life," Ves finished. He looked around the homey room, with its cheerful wallpaper, scattered toys, and other evidence of the family who filled it. "If not for me, then for my brother. I failed at that. I failed him, the library, Sebastian, even Fagerlie if you want to look at it that way."

"Normal?" Bonnie cocked her head at him. "What does that even mean, Vesper?"

"You know." He gestured vaguely around. "Normal."

She snorted. "I hope you aren't using me as an example. I assure you, plenty of people consider my arrangements anything but. Shall I go into the list of names I've been called over the years?"

"No need. But you don't understand." Just as Sebastian hadn't understood. "I can at least pass for human and walk the streets. But Noct doesn't even have that. I've been his only company since we ran away, at least until Fagerlie found us."

"How did he find you?" she asked curiously.

"He spotted Noct looking out a window during the day, while I was at work. Fortunately, instead of screaming or calling the police, he recognized Noct was one of the Dark Young and came upstairs to talk." Ves sighed. "When I came home that day, at first I was terrified we'd been found out. But when Fagerlie offered to help...I couldn't pass it up. Being condemned to hiding in our rooms, in the midst of society but utterly cut off from it...it was killing Noct slowly. He always had such a bright spirit, despite everything. But the isolation was wearing away what even our mother hadn't been able to destroy. Every day he seemed to slip further from me."

Bonnie put aside her cup. "Then bring him here."

Ves blinked at her. "What?"

"Everything you've done has been to save your brother," she said briskly. "Sebastian was a stranger to you at first—of course you didn't pour out a confession to him, not with so much at stake. But once you realized how dangerous Fagerlie is, you told him everything. I suppose you might have done it before sleeping with him, though."

Ves's face burned. "I—we—"

"Oh, don't bother, Vesper. I'm a grown woman. I know you didn't spend all night together playing tiddlywinks."

Unsure how to answer, he decided to ignore that part of the conversation. "He's no longer my friend, so I can hardly bring my brother to live under the same roof as him."

"It's my house," Bonnie said. Then her face softened. "Ves…none of us are perfect. But if our positions had been reversed, and Sebastian was consigned to the life your brother has been living, then I would have done anything to help him. I won't even pretend to imagine what it's been like to be you, always hiding your true nature, afraid to get close to anyone lest they find out. Believing yourself to be monstrous."

Emotion clogged his throat. Nothing in his experience had led him to imagine that there were people like Bonnie in the world. People who were simply *good,* who were able to forgive, who would hold out their hand to Noct and himself.

"Thank you," he said, emotion causing his voice to tremble. "But I don't know how to save Noct. When I don't give Fagerlie the map, he might kill him."

Bonnie nodded thoughtful. "Then it sounds like you'll have to give him a map."

"A map?"

She shrugged. "No one says it has to be correct. It isn't as though he'll know it's wrong until he gets there."

Ves's heart rose for the first time that day. "May I borrow some paper?"

"You're right. It's a spirit trap," Irene said, after studying the architectural plans for a number of minutes. "The entire library is a giant spirit trap, built to contain something in the very center. I can't believe I never noticed it before."

They stood in the head librarian's office. After Sebastian had informed Mr. Quinn of what he'd found, the head librarian had immediately summoned Irene.

"A spirit trap?" Sebastian asked. "I'm not entirely certain what that is."

"The name is a misnomer." Irene flipped through the plans. "They're meant to hold in entities able to extend their influence outside of themselves. Creatures, sorcerers, anything that can reach out to other minds. Most traps aren't nearly this elaborate." She pointed to the second floor, where the renovation had taken place. "And this broke the pattern. Or at least put a crack in it, as you guessed."

"To think it has been there all this time, trapped by our beloved library, and that the architect lost his sanity in the pursuit of containing it," Mr. Quinn said, almost dreamily. "What a noble end. If only my father's madness and confinement had come from such lofty work. Ah well, I suppose there's yet time for me to redeem the family name."

Irene's lips parted. "I'm…certain there is."

"How kind of you to say." Mr. Quinn turned to Sebastian. "Excellent work, Mr. Rath."

"Thank you, sir. Emeline Hollowell—or her book, assuming there's a difference—must be in there. She's already been reaching out—whispering to Mr. Rune and throwing things around with her power. Working with Mortimer." Sebastian glanced at Irene and saw her jaw go rigid, so he hurried on. "If Fagerlie was right and the comet will strengthen her, she might be able to use the break in the pattern to escape altogether."

"Then we shall not allow it," Mr. Quinn said firmly.

There came a brisk rap on the door. When Mr. Quinn called for them to enter, a young librarian by the name of Arno stepped inside.

"Message for Mr. Rath," he said, thrusting a folded piece of paper with Sebastian's name on it at him. "Your nephew said it was urgent."

"Willie brought this?" Sebastian asked in alarm. Had something happened to Bonnie? Or one of the children? Or Pete?

The note was short and read:

Sebastian,

I've sent a false map of the library to Fagerlie. He'll strike tonight, so alert the librarians to be ready for him. I don't think he has any more than eight men at the most, so it should be easy to overwhelm them. He has made a study of the arcane, though, so warn them to be wary of spells.

I'm going to use the opportunity to try and rescue Nocturn. I'd ask you to wish me luck, but I suppose you'd rather curse me, so I won't.

I am truly sorry for not telling you sooner. My whole life, Noct's whole life, we were told that if anyone learned of our nature, we'd be hunted and abused as monsters. I truly believed that if I explained things to you, the only result would be having to flee for my life, while leaving Noct behind. I can't express how much your acceptance meant to me. I should have told you last night, but I wanted to be absolutely certain I knew all the facts first. As soon as I did, I made my confession.

If we survive tonight, I'll leave Widdershins as quickly as I may. Just know I'll never forget you. You showed me a world I never thought possible.

Affectionately yours,

Vesper Rune

"Well?" Irene asked, when Sebastian didn't say anything.

He took a deep breath, then read the first paragraph aloud. When he was finished, Irene said, "No guns. If Fagerlie is a sorcerer, he'll be able to set fire to the powder inside."

"I am quite aware of the difficulties, Miss Endicott," Mr. Quinn said. "I have faced cultists before, if you recall. We will wait here tonight and defend the library against these interlopers."

Sebastian lowered the note. "Sir, I'd like permission to help Ves. He's going to try to save his brother, and I think his odds would be better if he wasn't alone."

Mr. Quinn's thin nostrils flared. "He became employed here under false pretenses and has now made his problem into ours. Why should I grant permission?"

"Because if it weren't for him, we wouldn't know what happened to Kelly. I'd likely be dead, and no one else would have any idea of the danger. Everyone would leave the library this evening as usual, at least until...forgive me, Irene, but until Mortimer returned to get the *Book of Breath*. Which I think, given Mortimer's behavior, we can all agree wouldn't be a good thing."

Irene clenched her jaw so hard he expected to hear a tooth crack. "You're absolutely right, Sebastian."

Mr. Quinn was silent for a moment. "For Mr. O'Neil's sake, then, I will allow it. But return here as soon as you may."

CHAPTER 26

"I f I had more time, I might be able to alter your shirt and vest," Bonnie said, frowning at the aforementioned articles of clothing. "For now I'll just cut a slit in the backs so you can use your tentacles without having to run about naked or in rags, but I'm sure I could sew up something better."

Ves's heart ached at her care. "Thank you for your kindness. I'm grateful for whatever you can do."

After sketching out a map of the library that was close enough to the real thing not to raise immediate alarm, he'd written up two notes. One to Fagerlie to include with the map, suggesting he'd wait at the library for him and help overcome any librarians or guards. The other he sent to Sebastian as a warning.

And a good-bye. Since Bonnie had so generously offered Noct a place to stay, he would bring his brother back here tonight. But he couldn't remain. How could he possibly face Sebastian ever again, knowing the hurt he'd caused? The affection that had slipped inevitably through his grasp?

He'd gone to his boarding house, packed up his things, and placed the mirrors back on the wall. For the first time, he'd made himself stand in front of one for more than a moment. Studying the features

Sebastian had found so pleasing, staring at the orange eyes the silver backing revealed.

Night drew in by the time he returned to the Rath house with his things. Somewhere around eleven o'clock, the earth would begin its pass through the tail of Halley's Comet. Fires would blaze around old stones, perhaps even atop Caprine Hill, if any were left who dared set foot there.

The evening edition of the newspaper was filled with stories of the wild extremes to which terror of the comet had driven people. Work stoppages, churches filled with terror-stricken parishioners begging to be saved, meteor showers attributed to the comet's influence, even strange multi-colored rings around the sun. A man in Alabama had taken strychnine and died in front of his wife and six children, screaming that the comet's tail would set the world aflame.

Once Ves returned, Bonnie took charge. While Pete and the children worked on dinner, she applied herself to a vest and shirt taken from Ves's bag, on the grounds he couldn't run about half-dressed after rescuing Noct. Ves was less certain her precaution was necessary, but it gave them something to do while they waited. It would be at least an hour or so before Fagerlie would reasonably make for the museum if he wished to arrive during the passage through the comet's tail.

"Here," she said, setting aside her shears and holding out the items. "Try these on."

He took them up the stairs and into the bathroom beside Sebastian's room. It was impossible not to think about what had passed between them, and by the time he walked back down the stairs wearing his altered clothing, he felt as though he'd swallowed a ball of lead. "It seems to work," he said, stepping back into the sitting room.

Bonnie wasn't there...but Sebastian stood in the center of the room, waiting.

Ves froze in the entryway. His heartbeat quickened, and an instant of gladness flashed through him, before he remembered. He'd thought Sebastian would remain at the library with his fellows, but it seemed he'd returned home instead.

"I-I'm sorry," he stammered, taking a hasty step back. "I didn't mean...I'll go."

He turned toward the front door, but Sebastian called, "Ves, wait."

Ves stopped, but didn't look back. His mind flailed for something to say, but what was there left to talk about?

The floor creaked as Sebastian took a step toward him, then stopped. "Can we...can we talk?"

He wanted to have a conversation? "About what?" Ves asked cautiously. "I lied to you. You were justly angry. I'm leaving town tonight as soon as I rescue Noct, and you'll never set eyes on me again. Doesn't that sum it up?"

"No, damn it. It doesn't."

Startled, he turned to find Sebastian wringing his hands, his mouth set in a line of distress. "I spoke before I had time to think," he said. "And I won't pretend I'm happy to know you applied for the job in the library under false pretenses. But I understand wanting to do your best for your family."

Ves laughed bitterly. "I abandoned our mother and grandfather. I doubt they'd say I did my best for them."

"They wanted to destroy the world!"

"That doesn't mean I didn't betray them."

Sebastian absorbed this. "I suppose you're right. But you didn't betray your brother."

Ves swallowed against the tension in his throat. "Bonnie said Noct could come here, afterwards. I'll stay away, of course, but...I trust you'll treat him well. You're a good man, better than I deserved, and—"

Sebastian crossed the space between them and seized Ves's arms with both hands. "Stop this," he ordered.

Then hauled Ves close and kissed him fiercely.

Startled, Ves returned the kiss. It deepened, and within moments they were clinging to one another. Sebastian's hands fisted in his hair, then slipped to his shoulders, down over his back, and found the slit in his vest and shirt.

"What the devil happened to your clothes?" Sebastian asked, startled. His face was flushed, lips reddened from the frantic kiss. Ves wanted to throw him down on the couch and see the flush on the rest of his pale skin.

Ves cleared his throat. "Bonnie thought I might want to fight without being rendered indecent."

"How inconsiderate of her. Inconsiderate to me, that is; I'd much rather have you indecent as possible. I'll have words with her."

Ves shook his head helplessly. "Sebastian…I don't know what's happening here. You haven't forgiven me, have you?"

Sebastian studied him for a long moment, until the faint flame of hope that had kindled in Ves began to flicker. Then he took Ves's hands in his. "I realized I could stew in my own unhappiness, cling to my hurt, and miss you. Or I could forgive you and not miss you." He held up an admonishing finger. "Not to suggest you won't have to make it up to me. I have a few ideas as to how you might do that."

"I'll bet you do," Ves said dryly, but an uncontrollable smile tugged at his lips. "Thank you."

Sebastian squeezed his hands and let go. "The librarians are preparing to defend the library against Fagerlie. I've come to help you rescue Noct. And *don't* tell me it's too dangerous—I have a plan."

Ves blinked in surprise. "You do?"

"Yes." Sebastian took a step back. "Oh, and I figured out where the *Book of Breath* is hidden in the library. I'll tell you about it on the way."

Sebastian and Ves lurked on the rooftop across from the house the School of Night had rented.

He'd explained everything to Ves as they made their way here. Ves's eyes lit up when Sebastian told him how the library rooms and levels fit together like a puzzle box, and his exclamation of "You're brilliant!" had sent a warm glow through Sebastian.

It was full dark when they arrived on the street, and lights still showed in the house that was their focus. Shapes moved back and forth, silhouetted against the curtains. "We'll need to wait for them to leave," Ves noted. "So we have to find somewhere to hide, where they won't notice us when they depart."

Sebastian cast about the dark street. Several of the streetlights had gone out, plunging the space between into shadow. The problem was less finding a place of concealment, and more of finding one where they could be assured to see the house clearly and not be spotted themselves, when Fagerlie and his minions eventually left.

Ves, it seemed, had already come to a decision. He caught Sebastian's arm, steering him toward the building directly across from Fagerlie's house. "Do you trust me?" he asked when they reached the moldering brick wall.

"Of course."

"Then hold on. I won't let you fall."

Before Sebastian could ask what Ves meant, the tentacles emerged from the back of his shirt in a slithering rush. He wrapped two about Sebastian, securing him against his back—then began to climb.

Sebastian bit back an exclamation when his feet left the ground. Ves clambered up the side of the building with ease, using tentacles and arms to grab any available hold. In the space of mere seconds, he deposited Sebastian gently onto the slate roof tiles.

"That was…impressive," Sebastian managed to say, when he had his breath back.

The waxing moon outlined the bare suggestion of Ves's features, but it was enough to see his brief smile. He caught Sebastian's hand in his, tugging him into a crouch, then crawling slowly along the roofline until they had a clear view of the house opposite.

The preparations inside appeared to be frenzied, with figures hurrying back and forth. Two men stood on the porch; at a glance, they would look as though they were simply enjoying the night air, but Sebastian had no doubt they were guards.

"Where is Nocturn?" he whispered.

Ves pointed to a shuttered window near the top of the house. Time and weather had warped the boards, so light leaked out from within. "The light is a good sign Fagerlie hasn't killed him yet. He wouldn't leave the room lit for a corpse."

God. Poor Ves, for even having to consider such things. "He probably means to keep you under his control, even after he gets the book."

Ves nodded thoughtfully. "I would make a useful soldier."

Sebastian reached for his shoulder, found a tentacle instead. He squeezed it in what he hoped was a reassuring manner. "You're a great deal more than that."

"I hope I am." Ves glanced at him briefly, then back to the house. "May I tell you something? I don't want you to think less of me, but…"

"Please tell me."

"I missed having a sense of purpose. The cult was terrible, and we suffered, but…there was a *reason* for it all. A grand destiny, which gave such a feeling of…I don't know, intensity, perhaps, to everything. Even on our most normal days, we knew our actions were building toward something amazing." Wistfulness touched Ves's words, and Sebastian wished he could see his face more clearly. "I know it sounds wrong, or mad, but I missed that. Fagerlie offered me a goal. A direction. A purpose, even if only a temporary one. I think I liked that, at least at first. Perhaps that makes me a bad person."

"No." Sebastian leaned against him, shoulders touching. "I understand. I mean, I can't truly know what you've been through, but it makes sense to feel that way."

"Thank you," Ves said. He might have said more, but his muscles went tense against Sebastian. "They're leaving."

The man who stepped off the porch and into the street might have been on his way to a costume party. He wore a close cap on his silver hair, and his attire consisted of a stiff ruffled collar and a fine black robe such as John Dee or the Wizard Earl might have worn in Elizabethan times. In his hand he carried a brass staff—his sorcerer's wand, no doubt.

"Mr. Fagerlie, I take it?" Sebastian whispered.

"He said he was a 'professor' in the School of Night. I suppose that's his regalia." Ves leaned forward as men in more ordinary clothing followed behind. Three carriages clattered up, and Fagerlie and his retinue climbed into them. Within moments, they were off, no doubt on their way to the museum.

"He had five men with him, and two remained behind," Ves sat back. "Not bad odds, at least for us."

Sebastian tried not to worry about his fellow librarians. Surely they could handle a mere six men, even if one of them was a sorcerer. They had Irene, after all, and had seen battle against far worse during the Dark Days of 1902. They'd be fine.

He hoped.

"All right, then," he said. "Let's get down off this roof and put my plan into action."

Sebastian raised his hand and knocked firmly on the door.

He strained his ears, but heard no sounds from inside. Curse it, surely his plan hadn't failed already. Swallowing back the nerves that threatened to choke him, he knocked again, more insistently this time.

The creak of footsteps across the rickety floor rewarded him. The door cracked open, revealing a sliver of dirty face and a glaring eye. "What d'you want?"

Sebastian plastered on his most affable smile. "Good evening, sir. I'm from First Esoteric Church. Have you heard the good news about—"

"Not interested," the man said, and attempted to close the door.

Sebastian had already stuck his foot in, though, so the edge dug into his shoe. "Just a few moments of your time," he said. "It won't take but a minute!"

"I said get lost," the man snarled, throwing the door open. He towered over Sebastian, and it was everything he could do to keep his back straight and his smile on.

"Azathoth cares for us all equally," Sebastian babbled, even as he backed toward the edge of the porch. "By which I mean not at all, as we're mere ants, unnoticed and unseen before his divine—"

"That's enough out of you, freak," the man began, raising his fist to pummel Sebastian.

A tentacle looped around his wrist, then another around his neck. Before he even had the chance to cry out, his head impacted with the sagging porch railing. He made an odd sound like a sigh and went limp, before his body was dragged out of sight and into the shadows.

"He's alive," Ves confirmed as he joined Sebastian. "Though he'll have a bad headache."

Sebastian nodded. "What about the other guard?"

"He must not have heard anything, or at least be assuming his fellow is taking care of us." Ves's orange eyes narrowed thoughtfully. "I'll look for him—we don't want him sending word to Fagerlie somehow. You get Noct to safety. The stair is there."

Sebastian ran up the steps. Unused to such exertion, he was soon gasping, and all but fell against the door when he at last reached it. A heavy bolt was thrown from the outside; he wrenched it back with a loud scrape, then pushed the door open.

A writhing mass in the center of the room shifted toward him.

For a moment, all that registered were the many black tentacles, the utter inhumanness of the outline before him. A cry of shock locked in his throat, behind his teeth.

Then he became aware of the human hand, the tattered smock, the face revealed in the light. The features were androgynous, olive-skinned and topped with dark hair, set with goat-like eyes that were blazing, icy blue.

Ves hadn't been lying when he said Noct was far less human than himself. The reason why he'd been so very desperate to help Noct, even if it meant working with Fagerlie, became blindingly clear in that instant.

Noct's eyes hardened. "Who are you?"

"A friend of your brother's," Sebastian said quickly. "Sebastian Rath. I've come to help."

Nocturn bowed his head slightly, revealing strange, twisted things that might have been horns and yet absolutely were not. "Then duck."

"What?"

"Duck!"

Sebastian hurled himself forward and down, even as Noct flung out his hand in the direction of the door. The syllables he spoke were meaningless to Sebastian—they might have been Aklo, or some other sorcerous language.

The man who had come up behind Sebastian shouted in pain and shock, frost racing across his skin. A fraction of a second later, Ves grabbed him from behind and threw him down the stairs.

"Noct!" Ves ran past Sebastian to his brother's side. "Are you all right?"

"Of course. I was just waiting for you." Noct moved upward, body —torso—supported by the many tentacles. "This man says he's your friend."

Ves caught Sebastian's hand in his own. "He is. You can trust him."

Then he casually brought Sebastian's hand to his lips, which…definitely would get his point across. But it also sent a flush of warmth through Sebastian. He'd had lovers before, yes, but never the sort of… well, *relationship* that lead to all the small gestures of affection people shared. Something in his chest seemed to melt, like warmed chocolate in an oven.

Nocturn, for his part, looked shocked, though only for a moment. "Then—then I do," he said staunchly. "We should leave before Fagerlie has the opportunity to come back."

Ves let go of Sebastian's hand. "You're right, but things have happened you don't know about. We need to get to the museum and help the librarians."

"Even though Mr. Quinn fired you?" Sebastian asked in surprise.

Ves met his gaze. "Fagerlie would likely have found his way in, whether or not I came along. I'm not the only bookbinder in the world, after all. But this is still my responsibility." He straightened. "Besides, I was raised with the purpose of bringing the age of mankind to an end at the hand of otherworldly horrors. I'll be damned if I run from some two-bit cult who doesn't even have enough ambition to destroy the world."

Sebastian let out a startled bark of laughter. "Well then, angel, we'd best get on our way."

Ves's cheeks pinked at the endearment. He turned his back to Noct, who immediately clambered onto it. Sebastian led the way downstairs, stepping over the groaning man at the bottom of the stairwell. It looked as though he had multiple bones broken, but Sebastian couldn't muster any pity for him.

As they stepped outside, Sebastian glanced around the poor neighborhood. "There's no chance of hailing a cab here."

"And we don't have anything to conceal me," Noct added from over Ves's shoulder. "I doubt any driver is going to stop for us."

"You go on ahead, Sebastian," Ves started, when the growl of an engine sounded from one end of the street.

Headlamps flicked on, and the automobile started toward them. Sebastian froze, heart pounding as it pulled up beside them. The top was folded back, so nothing blocked the sight of Mortimer Waite at the wheel.

CHAPTER 27

"What the devil are you doing here?" Sebastian demanded. Ves's hands curled into fists, and he moved to put himself between Waite and Sebastian. Noct was on Ves's back, so at least he'd be shielded if Waite had a gun.

Waite leveled a glare at Sebastian, then at Ves and Noct. "I'm trying to clear my name, you idiot. But perhaps you're the one who should be explaining himself, given you're consorting with other-worldly horrors."

"You poisoned me!" Ves exclaimed. Noct let out a gasp, and his tentacles tightened.

"I most certainly did not," Waite snapped back. "Of course I wanted the position for my cousin, but I wasn't about to start murdering people over it. Though obviously I didn't know you aren't a person."

"How dare you?" Sebastian took a threatening step forward.

Waite ignored him. "And I'd never heard of this *Book of Breath* until Mr. Quinn ordered us to search the library for it."

Ves grabbed Sebastian's arm, holding him back. "I poured my coffee myself. I brought it back to the bindery and put it down. The spirit conveniently caused a disturbance in the staff room, drawing me out of the bindery, and when I returned you were there waiting."

"And you had rat poison in your desk." Sebastian folded his arms over his chest. "How do you explain that?"

Wait rolled his eyes. "Obviously I was framed. Do you really think I'm stupid enough to hide a murder weapon in my own desk? And as for being in the bindery, I got there only moments before you returned. If you were gone long enough, someone else could easily have slipped inside, poisoned your coffee, and left."

"Do you think he's telling the truth?" Ves asked Sebastian. "Or is he just trying to trick us?"

"To what end?" Waite demanded. "It isn't as though the police are going to arrest me. Unless you want to appear in court and explain why the poison didn't so much as inconvenience you."

"He has a point," Sebastian said reluctantly. "But the engagement with Irene…"

"If I'd actually done what I'm being accused of, I'd be trying to convince her of my innocence, not you lot." Waite's lips curled in distaste. "Instead I'm following Sebastian around town, trying to find some way to exonerate myself."

Ves came to a decision. "All right. We need to get to the library as soon as possible, and Waite has a vehicle. If he tries anything, I can just strangle him from the back seat."

It was an empty threat, but Waite didn't know that. He went pale, but didn't object when Sebastian climbed into the passenger seat in the front, and Ves and Noct piled in the back.

They sped off down the street. Ves gripped Noct, and his brother held him in return, their tentacles intertwined. It was unspeakably good to have Noct back with him, safe and sound.

Even if they were heading into danger.

Meteorites streaked the sky above, flaring bright for a few seconds as they tumbled toward earth. Auroral colors licked the northernmost edge of the horizon, there and then gone.

"It's starting," Ves said.

The museum at last came into view. The auto slowed as it approached the marble stairs and the main entrance. Light streamed from within, and the banner announcing the comet lecture and fundraiser flapped in the wind. Attendants helped men and women into and out of carriages and autos. The male guests wore fine tuxedos, and the women dripped with diamonds and furs. Ves couldn't even imagine what their lives must be like.

"We can't go in that way," Sebastian said. "We'll need to use the staff exit."

"It'll be locked," Waite pointed out.

"Then I'll break it down if I must." Ves met Sebastian's gaze. "Fagerlie had to get in somehow. He wasn't exactly dressed subtly, so I'd guess he didn't use the main door."

Waite guided the auto around the side of the museum and down an alleyway mostly used for service. The staff door swung open in the breeze, creaking back and forth.

Waite brought the automobile to a halt and shut off the engine. Ves got out and waited while Noct clambered on his back. Sebastian led the way to the door, and the rest followed.

The corridor beyond was plain in appearance and lined with specimen cabinets along the walls and pipes on the ceiling. "Is this the storage area?" Ves asked.

"One of them." Sebastian started off confidently down the hall. "We shouldn't run into anyone at this time of night, with the comet lecture confined to the front of the museum. If we do, I'll signal you to hide while I deal with them."

They made their way through a bewildering maze of stairs, halls, and doors. Though the layout of the library had a known purpose now, there was no obvious reason the rest of the museum should have been so bizarrely designed. Had the strain of the books bound to him cracked Dromgoole's mind and led him to create such a distorted structure?

Fortunately, they saw no one else in the shadowy corridors as they made their way to the library. Unfortunately, the same held true when they stepped through the doors. Where Ves had expected to hear the sounds of conflict, or—if they were lucky—its aftermath, there was only silence. Most of the lights had been shut off, leaving the stacks in darkness, but his keener-than-human sight showed nothing lurking there.

Waite put his hands on his hips. "So where the devil is everyone?"

⁂

"I-I don't know." Dread turned Sebastian's blood sluggish in his veins. "The first line of defense should have been here, while other librarians waited in the stacks in case the intruders got past. Or at least, that's what I'd imagine, though obviously I didn't attend Mr. Quinn's emergency briefing."

"Would that have been in the sword room?" Ves asked. He stood taut and alert, hands curled into fists, his orange eyes sharp. He looked magnificent, and the sight of him stole Sebastian's breath away.

"Yes. You said you gave Fagerlie a fake map?"

"It was somewhat close to reality on the first floor, so as not to raise suspicion. If they've gotten any further, they'll be hopelessly lost at this point. With any luck, Fagerlie is stumbling around cursing my name."

Sebastian nodded, his mind racing. "I'll go to the sword room and see if anyone is still there, or if there's any indicator as to where they went, while you look for Fagerlie."

"I don't want you to go alone," Ves said reluctantly. "But I'd rather have Mr. Waite where I can keep an eye on him."

"Excuse me," Mortimer protested. They both ignored him.

"If I see or hear Fagerlie, I'll hide," Sebastian said.

"And if they see you first?"

"Then I'll run. I know this library, and they don't. It shouldn't be difficult to lose them."

Ves looked concerned, but he said, "Very well. Stay safe, Sebastian."

"And you, angel."

Ves's smile bloomed like the sunrise at the pet name. "I'll see you on the other side."

They made their way through the stacks, listening intently. The air felt odd: heavy, as though it had gained a strange density. It lay on

Sebastian's skin with a palpable weight, and every exhalation seemed to take more effort than usual.

There was no sign of anyone on the first floor. Once they reached the second level, they split up before reaching the sword room. Moving as quietly as possible, Sebastian slipped into the labyrinth. Despite his bold words to Ves, his heart rabbited in his chest, and he jumped at every creak from the laden shelves. The air seemed to be growing thicker and more humid, the atmosphere turning oppressive.

There—the door to the sword room. Shut tight, with a chair jammed below the knob.

What the devil? Sebastian cast about, but saw no one. Had the librarians trapped Fagerlie's bunch inside? But if so, someone would have been left to stand guard.

Something was very, very wrong.

He yanked the chair free and threw open the door. The sweet scent of chloroform wafted out to greet him.

The librarians lay around the room, in varying states of sleep or grogginess. Irene sprawled by the door, the wood beneath her hand scorched, as though she'd been trying to cast a spell and burn her way out when the gas overcame her.

Holding his breath, Sebastian rushed inside, grabbed her beneath the arms, and dragged her into the clean air. He straightened, ready to run back in, when something struck him from behind.

CHAPTER 28

The blow caught Sebastian on the shoulder, sending him crashing into a bookcase. Though glancing, a shock of pain went through him, and he cried out in surprise. He spun, putting his back to the shelves, expecting to find himself confronted with one of the School of Night's lackeys.

Arthur stood there, a look of fury on his face and a hammer in his hand.

Sebastian gaped at him, his brain refusing to comprehend what his eyes saw. Why had Arthur hit him? What was he doing with a hammer?

Oh God. Mortimer's innocence meant someone else had tried to poison Ves and sent hired killers after Sebastian. But there hadn't been any time to consider who the real culprit might be.

And even if there had been, Sebastian would never have considered Arthur. They were friends. Arthur was a good man.

There had to be some other explanation. Had to.

Arthur stepped past him, slammed the door, and shoved the chair back into place. Almost immediately, someone began to pound on it—the natural flow of air had revived at least one of the librarians, it seemed.

Not that it did much to help Sebastian, stuck on this side of the door with a murderous Arthur.

Sebastian held up both hands as his attacker advanced on him. "Wh-what are you doing? We're *friends*, Arthur!"

"You just couldn't leave well enough alone, could you?" Arthur's voice shook. "Going on and on about O'Neil, refusing to listen even when everyone told you to stop. Even when I pretended a book from my own collection had been stolen, you refused to accept the story I gave you."

Sebastian's mind spun, like a machine with a slipped gear, going nowhere. He could only think of all the nights they'd retired to The Silver Key, celebrating or commiserating over drinks as the situation warranted. "I've known you for almost eight years. I danced at your wedding!"

Anguish twisted Arthur's features. "That's why I didn't want to hurt you. The bookbinders had to go, but I did everything I could to dissuade you from looking too closely into O'Neil's death. If you'd only listened, everything would be fine!"

"You killed him, didn't you?" Sebastian's fingers went numb, and he barely felt the pain in his shoulder. "You murdered O'Neil and poisoned Ves."

Arthur gestured impatiently. "Obviously I misjudged the dosage, since Rune was in fine health the last time I saw him." As though Ves's survival absolved him of any guilt.

The hammering on the door turned into repeated blows, as though more than one person was throwing themselves at it. The chair shuddered, and Arthur started to turn in that direction.

"Did you hire the men who threatened my family?" Sebastian demanded.

"I didn't mean for you to get caught up in this," Arthur protested, his attention diverted back to Sebastian. "But I couldn't risk you ruining everything at the last moment. You have to understand that."

"But why?" Sebastian asked. "Arthur, if you ever counted me as your friend, at least tell me that."

"You know we lost everything in the crash of 1907."

Sebastian swallowed, but his throat was too dry for it to do any good. He had to keep Arthur talking. "Of course I know. I paid your bar tab for the rest of the year, because it was the only thing I knew to do to help you."

"I remember," Arthur said raggedly. "And I appreciated it, because you didn't make me feel like a beggar. But my wife's relatives…I've had to plead for handouts from them for the last three years, just to make ends meet. They look down their noses and never let me forget that I'm a failure. My own wife says it's a good thing we don't have children, because I couldn't provide for them. Do you know how humiliating that is?"

"Humiliating enough to murder your fellow librarians?" Sebastian exclaimed. "Your friends? What do you mean to do, sell the *Book of Breath* for money? That won't get you back on your feet. You'll have to flee Widdershins at best and set up elsewhere, always knowing the law could be one step behind you."

Arthur shook his head. "No. The book is *mine*. Emeline—the woman bound to it—already helped me. Told me where to find gold among the dead."

The unexpected bequest Arthur mentioned hadn't come from a relative after all. "It told you to rob a grave?"

"She did more than that," Arthur snapped. "She was kind to me. She didn't—didn't pity me, like the rest of you. She doesn't see me as a failure the way my wife and her family do. She wants to help me become the man I would have been if bad luck hadn't dogged my footsteps."

"Perhaps it was bad luck and not bad decisions before," Sebastian said, wondering how he could possibly get through to Arthur. "But this *is* a bad decision. This dead necromancer is lying to you."

"You're wrong." Arthur straightened his shoulders. "If I unbind her tonight, beneath the comet, she will give me everything I could ever wish for. Everything I deserve. I won't be a failure anymore. Now get out of my way, Sebastian."

The wood of the door was beginning to crack. Sebastian clenched his fists. "No. I'm not letting you unleash some horror on the rest of us. You'll have to go through me."

"Then I will," Arthur said, and lifted the hammer high. He made as if to step forward—then let out a startled cry.

"I don't think so," Irene said from where Sebastian had left her on the floor.

Arthur jerked frantically, but the very stone of the floor had molded itself around the toe of one shoe, pinning him in place. "Damn it! Let me go!"

The door to the sword room burst outward in a shower of breaking wood. Mr. Quinn stepped through, tossing down the marble bust of Paracelsus he'd used to batter his way through.

Arthur snarled and wrenched his foot free. He barreled into Sebastian, shoving him hard against the wall. Sebastian tried to grapple with him, but was forced to duck as the hammer whistled past his ear. A moment later, Arthur was free, his footsteps receding as he fled into the labyrinth.

Curse it.

Sebastian bent to help Irene up. "How long were you awake?"

"Long enough." She dusted off her skirt. "I heard Arthur's attempts to excuse his betrayal. If I'd been less groggy, I might have gotten hold of him better with the stone shaping spell, curse it. I wish magic came as easily to me as it does to some of my family members." She paused. "Does this mean Mortimer is innocent?"

"It does."

"Then I shall offer Mr. Waite an apology," Mr. Quinn said. He clutched his old, blood-stained dictionary in his hands. "I made the rare mistake of overestimating one of the old families and assumed his ambition matched his name."

"Er, that's certainly one way to put it," Sebastian said. "He's here to help us, along with Ves and his brother. If you see a lot of tentacles, their owner is probably on our side."

"And Mr. Fairchild has broken his oath and betrayed us." Mr. Quinn's voice remained level, but the chill in his silvery eyes made the hairs on the back of Sebastian's neck prickle.

"He might be partially under control of the *Book of Breath*," Sebastian said. "It's been talking to him. Pretending to be on his side."

"Or he might simply be a colossal prick who has decided he feels emasculated because he has to ask for money," Irene replied. Turning to Mr. Quinn, she added, "He admitted to killing Mr. O'Neil. I suspect the body is concealed somewhere in the Physics and Astronomy Collection, since that's where Arthur works."

More and more librarians emerged from the sword room. One of them carried a metal cylinder in his hands, which he held up as he approached. The label read CHLOROFORM. "I found this behind one of the ventilation grates."

Mr. Quinn hefted his dictionary. "Anyone who needs to recover, please remain here. The rest of you—follow me." He paused, then turned to Sebastian. "Actually, Mr. Rath, I have a special task for you."

Ves hurried through the maze of the library, aiming for the sheep room, where the alteration had been made that weakened the spirit's prison. He could leave Noct on guard there, then he and Waite would try to find Fagerlie, assuming he was still wandering lost in the labyrinth.

Unfortunately, light shone from the sheep room already. Despite the false map, Fagerlie had beaten them there.

"Who would have started knocking down the wall?" a male voice asked from inside.

"I don't know," Fagerlie replied, "but it's a good thing they did, or else we might never have found this place. The Young will pay for its treachery."

Ves ground his teeth together. But insults didn't matter right now. Someone else clearly knew about the *Book of Breath*—and had felt confident enough of not being disturbed that they'd started to try and get through the wall to where it lay concealed. Which meant none of the librarians had been around to stop them.

He really, really wished he hadn't suggested Sebastian find the librarians alone.

Ves signaled to Noct, who uncurled from around him, using his strong tentacles to climb up the nearby shelves. The sound of a mallet striking masonry rang from inside the room. "Stay back here," he ordered Waite, his words covered by the loud demolition of the wall. "I'll try to draw them out of the room and away from the book."

Waite scanned the shelves and took down the heaviest volume in easy reach. "I'll hide and whack anyone who comes close."

Ves crept nearer to the doorway. One of the men stood guard, peering straight out into the darkened stacks.

Time to go up.

He followed Noct's example, grabbing hold of anything he could use to lift himself up: shelves, lighting fixtures, decorative elements, anything to move him ever closer to the oblivious guard.

When he was in striking distance, he didn't hesitate. His tentacles lashed down, grabbed the man around the chest, and hurled him in the direction of the stacks. Hopefully Waite would take care of him there.

Either someone inside saw Ves grab the guard, or heard his body hit the stacks, because a cry of alarm immediately rang out.

"Keep working, curse you!" Fagerlie ordered.

Damn it.

"Vesper, Vesper," Fagerlie called sadly. "I'm very disappointed in you. I thought you'd come around to my way of thinking. A shame."

They were going to have to fight. But at least Ves was more or less impervious to sorcery. Fagerlie had to be his target.

He swung from the shelf he perched on and through the door.

A small hole had been knocked in the wall opposite, using what looked like a hammer or some other instrument not as well suited to the job as the big mallet one of the men wielded now. Even as Ves entered, he swung it one last time, and the masonry crumbled to reveal a hollow space beyond. "There's a hidden room!"

"Open it!" Fagerlie roared.

Ves charged the nearest man, slamming him down. Another slashed at him frantically with a knife—and left a line of stinging, blazing pain on one of his tentacles. Ves recoiled instinctively, and Fagerlie laughed.

"What?" he said. "You think I would work with two of the Dark Young and not have any sort of defense against them handy?"

Ves grabbed for the wrist of the man with the silver-plated knife, but it was only a feint. Another tentacle swept down, wrapped around the man's ankles, and yanked him off his feet. Unexpected satisfaction shot through Ves, all of the old training coming back, even though he'd never truly used it in a fight like this.

Then Waite charged in, and Noct swung down, hovering at the entrance, his blue eyes burning like cold fire. While Waite laid into the first lackey he saw, Noct's tentacles wove a hypnotizing pattern, creating a spell without words.

The wooden shelves suddenly burst into verdant life. Branches exploded outward, knocking men down or else impaling them on jagged thorns. The wild scent of spring in the deep woods filled the air, and Ves laughed from the joy of it.

All of the men who still could run, did so. Noct whipped up out of the way of a silver dagger, and they fled into the stacks. Fagerlie ran after them; Noct made a grab for him, but only succeeded in tearing the staff from his hand.

"I'm resistant to magic—I'll get him," Ves called to Waite. Hopefully Sebastian would show up with the rest of the librarians before any of the others could escape.

Hopefully Sebastian and the librarians *could* show up.

Ves chased Fagerlie through the maze of rooms. At first, it seemed as though Fagerlie would find his way up, toward the top level where the only escape waited. But he took a wrong turn, and within moments fetched up in front of the doors leading to the bat room. He tried to open them, but found them still locked.

Fagerlie turned and put his back to the doors. "I'm disappointed in you, Vesper. Though not nearly as disappointed as your mother is."

Ves walked slowly between the imposing towers of shelving. His tentacles flared around him, and he saw a flicker of fear on Fagerlie's face. "I doubt she could be all that disappointed, considering she's rotting in whatever hell her gods consigned her too."

The fear was replaced by a look of smug superiority. "Foolish child. Do you really believe that?"

The words stopped Ves in his tracks, as surely as if he'd walked into a wall. "She's dead. She and Grandfather both. The world wasn't remade."

"Failure doesn't always equal death, my boy." Fagerlie lifted something in his hand. "Although in your case, it does. Have you ever heard of the Beast of Gévaudan? One of the few Young to reach infamy outside of arcane circles. Impossible to kill, until a hunter finally realized its nature and shot it with a silver bullet."

Ves's breath froze in his lungs as Fagerlie leveled a revolver at him. "Your brother could have exploded this in my hand, but you have no sorcerous ability. No wonder your mother felt so let down by you. Good-bye, Vesper. You really should have known better than to cross me."

CHAPTER 29

*V*es stared at the black bore of the gun. He had no doubt the silver bullet in the chamber would kill him if it struck. His only hope was to somehow move fast enough to get out of the way before Fagerlie shot him. An ordinary bullet might have to be a very direct hit to kill him, but a silver one?

The doors behind Fagerlie burst open. "Forward, bats!" Sebastian shouted.

A stream of chittering brown bodies hurtled out the open doors. Fagerlie let out a wild cry and ducked, flinging up his hands to protect himself from the unexpected flood of winged creatures. Taking advantage of his distraction, Ves grabbed him by waist and wrist, and slammed him into the floor. Fagerlie cried out, so Ves repeated the movement. This time, the sorcerer remained still and silent.

The last of the bats dodged Ves's head. Sebastian stared down at Fagerlie in horror—then flung himself on Ves. "Are you all right?"

Ves hugged him tight. "I am. It looks like it was your turn to save me," he said against Sebastian's hair.

Thumps and shouts sounded from other parts of the library, intermixed with startled screams as the bats swooped past Fagerlie's henchmen. "You found the librarians, I take it?" Ves asked.

"Yes." Sebastian stepped back and pulled off his tie. Kneeling, he began to bind Fagerlie's hands with it. "Arthur was the one to betray us. He murdered Kelly and tried to do the same to you."

Gods of the wood. Ves joined Sebastian on the floor and began to do a hasty search of Fagerlie's pockets. "I'm sorry."

"So am I." Sebastian's mouth tightened. "He got away, so he's somewhere in the stacks. Or has fled the library, if he has any sense."

Ves found a silver-plated knife in one of the robe's pockets, which he picked up gingerly by its pearl handle, before passing it to Sebastian. Also in the pocket was a coarse gray thread.

"What the devil is that?" Sebastian asked.

Ves inspected it closely. "It's the thread made from Fagerlie's hair, that he meant to have me use to rebind the book. It would give him some sort of mastery over it, though how or what I can't imagine."

"It drove Dromgoole mad," Sebastian said. When Ves gave him a quizzical look, he shrugged. "I read another letter. You can read it yourself later, but it made me realize…well, the way Ladysmith talks about his hopes that they can be together again, all the while knowing their reunion never came…" He offered Ves a wry smile. "That's what brought me to my senses. Life's too short, and I didn't want to miss the chance to be with you."

Warmth filled Ves's chest, and he embraced Sebastian again. "I'm glad."

"So am I. I'm also glad Fagerlie didn't get the chance to bind the book to him. And Arthur didn't free it."

The hair on the nape of Ves's neck pricked. "You said he escaped."

"Yes, but…" Sebastian trailed off, meeting his gaze. "Fagerlie…did he find the right room?"

"Unfortunately. He said it looked as though someone had already been trying to get inside."

"Arthur had a hammer." Sebastian rubbed at one shoulder. "But it would take him hours to get through a masonry wall with it."

"Fagerlie had more than a hammer. They managed to break through."

Sebastian swore and sprang to his feet, off and running in an instant. Ves caught up easily, and they reached the room at the same moment.

It was empty now, just dropped sledgehammers and the body of one of the henchmen, hanging from a broken branch. Sebastian stumbled at the sight of the verdant shelves. "What—"

"Noct's work," Ves said. "I told you he was more competent at sorcery than me."

Sebastian only shook his head. They approached the hole in the wall warily—until the glint of a flashlight showed from the darkness beyond.

Ves snarled a curse and ran for the hole, scrambling through and hitting the floor prepared to fight.

The room was small and strangely angled, with the walls meeting the floor in ways that made no sense to his eyes. Symbols he didn't recognize were carved into each surface. The space was empty, save for a single plinth in the middle of the floor.

No doubt the *Book of Breath* had been on the plinth. But now, it was in Arthur's hand.

He'd set the flashlight on the plinth in order to do his work, its beam focused directly on the book. The leather cover was cracked and dry-looking, and had clearly not been made from the skin of a calf or goat. The ivory curve of a hyoid bone decorated the front, along with the dried cartilage of a trachea. The thread used in the long-stitch binding resembled the hair in Ves's pocket, in texture though not color.

And Arthur had just slipped the edge of a pen knife beneath the thread.

"Don't!" Sebastian shouted as he clambered through the hole.

Arthur didn't look at him, didn't so much as flinch. Instead, faster than Ves could move to interfere, he slashed through the hair thread and unbound the book.

"No!" Sebastian shouted. His heart pounded in his throat, the air so thick it felt more like liquid, and the sound died almost as soon as it left his mouth.

Ves slapped the book out of Arthur's hand, but too late. It fell to the ground and skidded away, shedding folios as it did so.

Wind roared through the room, tearing at Sebastian's hair and nearly hurling him off his feet. The thick air made it feel as though he'd been caught in a whirlpool rather than a whirlwind. Arthur threw back his head and stretched out his arms, welcoming the blast.

And something began to coalesce, rising like mist from the unbound book.

Ves stepped back, moving protectively between it and Sebastian. Sebastian grabbed one of his tentacles, and the air seemed to grow thinner, so that it was less like being battered by a current of water and more like a strong wind. Something to do with Ves's magic resistance, perhaps?

The form that gathered in the air was a horror. For the first time, it occurred to Sebastian that incorporeal creatures, even those that had once been human, wouldn't be limited in their shape by either physics or imagination.

She—it—might have once been the woman called Emeline, but either death or the process of being made into a sentient book had stripped away any semblance of humanity. The very sight of her made Sebastian's brain ache, as his mind sought to find some order amidst the tangled limbs, loose skin, and slavering mouths. They opened and closed, devoid of either teeth or tongue, and the lungs that pumped air into them dangled on the outside of her body. Bile stung Sebastian's throat, and it was all he could do not to retch.

"Free," said a thousand voices, some whispering, some shouting, some raggedly screaming in pain.

Arthur's face had gone the color of spoiled milk at the sight of what he'd unleashed. But still, he braced himself and said, "I kept up my part of the bargain! I freed you at the proper hour, while the tail of the comet you died beneath enshrouds the earth. Now it's your turn to help me."

A horrid, creeping laugh seemed to crawl around the floor. *"No."*

Arthur's mouth worked. "But—"

"Why should I do the bidding of something like you?" The words were

hot in Sebastian's ear, then far away. *"The comet has given its power to my brothers and sister, as well as myself. They will feed until they grow strong enough to be unbound. But for now, I shall feed on* you."

Arthur grabbed at his throat, alarm spreading over his face. "It's killing him!" Sebastian said, grabbing Ves's arm.

Ves's eyes were desperate. "Get out of here before she does the same to you! I'll try to bind her book."

Sebastian tightened his hold. "I'm not leaving you. I can help. I'm *going* to help."

He'd failed to save his mother, when she'd died screaming in the flames. But he'd be damned if he failed Ves.

Ves hesitated, then nodded. "Don't let go of me."

"I won't. But we need something to distract it."

"Leave that to me," Irene called from the hole in the wall.

Irene's round face was slick with sweat, and the wind had torn off her hat and left her short hair in disarray. The fashionable skirt twisted around her legs, and the arm of her coat had ripped at the seam.

In her hand she held Fagerlie's staff. The gemstones embedded in it glowed with an inner light as she drew magic through it. She thrust the staff in front of her, chanting in the language of sorcerers in a clear, commanding tone.

Sebastian didn't know enough about magic to guess what she was doing, but it enraged Emeline. She let Arthur's corpse fall and unleashed a scream that made Sebastian's ears ache.

Ves tugged on him, and they both ran, while Irene kept the spirit's attention on her. They grabbed up the loose pages; the paper looked like vellum and had a greasy feel that turned Sebastian's stomach. He didn't dare do more than glance at what was inscribed on the paper in spiky handwriting, every line like the slash of a knife.

When Ves's hand closed around the leather cover, Emeline finally seemed to become aware of what they were about. She turned away from Irene, mouths flopping as a thousand voices whispered or spoke or screamed: *"No! I will not be bound again; not to you; not to anyone."*

A wall of wind slammed into them. It tore Sebastian's hand from Ves's tentacle, sent him hurtling into the wall—

Then there was no air. None at all. Sebastian's lungs heaved, but failed to inflate, because there was nothing to fill them. His hands flew to his throat instinctively, scrabbling at nothing.

He was dying. Just as Arthur had died. And there was nothing he could do to stop it.

Blackness spangled the air in front of Sebastian's eyes. He fell to the floor, but the pain seemed distant, unimportant compared to the agony in his heaving lungs. He needed air, but there was none, stolen away by the monstrous undead thing before him.

Then a host of tentacles wrapped around him: arms, legs, chest. A thin thread of air passed his lips, and he gulped it down, again and again. It wasn't much, but it was far better than nothing. His vision cleared, and he looked up, expecting to see Ves.

Instead, it was Nocturn who bent over him with worried eyes. "Vesper!" he called. "Get over here—now!"

The blasphemous thing that had been released from the book screamed her rage. But Irene now stood between her and Sebastian, weaving a spell which apparently protected her from Emeline's breath-stealing power.

Then Ves was there, and Noct handed him over. Ves's human hands clutched the unbound book, but he hauled Sebastian close with his other arms. "Are you all right?"

Sebastian's breath eased even further, enough to say, "It doesn't matter! Get binding, now!"

Noct had moved to support Irene, chanting rapidly alongside her, his hand also resting on the staff. The gemstones glowed like Christmas lights now, afire with the magic they both channeled from the great arcane vortex beneath Widdershins.

Ves pulled his own binding kit from his pocket, but hesitated. "I think...I could be wrong, but from what you said about Dromgoole, I think these spirits have to be bound to someone."

Sebastian began to reassemble the book, thrusting the folios in where they seemed to belong. The writing made his brain itch, and he hoped it wouldn't spoil everything if one or two pages were out of order. "Alexander Dromgoole bound them all to himself and they drove him mad."

"He made that sacrifice for a reason," Ves said. "It wasn't enough just to wall them away, though once they were walled away, clearly the spirit traps held even after his death. Though maybe that was because his hands were the ones to create the traps in the first place."

"What are you saying?"

"We need to bind it to someone. By using some part of them, I assume, given the hair thread."

"We hardly have time to make thread!" Sebastian snapped. "And we certainly can't use Fagerlie's!"

"Blood on thread might work," Irene called over her shoulder.

Ves hesitated. "I'll try mine, but I'm resistant to sorcery, so it may not work."

Sebastian met his gaze. "But mine will."

Ves's eyes widened in alarm, their strange goatish pupils dilating. "You can't. Sebastian, these books drove Dromgoole mad."

An odd sense of calm settled over Sebastian. "It took all four of them to do it, at least according to Ladysmith. So we'll just have to find some way to destroy the books before it comes to that, won't we?"

A desperate look came into Ves's eyes, as though he wished to object. But instead, he silently threaded the heavy needle and handed it to Sebastian. "Pass it through your flesh, then hand it to me."

Sebastian swallowed—but this was the only way to be sure his blood covered absolutely every inch of the thread. He took the needle and held it over his arm, hands shaking just a little.

Irene stumbled. Noct's tentacles shot out, supporting her.

They were all going to die if he couldn't do this.

Sebastian stabbed the needle into his forearm, going deep enough to make sure he hit the bloody meat of the muscle, and came out the other side.

It hurt—the needle was no small thing used by doctors on their patients, but thick and tough. He gritted his teeth when Ves grabbed it and yanked it through to get enough bloodied thread to begin.

He felt each tug as Ves ran the needle through the holes punched into the book seventy-five years ago, when the same comet that now bathed the earth in its tail had also been ascendant. The thick thread sent a fiery pain through him with every one of Ves's movements, as inch after inch was dragged through the wound, going in white and emerging bathed in blood.

Stitching a part of Sebastian into a part of someone else.

The long-dead necromancer's rage boiled through him, then calmed. The howls and cries died away, and in his mind's eye, he suddenly saw it. No, saw *her*.

Emeline.

She wore the dress of a long-past era, mutton sleeves and full skirts meant to emphasize the slimness of her waist. Her blond hair was curled to either side of her face, the bulk of it mounded up into an elaborate, braided bun. Her hazel eyes burned with a cold fire, and the smile on her face struck him as genuine as that of a shark.

"Please help me, sir," she simpered. "I only wish my freedom—is that too much to ask?"

"I...yes," Sebastian objected.

Ves's head snapped around. "Who are you talking to?"

"Keep going!" Noct shouted.

Ves bent his head and went back to the binding. The pain flared again in Sebastian's arm, and he blinked, but she was still there. In his head.

"Of course," Emeline went on, "I don't wish freedom from *you*. Not at all. Stop this, and I'll be so grateful, sir, I'll do whatever it is you wish." Her icy eyes blinked in an attempt at coyness. "You desire to be useful, don't you? Not to let down any of those who depend on you? To save them?"

"Yes," he said, though he didn't want to.

"I can help with that. I can give you riches enough to make your sister wealthy beyond her wildest dreams. Send all of her many children to university for a good education, rather than the life of manual labor that awaits them." She loomed larger in his mind. "More...if you say the word, I will make your lover a normal man."

"No!" Sebastian shouted. "I love Vesper for who he is! So go to hell, you damned thing."

Ves pulled taut the final stitch, knotted it—and severed the thread.

The spirit screamed her fury, but the sound was impotent. Even as the winds died, the thick mist forming her horrifying shape streamed back into the book. The pressure in the room fell, Sebastian's ears popped—and then there was stillness.

"Oh thank God," Irene mumbled and promptly collapsed.

Noct caught her before she hit the floor. A startled look crossed his face as he cradled her in his tentacles and arm alike. "Oh. Oh dear."

She blinked. Then for a moment, her eyes seemed to fix on Noct's face. "You..."

At that moment, Mortimer entered through the hole. "Irene!" he exclaimed, running to her. Noct hastily lowered her to the ground and squirmed away.

She lifted her arm to touch Mortimer, then frowned. "My coat is ruined."

He pulled her close. "I'll buy you a new one, darling. I'm just glad you're all right."

Sweeping her into his arms, he carried her out of the now-silent chamber. Noct watched them go in silence.

Ves rose to his feet and set the book on the plinth. Then he turned back to Sebastian, caught sight of his bleeding arm, and dropped to his knees. His hands gentle as possible, he pulled out the last of the thread. Then he wrapped a tentacle around the arm to put pressure on the bleeding.

"We need to get you properly bandaged," he said. "But otherwise...are you all right?"

Sebastian nodded tiredly. His head ached, and he felt as though he could sleep a week. "I'm fine. The spirit touched my mind and tried to persuade me to stop binding her, but she didn't have time to figure out the right approach the way she did with Arthur."

"Still, I imagine your connection was far more intense." Ves gently cupped Sebastian's chin. "And what was that about loving me as I am?"

Heat rushed into Sebastian's face. "I...that is...I know it's a bit soon..."

"Really?" Ves bent closer for a kiss. "Because I feel like I've been waiting my entire life."

CHAPTER 30

"In light of your actions," Mr. Quinn said to Ves, "I've decided to rehire you. Though you came here under false pretenses, Erasmus was correct in his judgment to add you to our numbers. And of course, Widdershins always knows its own."

Ves stood very straight, hands clasped respectfully behind him. Mr. Quinn's dictionary had been returned to its place of honor with a few additional bloodstains, and the library put back in its usual order. "Thank you, sir. I promise, I'm not hiding any more secrets."

"I would hope not." His thin lips pursed. "I understand that there are more of these infernal books scattered about in Widdershins?"

"Yes," Sebastian said, who'd been summoned along with Ves to the head librarian's office. "Three more: blood, flesh, and bone."

Mr. Quinn steepled his spidery fingers in front of him. "We are the Librarians of Widdershins. Our task is to watch over the town, in whatever way we are able. This is a task that seems uniquely suited to us. Therefore, I would like for the two of you to continue Mr. O'Neil's work and attempt to find the rest of the Books of the Bound, before they can cause any further trouble."

"Of course," Ves agreed, the same moment Sebastian said, "It would be our honor, sir."

"Excellent." Mr. Quinn sat back in his chair. "Oh, Mr. Rune, I would very much like to speak to your brother about a possible position in the library. Behind the scenes, naturally; I wouldn't wish to burden him with Dr. Leavitt or Dr. Norris."

Ves's heart quickened, and he exchanged a glance with Sebastian, who inclined his head slightly.

"I…I think he might like that," Ves said. "I'm not certain how he would come to work, though. He can't pretend to be completely human the way I can."

Mr. Quinn waved one thin hand. "A matter to be worried about should he accept my offer. Where are you staying?"

Bonnie had proved as good as her word. "We're both staying with Sebastian's family, for the time being."

"Excellent. I shall call upon you tonight, if that is convenient."

"It—it is." In his wildest dreams, Ves had never thought such a thing might happen. "Thank you for your generosity, sir."

Mr. Quinn's smile was a tad unsettling. "Oh, I assure you, this is not charity, Mr. Rune. Now, I shall let you return to your work."

They both nodded, but as they turned to the door, he added, "One more thing, gentlemen. Though thankfully I myself experience no such attractions, I am not insensible to their existence. So I shall tell you what I told Miss Endicott and Mr. Waite: there is to be no…*high spirited behavior*…in the library. Do I make myself clear?"

Ves's cheeks burned with embarrassment, but Sebastian grinned. "We're professionals and will comport ourselves as such, Head Librarian."

"See that you do."

As soon as they were safely out of the office and hurrying down the corridor, Sebastian bumped his elbow against Ves's. "This is wonderful! And Noct will be able to work here too!"

"Yes." Unease touched Ves when he remembered Mr. Quinn's smile. "Though…why? He's intelligent, and more knowledgeable than I when it comes to the arcane arts, but he has no experience working as a librarian."

Sebastian shrugged. "I've learned it's best not to ask why Mr. Quinn does anything. Possibly he can't pass up the chance to have another sorcerer on staff. Or maybe he just thinks all those arms will come in useful sorting books."

"Honestly, that does seem likely." They came to the bindery door, and Ves slowed. "I'd like to speak with Irene. Do you know where she is?"

Sebastian nodded. "She's with the rest of the Endicotts, sealing the *Book of Breath* back in where it belongs. Come on—I want to see how they're doing."

It had been five days since he'd bound the book to Sebastian. A doctor had treated the wound in his arm, and it didn't seem to pain him much. Or at least, it hadn't when they'd made love last night.

Ves stopped that train of thought before it distracted him too much. "How are you feeling?" he asked as they made their way through the maze of the stacks. "No untoward side effects of having a murderous book bound to you?"

Sebastian shook his head. "No. None I've noticed so far, at least."

Hopefully it remained that way. Whatever happened, Ves wasn't going to see Sebastian go down the same road as Dromgoole.

"Do you think we'll see Fagerlie again?" Sebastian added.

After they'd bound Emeline, it had taken a while for anyone to remember Fagerlie. When three librarians had gone to secure him, they'd found only the tie Sebastian had knotted around his wrists. In the midst of the commotion, he'd somehow slipped out of the library and vanished.

"If he values his health, he'll stay far away," Ves said darkly.

They reached the Astronomy and Physics Collection. Over the weekend, Kelly O'Neil's body had finally been located, stuffed behind a shelving unit. Arthur had poured plaster over the corpse in an attempt to seal in the smell, which had worked well enough to convince the junior librarian who admitted to asking about it that it was just a dead rat in an inaccessible place.

The *Book of Breath* had been replaced on its plinth and the wall rebuilt under the direction of the Endicott sorcerers. The alteration had also been removed and reconstructed, so the spirit trap should work properly again.

The small group currently gathered in front of the rebuilt wall had apparently just finished some sort of ceremony, based on the smell of incense and the symbols chalked onto the plaster. Their leader was a distinguished Black man; the Endicotts must acquire new blood wherever the British Empire went in the world. Irene was easy to spot amidst them in her plumed hat and silk dress.

She turned as they approached. "Well, that's done with," she said. "Hopefully we won't hear another peep out of her."

"I certainly hope not," Ves agreed. "May I speak to you for a moment?"

She arched a brow, but followed him a short distance away. When Sebastian hesitated, Ves beckoned him over. This involved him as well, in a way. "I just wanted to know...Fagerlie promised Noct and me that he would lift the curse of our blood. I thought perhaps your family could help us? I'm not certain how I'd repay you, but..."

He trailed off as Irene shook her head. A gentle expression came over her features, and she patted his arm. "I'm sorry, Vesper. But there is no 'curse of your blood.' There's just...you. As with any child, if there was a way to take away half of what makes it alive, all you'd have left would be a messy pile of bits."

"Oh." A part of him had suspected the answer, but even so, hearing it spoken aloud felt like the final nail in a coffin.

Sebastian put a hand on Ves's arm. "Come back to my office with me. We can start looking for the next Book of the Bound."

"I'd like to stop in the bindery first, actually."

They walked back in silence. Once they were inside, Sebastian shut the door and pulled Ves into a hug. "I'm sorry, angel."

Ves hugged him back. "So am I." He let out a long breath. "But... it's all right, I think. Up until now, Noct and I really never had anyone but each other. Now we have you, and Bonnie, and the children, and the librarians. We might be monsters, but we're monsters who belong somewhere."

Sebastian kissed him softly. When the skin along Ves's spine began to tingle, he pulled away. "No 'high spirited behavior,' remember?"

"I remember." Sebastian kissed him again, swiftly. "Now, what did you want from here?"

Ves walked slowly to his desk and removed the secret document drawer. The aged slip of paper with its signatures in blood was still inside.

To whomever comes after me: I charge you to continue our sacred work. To stand against necromancy and things from the Outside, and bind them so they cannot exert their will on our world.

Nathaniel R. Ladysmith, December 13, 1859
   Thomas Halliwell, February 10, 1864
   Rebecca Rath, October 31, 1882
   Kelly O'Neil, January 28, 1905

Ves took out his bookbinding kit and removed the same needle that had passed through Sebastian's arm not long ago. It had been cleaned, and its sharp point gleamed as he pressed it to his own finger. Below O'Neil's name, he wrote:

Vesper Rune, May 23, 1910

He didn't know what effect it would have on him, if any, given his magic resistance. But it was an Oath, a Binder's Oath, and if nothing else a visible mark of his commitment.

He set it down to let the blood dry, then turned to Sebastian and found him smiling. "You're one of us, now," Sebastian said. "A part of the library."

"I just signed an oath in blood. You don't need to make it *more* ominous."

Sebastian laughed and kissed him on the cheek. "Come on. Let's get to work."

Once in Sebastian's office, he retreated to the pile of architectural drawings. "We have the letters, and we have these. I wonder if going through the drawings with an eye toward any that have built-in spirit traps would help?"

"Are those all of Dromgoole's buildings?"

"I don't know." Sebastian frowned as he began to shuffle slowly through them. "I don't think there's a record of everything he designed…but how many could there be?"

Ves shrugged. "I haven't the slightest idea. Fewer than if he wasn't chasing down murderous books, I should think."

Sebastian chuckled. "You're not wrong. I…"

The words faded, and his skin went chalk-white. Ves hurried to his side. "What's the matter? Are you all right?"

Sebastian swallowed forcefully. "This set of drawings. I know this place." He slowly looked up and met Ves's eyes. "This is the house I grew up in."

The adventures of Sebastian and Ves will continue in Unseen, Rath & Rune Book 2.

SHARE YOUR EXPERIENCE

If you enjoyed this book, please consider leaving a review on the site where you purchased it, or on Goodreads.

Thank you for your support of independent authors!

END NOTES

Huge shout-out to all of my Patreon patrons, especially Dusk T., Robin H., and Shane M. Thanks also to patron Colette for naming the bar the librarians hang out in, The Silver Key. If you'd like to join them, check it out here: https://www.patreon.com/jordanlhawk

For anyone interested in learning more about turn of the century libraries, it is my true pleasure to direct you to *A Book for All Readers* by Ainsworth Rand Spofford, which is in the public domain and can be downloaded from Project Gutenberg (http://www.gutenberg.org/ ebooks/22608). Spofford was the Sixth Librarian of Congress and an incredibly entertaining writer, whose deep passion for his subject shines forth in every paragraph. Much like Vesper, I think it's fair to say Mr. Spofford was literally ready to die on the hill of proper margin width in rebinding.

By 1910 large institutions such as the Boston Public Library had sizable binderies, staffed with numerous people and equipped with machinery to make the job quicker and easier. Such a setup seemed impractical for a smaller institution such as the Ladysmith museum. I also couldn't see Mr. Quinn sending any of his beloved books, but especially cursed or rare tomes, out to a commercial bindery. Hence the decision to set up the bindery and conservatory of the museum's library as I did.

The rare book trade flourished in America from the late 1800s up until the Great Depression. Much as with tulip bulbs during "tulipomania" in the 1600s, or Beanie Babies in the modern era, rare books were considered a solid investment whose value would only ever go up, never down. Though some were sought out by genuine book lovers, their status as an investment not only led to wildly inflated prices, but to a high demand from those rich enough to afford them not as important cultural artifacts, but as something to be acquired the way one might acquire stocks and bonds. The true victims of the rare book trade were public and university libraries. Small, rural public libraries, which might have ended up with rare volumes purely by chance, and which lacked the means to keep them secure, suffered the most. Libraries big and small were stripped of any book considered valuable by unscrupulous men, who would then remove as many marks of ownership as possible so they could be sold on to "collectors" who cared less for the books than for their perceived investment value. The trade finally collapsed along with the stock market.

The panic surrounding Halley's Comet really happened, and every news story mentioned in this book is based on actual newspaper articles, as are the "comet pills." And yes, that includes the article about planned human sacrifice, where a man named Henry Heineman and his cult the Select Followers apparently attempted to sacrifice a Miss Jane Warfield to stop God from destroying the cosmos.

In addition to the usual apocalyptic fears surrounding comet sightings throughout history, science stepped in to further whip everyone into a frenzy. After the presence of cyanogen gas was discovered in the comet's tail, French astronomer Camille Flammarion stated the gas would wipe out all life on earth when the planet passed through the comet's tail shortly after transit. Though other astronomers immediately discredited this view, it stoked public hysteria even higher.

Halley's Comet wasn't the only celestial visitor in 1910. An even brighter comet unexpectedly appeared on January 12. Called the Daylight Comet or the Great January Comet, it was already visible to the naked eye when first noticed by diamond miners in the Transvaal.

The first scientific observation came on January 17, by which time it was bright enough to be seen during the daytime. When Halley's Comet returned in 1986, some eyewitnesses of the 1910 visit reported having viewed it previously in the daylight; as Halley's was visible only around dawn and dusk in 1910, it's thought they conflated the memory of the two comets.

The New England vampire panics occurred sporadically from the late 1700s until the 1890s. The romantic literary vampire notwithstanding, the vampire myth originated as a pre-germ-theory attempt to understand the spread of disease, especially through close-knit families. In the New England panics, tuberculosis would strike down one member of a family at a time; the explanation was that the first sufferer had been a vampire, who now returned to feed on their kin. The body would be exhumed, and various organs (usually the heart, but records also show the liver on at least one occasion) were burned. The ashes would then be fed as a cure to any sufferers.

The School of Night is inspired by a wild theory concocted by Arthur Acheson in 1903, based on the line from *Love's Labours Lost* that Ves quotes. It's the modern name for an Elizabethan-era conspiracy theory of a "School of Atheism" used to accuse and discredit Sir Walter Raleigh and some of the poets and scientists he patronized. Sad as it is to say, there is absolutely no evidence that Shakespeare, Marlowe, Raleigh, and the Wizard Earl ever belonged to a secret occult cabal.

The use of silver in folklore has a very old pedigree. It should be noted that evil creatures such as vampires could not be seen reflected in mirrors not because they have no reflections at all, but because the silver used to back mirrors was too "pure" to reflect such corruption. The Beast of Gévaudan—whatever it or they might have actually been—supposedly could not be killed until it was shot with a silver bullet created by melting down amulets bearing the image of the Virgin Mary. Though Vesper and Nocturn aren't old-school monsters, it was nevertheless fun to give them an old-school weakness.

ALSO BY JORDAN L. HAWK

Dangerous Spirits
Guardian Spirits

ABOUT THE AUTHOR

Jordan L. Hawk is a trans author from North Carolina. Childhood tales of mountain ghosts and mysterious creatures gave him a life-long love of things that go bump in the night. When he isn't writing, he brews his own beer and tries to keep the cats from destroying the house. His best-selling Whyborne & Griffin series (beginning with *Widdershins*) can be found in print, ebook, and audiobook.

If you're interested in receiving Jordan's newsletter and being the first to know when new books are released, please sign up at his website: http://www.jordanlhawk.com. Or join his Facebook reader group, Widdershins Knows Its Own.

Find Jordan online:

http://www.jordanlhawk.com

https://twitter.com/jordanlhawk

https://www.facebook.com/jordanlhawk

Printed in Great Britain
by Amazon